To three amazing women who made this rewrite possible,
and helped me breathe new life into an old story—
Natashya Wilson, Gabrielle Vicedomini and Kristi Yanta!

GENA SHOWALTER

Oh My Goth

HARLEQUIN® TEEN

ISBN-13: 978-1-335-13972-6

Oh My Goth

This is the revised text of the work first published by Simon & Schuster in 2006

This edition published by Harlequin TEEN, 2018

This edition published by arrangement with Harlequin Books S.A.

For questions and comments about the quality of this book, please contact us at CustomerService@Harlequin.com.

Printed in U.S.A.

Chapter 1

Outward beauty will fade,
but the things we do—our cruelties or
simple kindnesses—will live forever
in the people we hurt or help.

—From the journal of
Miranda Beers

My name is Jade Leighton, and this morning I staged my own death. Fiona, my stepmom, walked in and just about screamed the house down.

First: *knock, please!*

Second: I think she screamed louder when I opened my eyes.

Third: I'm pretty sure she'll need therapy to recover.

I know, I know. How morbid of me. My actions must have been a cry for help, and I should see a doctor. Why focus on death when life is what matters, right?

Here's the deal. I never wanted to be discovered. I'd planned to snap a few photos of my "corpse" to study later—at the suggestion of *my* therapist, thank you very much.

Okay, okay. He didn't suggest I stage my own death... exactly. He said I should face my past head-on so that I can let it go, move forward, and embrace a bright future.

My interpretation? Re-create my mother's death—the most defining moment of my life—and find whatever shred of beauty was hidden in the darkness.

Her name was Miranda.

When my parents got along, my dad called her Randy, a nickname she claimed to hate. He would say it with a twinkle in his eyes, and Mom would protest while fighting a smile.

I was five years old when she enrolled me in a ballet class. The day of my first lesson, I remember wearing a pink tutu and feeling like a princess. I twirled all the way to the car and begged Mom to let me sit in the front seat like "a big girl." The studio was only a few miles from our house, so she decided to humor me. That's my best guess, anyway.

I don't remember what happened to us. I'm told another vehicle slammed into ours halfway to the studio, propelling us off a bridge, that we landed upside down next to a river.

I *do* remember opening my eyes and hearing the thunder of my heartbeat as blood rushed in my ears. I remember the scent of old pennies and fuel thickening the air... the feel of my seat belt pinning me in place, the strap cutting into my tiny chest.

I remember panicking, fighting to straighten as warm blood trickled down my face and splashed onto my mother...who lay beneath me, splayed across the minivan's dash, surrounded by broken glass.

One of her eyes had been gouged out, while the other stared at nothing. A metal spike protruded from her torso, and bones stuck out of her collar, an arm, and both her legs.

Hours passed. An eternity. Later, Dad told me the car responsible for our predicament had taken a dive on the other side of the bridge, and the only occupant had died on impact. No one witnessed the collision, so no one called for help.

By the time we were found, I'd screamed so loud and long that I'd permanently damaged my vocal cords.

Dad says I quit being me that day, that I completely shut down.

He isn't wrong.

I'm seventeen-years-old now. Since the accident, I haven't shed a single tear or laughed. According to Fiona, I suffer from permanent RWF—resting witch face. (She refuses to curse.) I also haven't thrown a temper tantrum, or argued about…anything. I haven't cared enough. I don't even get excited when good things happen to me or anyone else.

Why should I? Good things never last.

I spent many years in counseling. My therapist says my emotional detachment is a protective measure I use to shield myself from a trauma I'm not yet able to handle. He isn't wrong, either.

I choose not to feel. I *like* my numbness.

My dad isn't so enamored of it. Last year, he asked me to give him a genuine smile for his birthday. I faked it, and he sighed. Then he said, "There's no sparkle in your eyes," all kinds of depression in his voice.

For a short window of time afterward, he tried telling me jokes to "earn" a laugh.

Where does a sheep go for a haircut? To the baaaa baaaa shop!

How do you make a tissue dance? You put a little boogie in it.

What time did the man go to the dentist? Tooth hurt-y.

Another failure. His depression deepened, and finally he gave up.

I don't enjoy hurting him, but I'm not going to change just to please him. My life, my decision.

The bell for first period rings, drawing me from my thoughts and signaling the start of a new school day. I've been seated for over ten minutes. I'm not eager, trust me—I'm just punctual. If you aren't early, you're late.

Mr. Parton takes attendance. He smiles sweetly at Mercedes Turner, teacher's pet, and glares daggers at me, teacher's nightmare. When he begins his lecture, comparing triangles, drawing tangents to circles, I hear *blah, blah, blah.*

I've never liked sitting for long periods of time as someone who hates me explains the ins and outs of a subject I'll never actually use in the real world. Go figure. The only classes I find the least bit interesting are creative writing, art and anatomy. For all others, I spend my time doodling different parts of the skeletal system in a notebook.

Today I've done a femur, metacarpals and phalanges, a radius and an ulna. Things guaranteed to creep out Mr. Parton if he demands to see what has me so enraptured.

A douche move on my part. I kind of suck. Maybe my friend Linda "Linnie" Baker is right: *How do you know someone has spoken to Jade? They're crying!*

Linnie offered the quip after I made a junior sob for giving her the stink eye. At school the only people I talk to—besides my friends—are the students who *insult* my friends.

I never shout, only warn, but for some reason my calm

tone elicits fear. *Apologize now, or I'll cut out your tongue so you're no longer able to speak such ugly words.*

The thing is, my warnings are not threats but promises. One day I'll probably end up in jail.

"Tsk, tsk, Jade. Touching yourself in class," Charlee Ann Richards says, her voice soft. She's seated next to me. "How scandalous."

I realize that I stopped drawing in favor of tracing my fingertips over the plethora of scars at the base of my neck, courtesy of the car wreck and my seat belt. Thanks to shards of glass, more scars decorate my abdomen and legs.

Ignoring Charlee Ann, I pick up my pencil and draw a sternum, then a rib cage. Soon I have an entire skeleton on the page, though the bones are scattered like puzzle pieces that need to fit together.

As if offended by my lack of concern, Charlee Ann confiscates the paper and mutters, "You are *such* a freak."

I run my tongue over my teeth. I choose not to feel, yes, but I do *not* like having my things taken from me. However, I remain mute. The moment I speak up, she'll know how to strike at me next time.

She learned from a master, after all. Her mentor, Mercedes. According to Linnie, Charlee Ann is Mercedes's clone, and together the two are the most popular girls at Hathaway High.

I know Mercedes well. Her mom, Nadine, used to date my dad. In fact, Nadine was his first serious girlfriend after my mother died. Dad and Nadine were serious enough to shack up together. Mercedes and I became friends; in elementary school, we were never far from each other's side. Then, right before our first year of junior high, Nadine broke up with my dad and moved out.

Like the car accident, the day is forever burned into my mind. Nadine held her bag in one hand and Mercedes's hand in the other. She looked at me dead-on and said, "*You* are to blame for this. You're a bad influence. A budding sociopath!"

I think my dad agreed with her. That same night, he had a few too many beers and said to me, "Did you really have to ask Nadine how she wanted to die—then explain in minute detail how other people have died? You frightened her."

Mercedes and I were never friends again. In fact, we became target practice for each other.

"Nothing to say?" Charlee Ann asks with a smirk.

Again, I ignore her. To the rest of the world, I'm weird. So what? So I wonder how people are going to die. Again, so what? The opinions of others mean nothing to me.

I wish my friends felt the same. Linnie, Kimberly Nguyen and Robb Martinez care a little too much.

Insults cause Linnie to spiral and seek praise in all the wrong places. Kimberly adds another layer of sass to her attitude, as my dad would say. Robb often sinks into a deep, dark depression and goes mute.

I might not know how to help them, but I do know how to threaten their tormentors.

Charlee Ann hands my paper to Mercedes, who is sitting directly behind her. "Look at this," she whispers. "We should schedule an intervention, yeah? Before she murders us all."

Charlee Ann is probably going to kill someone, hide the body but get caught, anyway, and die in prison when another girl shanks her. Mercedes is probably going to have a heart attack at thirty and never recover.

Mercedes studies my artwork and shudders. "I doubt it will help," she whispers back. From her coiffed blond hair to her fit-and-flare buttercup-yellow dress, she is the epitome of perfect. "The crazy is strong in this one."

Charlee Ann chortles.

Mercedes knows I'm forced to go to therapy, but she's never told her friends. Not out of the goodness of her heart. (Does she still have a heart?) She keeps quiet because I have dirt on her, too. For years I've watched her struggle with an eating disorder. Whatever goes in soon comes right back out.

I blame Nadine. (Who is probably going to outlive us all.) The woman constantly criticizes her daughter; nothing Mercedes does is ever good enough. Even I admit she's smart and beautiful—on the outside.

I should probably feel sorry for her, but sympathy is beyond me. Like her mother, Mercedes tears down others in an attempt to feel better about herself. I think that's why she's my only no-emotion exception. I kinda sorta enjoy tearing *her* down.

"Keep the paper," I say just as softly. "It can pass as your new student ID. The resemblance is uncanny, don't you think?"

Shock and horror flare in Mercedes's blue, blue eyes—eyes that quickly well with tears. She blinks rapidly, and the tears vanish. Hey, maybe I imagined them.

"Shut your mouth," Charlee Ann snaps, earning a disapproving glance from Mr. Parton, Oklahoma's worst teacher. She shrivels in her seat. "Sorry. My bad."

He nods and continues his lecture. To him, she can do no wrong.

As cochairs of Make a Difference—or, as I liked to call it, MAD—both Charlee Ann and Mercedes are considered earth angels. They spearhead most school fundraisers and throw parties to encourage students to support each other, no matter their race, religion, gender or sexuality.

Their next event—Light Night—is three or four weeks away. (I don't know the exact date because I tune out every time someone starts talking about it.) Tickets are twenty dollars a pop. Twenty dollars to dress up, stand outside during a heat wave, eat crappy hors d'oeuvres and light a candle at the same time as other people? No, thank you.

Take my money. I'll keep my time. What Mercedes and Charlee Ann don't seem to understand? You don't need to light a candle to prove you support other people, whatever their race, religion, gender or sexuality. You just need to be kind on a day-to-day basis. Yeah, I know. What a shocker.

And yeah, I get that I'm not always kind to others. I like to think I'm a little less of a hypocrite, though, since I get my jollies from bullying the bullies. Or is a hypocrite just a hypocrite no matter the circumstances? Oh, well.

Eyes narrowing, Mercedes leans toward me. "My mother says you're so heinous because you're jealous of me. What does your mother tell you about me?" She fluffs her hair. "Oh, that's right. She can't tell you anything. She's dead."

Charlee Ann offers me another smirk, clearly assured I've been put in my place.

Why would I be upset? Mercedes spoke the truth. My mother *is* dead, and she *can't* tell me anything.

Uh-oh. Mr. Parton looks ready for war as he stomps toward us. Both Mercedes and Charlee Ann sit up straighter and gaze at him with adoring eyes, as if caught up in the wonders of his lecture. Talk about false advertising. The only person who adores Mr. Parton is *Mr. Parton.*

He stops to pat Mercedes on the shoulder, all *You're such a good girl.*

This world isn't fair, so he'll probably die of old age, in his sleep, while having an X-rated dream.

As soon as he passes her, she withdraws her cell phone to sneak a selfie with Charlee Ann as the two pretend to gag. I'm sure the caption will mention me.

I've never understood the "art" of the selfie or how and why so many people morph into a philosopher on the internet. Every day people post pictures of their faces and caption each photo with "words of wisdom."

Can't let life's cares get you down.

Really? So you aren't obsessing about the number of likes and shares you're getting?

Look at this big, beautiful world. Good job, God!

Problem: your ginormous head is obscuring the beautiful world around you.

Take time to enjoy every season of your life, guys. Even the storms. Without rain, we wouldn't have flowers.

And we can't understand the profound nature of your advice unless we see you sitting in your car with your hand resting in your hair?

Why not post pictures with a statement of fact: Look at me. Look at me right now! I look AMAZEBALLS. Sidebar: I'm super-duper smart, right?

I sigh. Linnie says my name suits me perfectly. Jade is jaded, yo. Maybe she's right. Again. She also says I was born in the wrong century. While my friends consider their cell phones an extension of their hands, I use mine only to send my dad proof-of-life texts.

To me the internet sucks. There are far too many trolls—fools who think cruelty is hilarious and their opinion is the only right one, who forget that the person they are calling terrible names has baggage, too. Cowards who think they are protected behind their screen, because the other person isn't nearby to gut-punch and junk-slam.

Linnie once posted a picture of us eating lunch together, and no joke, someone legit told us the world would be a better place without us, that we should just go ahead and kill ourselves.

She cried for weeks, nothing I said was able to comfort her. Unlike me, she still loves the internet. If she's not in class, she's on her phone.

"If Miss Baker will give me the honor of her attention," Mr. Parton snaps, "I'll explain the relation between sine and cosine."

All eyes zoom to Linnie. Her cheeks turn bright red as she shifts in her chair. I think she'll die of some rare disease, but only after she's traveled the world and left her mark.

She sits several rows ahead of me, at the front of the class. At the beginning of the school year, Mr. Parton separated us so we couldn't "plot the downfall of the world." Yeah. He really used that phrase.

I'm not surprised he's singled her out today. He tends to focus all his negative energy on one of us each and every day.

I don't hate him, but I might cheer if Wolverine smashed through the door and gave him a prostate exam. When we ask questions, he sneers as if we're dumb for not already understanding something we've never before studied.

To draw attention away from her, I say, "You have my permission to continue, Mr. P.," and give a royal wave of my hand. "Unless *you* don't know the relation between a sine and a cosine?"

A chorus of chuckles abounds.

He scowls at me, a vein throbbing on his forehead. I think he secretly hopes I'll cower in my seat. Too bad, so sad. Fear of him is as foreign to me as happiness and hatred.

Mercedes raises her hand. She doesn't wait to be called on but says, "If Jade insists on being disruptive in class, perhaps you should make her stand in the corner by herself. Except then we'd have to look at her, and everyone would probably lose their breakfast."

More chuckles abound.

Mr. Parton smiles before masking his amusement with a stern expression. "That was beneath you, Miss Turner. We must be kind to others, even when our kindness isn't deserved."

Barf. "You'd lose your breakfast? Really?" I ask her. "No wonder you look at me so much. No one enjoys losing a meal more than you, eh, Mer?"

The color drains from her cheeks.

"Enough." Mr. Parton claps his hands once, twice. When I meet his gaze, his too-thin lips press together even as his eyes glow with triumph—as if he's won some kind of war against me. Silly Mr. Parton. "We're here to learn."

If that's true, we need another teacher.

Mercedes raises her hand a second time. "I have an equation, Mr. Parton. May I share it with the rest of the class?"

"Of course."

She sneers at me. "You dress like a Goth to set yourself apart from others, to protest conformity, and yet you conform to the image of other Goths. Explain that."

Hello, stereotype. "Your equation is flawed," I say. "You assume I am what I am as an act against some type of conformity. The truth is, I simply am what I am."

Most people are afraid of death. Not me. I'm curious about it. I know the body dies—does the soul die, as well? I accept the fact that we are all bound for the grave, and I find beauty in things other people consider doom and gloom. Like a withered tree, or a broken mirror. Even a pile of debris. In books and movies, I tend to sympathize with the villain.

I'm not normal, and I don't want to pretend otherwise.

"You're a freak, plain and simple," Charlee Ann says.

I meet her gaze, unwavering. "Again, there's a flaw in your reasoning. There's nothing wrong with being a freak. However, there *is* something wrong with being a fraud."

Her jaw drops. "I am *not* a fraud!"

Linnie gives me an *I adore you* smile.

Doing my best impression of Charlee Ann, I flip my hair over my shoulder. "I'm so kind and compassionate. I love and support everyone always." As she glares at me, I add, "What a person looks like isn't what determines your treatment of them—the blackened state of your heart is."

Once again Mr. Parton claps his hands. "All right. That's enough, Miss Leighton."

Me? I wait for him to call out Charlee Ann or Mercedes.

Still waiting…

Waiting…

Wow. Okay, all right. "Here's a problem I'd love for you to solve for the class." I lift my chin, square my shoulders. "There are twenty-one kids in this room, and not one of them has learned anything but the consequences of having a bad teacher. How do you explain *that*?"

Everyone snickers, even Mercedes and Charlee Ann.

The vein in Mr. Parton's forehead throbs *faster.* "One more word out of you, Miss Leighton, and you'll spend a week in detention."

Is he kidding? I might have just won the lottery. Detention lasts for an hour after school. The longer I can avoid Fiona and a new lecture from my dad, the better.

"Word," I say.

His eyes narrow to tiny slits and his face darkens to lobster red, clashing with his white button-down shirt and brown dress slacks. He's so neat and tidy; he obviously prizes order.

To him, I must look like chaos. My clothes are usually torn. I have a silver hoop in my nose and two eyebrow rings. One of my arms is sleeved in tattoos. My back is also covered.

Part of my armor, my therapist says.

He's wrong. They are my memorials.

Robb gave me my first tattoo—a broken heart on my wrist. Of course my dad flipped out. What he didn't understand, then or now? The image reminds me of my mother, forever and always.

I told him I would be getting other tattoos with or without his approval. Rather than "putting my health at risk," Dad shocked me by hiring a professional to do the rest of the work. We had to travel out of state, and he had to sign paperwork to grant his permission, but each and every time he did it with only a handful of complaints.

"If you want detention so badly, I'll give it to you—for the rest of the month." Mr. Parton crosses his arms, clearly expecting me to rush out an apology. "How does that sound?"

When will he learn I'm not like other kids?

"Mr. Parton," I say, picking a fleck of black nail polish from my index finger. "Have you noticed you're the one being disruptive, wasting everyone's time? You offered detention. I accepted. Can we move on, please?"

Rage detonates in his eyes as a chorus of "Oooh" and "Aaah" rings out.

"That's it! I want you gone." He closes the distance to slap his hands against the sides of my desk. The metal legs vibrate. If he doesn't learn to control his stress levels, that vein in his forehead is going to burst. "You are nothing but a nuisance. At this rate, you're going to fail my class. Probably *all* your classes."

If I hadn't taught myself to shut down emotionally, I might have erupted just then. He's not supposed to discuss my private business with others. But all I feel is more nothingness. "You're wrong about my grades," I inform him. "I'm passing every class...that has a decent teacher."

He jerks a finger toward the door. "Get out of my classroom. Go straight to Principal Hatcher's office. Do not talk to anyone along the way. Do not stop in the bathroom."

Tomb-like silence slithers through the room.

"May I collect two hundred dollars for passing Go?" I say as I bend down to retrieve my books and bag from the floor.

"Out!"

"Happy to go just as soon as you write me a note."

His nostrils flare before he stomps to his desk, scribbles something and throws a piece of paper at my feet.

I may be indifferent, but I'm not stupid. This is a power play. One of many. Mr. Parton has always enjoyed taking his frustrations out on his students. If he spills coffee on his shirt, we get a quiz. If he locks his keys in his car, we get ten pages of homework.

I remain beside my desk, stiff as a board. I will not pick up that paper.

On my sixteenth birthday, my dad gifted me with two of my mother's journals. One she'd written before her marriage, the other she'd written after. I've read every precious word more times than I can count. One of my favorite passages plays through my mind.

If I don't stand up for myself, I will fall. I must be strong, and I must be brave. I must be me. If I fall, how will I ever have the strength to carry my little girl when she needs me most?

At one time she was the head cheerleader, a position she lost when she got pregnant with me. My dad, the football star, had knocked her up.

As soon as she hit her second trimester, she was kicked off the cheer squad. Kids called her a slut and a whore, and she lost many friends.

Although I suppose they weren't really friends. Arguably not even people worth knowing.

I wish I could read Mom's other journals and discover more pearls of wisdom from her, but my dad said the rest were lost when we moved out of my childhood home and into the one we now share with Fiona.

"Miss Leighton!" Mr. Parton's voice yanks me from my thoughts. "Pick up the pace. The sooner you're gone, the sooner the rest of the class can enjoy the lesson."

I stand and adjust the strap of my bag on my shoulder. "I don't think you have to worry about anyone enjoying it."

I don't mean the words as a taunt but a simple truth. Still, students laugh.

He closes in on me once again, and he looks ready to snap—my neck, that is. I remain in place, forcing him to peer up at me. At five-ten, I'm two inches taller than Mr. Parton.

When he realizes I can't be intimidated, he balls his fists. "Don't you dare come back in here. You do, and you'll be punished. Do you understand me?"

"Of course. Your lectures are always punishment." I step past him, past the paper he threw, and nod goodbye to Linnie as I stroll into the hall.

Chapter 2

Sometimes you have to see yourself through someone else's eyes in order to see the real you.

—*Miranda Leighton*
(formerly *Miranda Beers*)

The next morning, I walk to school, as usual. My dad bought me a car, oh, about a year ago, but I refused to drive it so he finally sold it. I'm not afraid of cars, per se, but I'm not eager to sit behind the wheel of one either, responsible for the life of everyone on the road.

I'm proactive, I guess. And I'm early again—as usual. I spot Mercedes's car in the lot. Hard to miss it, considering it's the only one here. She's slumped over the wheel, her body heaving as if she's sobbing.

Well. That's new. Nadine must have given her crap again. As a kid, when someone hurt her, Mercedes always waited until she was alone with me before she broke down. I calmed and defended her and, in return, she adored me. Now I perch under a tree, hidden in the shade, and watch her. Would other people feel sorry for her? Maybe wonder just how deep her internal wounds run?

I can hear my therapist: *Wounded animals lash out. This girl...her pain...it has made her an animal.*

I can even hear my response: *Are you talking about Mercedes, Dr. Miller, or me?*

Why can't I talk about you both, Miss Leighton?

I don't care if she's wounded. If she insults my friends today, I won't go easy on her.

By the time the first car arrives, Mercedes has calmed and righted her makeup. She looks as perfect and snotty as always, and the transformation stuns me. I'd swear there are two Mercedes: Miss Vulnerable and Her Majesty the Witch of Hathaway High.

I stay put until Kimberly, Linnie and Robb emerge from a rusty sedan.

The rough, tough Kimberly is wearing a ripped black T-shirt with a matching tank underneath. And matching skinny jeans, I guess, since they are equally ripped. Those jeans might get her sent home for violating the school's dress code. Not that she'll care. The dark color complements her golden skin while the harshness of her clothing presents the perfect contrast to her fine-boned features. A metal belt circles her waist, a shiny silver skull and crossbones in the center. Rings decorate each of her fingers, and bracelets clink together on her wrists.

Redheaded, freckled Linnie looks like a doll in a black shirt covered in ribbons and bows, a ruffled black skirt and a pair of lacy black hose. Her makeup is thick, giving her long-lashed Barbie eyes and bloodred heart-shaped lips and adding color to her porcelain skin. Her hair is anchored in twin pigtails with big, sweeping curls.

Robb is tall and thin, with brown skin, black hair, and eyes a shade in between. He's the only one wearing colors, and they look good on him. His hair is tipped in neon green, and his pants are red-and-black plaid. And yes, the rest of him is draped in black.

Some people consider us "typical Goth." Those same people think we worship Satan (no thanks), cut ourselves (ouch) or cast black magic spells (I'm fresh out of magic).

Kimberly is rocking out to a song on her iPhone. In junior high, music brought her, Linnie and Robb together. My tastes are different. I prefer classical music. They love me, anyway.

Linnie is chewing gum while typing fast as lightning on her phone, and Robb is picking up a book some girl dropped. The girl doesn't thank him; she rushes off, her gaze darting around the parking lot, and it's clear she hopes no one witnessed her interaction with the Goth boy.

Next time I see her, I'm going to hurt her. Robb is one of the kindest people I know. He runs the website for a local food bank, free of charge. If ever he drives past a homeless person, he stops at the nearest gas station to buy the person whatever food and water he can afford. He rescues stray dogs and cats, too!

He cares about the world around him and the people populating it. And some girl at our school looks at him as if he's garbage?

My blood begins to boil. My hands curl into fists.

Inhale, exhale. Again. In, out. I shove, punch and kick the rage deep, deep inside a hidden corner of my heart where I've buried a thousand other emotions. My blood cools, and my hands uncurl. Out of sight, out of mind.

No emotions, no problems.

I suspect Robb will die in his sixties. He'll get so

wrapped up in a video game—because yes, the addiction is strong in this one—that he'll forget to eat. Oh! Or maybe he'll marry a guy totally devoted to him who remembers to feed him. Aww. I'm enamored of their relationship already.

I notice a group of kids snickering as they draw closer to my friends. One of the kids even withdraws a key—to add another scratch to Linnie's rust bucket of a car? Not on my watch.

Their deaths: by my fists if they aren't careful.

My friends haven't noticed me yet. That changes when I step in front of Keys and cant my head to the side. That's it, that's all I do. He loses his smile, and the rest of his group goes quiet.

If he wants to take a swing at me, fine. Go for it. He won't emerge unscathed.

"Move along," I command. "Now. Before I treat your face like you planned to treat her car."

He hesitates. Then one of his friends tugs on his shirt, and the group steps back. I think I hear one of them say, "They aren't worth it." *Then* they scramble away.

My reputation precedes me. "*You* aren't worth *anything*," I call.

Linnie bumps my shoulder, one of her bows tickling my skin. "You weigh...what? A buck two? Yet you can scare a boy who weighs three hundred pounds."

Robb pats the top of her head and offers her a sad smile. His smiles are *always* sad, and I don't know why. I've never asked, and he's never volunteered the info. "Look at the pretty, trying to math," he says. "You, my dear, would have better luck growing a tail."

"Why add a tail to perfection?" She spreads her arms wide and twirls. "I'm *amazing*!" She's also high as a kite, her pupils the size of saucers.

"No, you're embarrassing." Kimberly is the mother hen of the group, always trying to keep her chicks in line. She flips her long, dark ponytail over her shoulder and studies me. "Sadly, you look as cheery as usual. Meaning not at all. Inform your face you're with friends."

I take no offense. She believes in honesty at all costs.

From what little she's admitted about her past, I know her life has been rougher and tougher than most. She never knew her dad and lost her mom early on. For nearly ten years, she bounced between foster homes, some good, some really, really bad. At thirteen, she moved in with her aunt, where she's lived ever since.

"Don't listen to her." Linnie gives my shoulder another bump. "You look tragic but beautiful."

Tragic? Really? I'd use the word to describe *her*.

Sometimes, when I peer deep enough, I see past her smile to the injured girl within. Not that I know *why* she's injured or why she does some of the things she does. Again, I've never asked. Perhaps she lacks affection at home? She's the richest girl at Hathaway High and lacks for nothing monetarily.

For her sixteenth birthday, her parents gave her an Aston Martin. Has she driven it even once? Nope. She worked at a movie theater for a year and used her own money to buy the Rust Bucket.

Every so often the plump redhead sleeps with a boy who shows interest in her, even though she suspects he's pretending. The next day he calls her terrible names as if she made a mistake but he's a god for nailing her.

Riddle me this. Who cares more about his reputation than another person's feelings, and sucks in bed? An asshole.

Linnie is wonderful. If I wanted to love, she would be first in line. I just wish I could protect her from idiot boys. She's always cut to the core by the rejection—which makes her even more vulnerable to anyone who hopes to use her. It's a vicious cycle.

My hands are curling into fists again. Inhale, exhale. *Good, that's good.* I relax.

What's wrong with me today, anyway?

"Lin's right. You're beautiful just the way you are," Robb says, and gives me a hug.

I go stiff. It's an automatic reaction, one I can't stop. Any display of affection makes me uncomfortable—makes me *want* to feel. I don't want to want to feel. According to Dr. Miller, someday I'll have to deal with all the rage and pain I've buried, all the agony and anguish, before I can get even a glimmer of happiness.

I step from Robb's embrace as a cold sweat beads over my forehead. His shoulders roll in. He stares down at his feet. Ugh. I've hurt the nicest person in the world. I suck. It's just… I don't want to get attached to him, or to anyone. I don't *let* myself get attached. People are gonna die. It's a simple fact of life. If you don't get attached, you don't have to mourn.

Apologizing to him won't do a bit of good, though. Words don't mean jack if you have no intention of changing.

I'll make it up to Robb some other way.

"Guess what?" Linnie drops her cell phone in her bag—a bag that resembles a corset—and heads to the front doors, forcing us to follow or be left behind. "I hear we're getting a new student today."

"Boy or girl?" Robb asks, intrigued.

"Boy," Linnie wiggles her brows. "A *cute* boy."

Interest gleams in Kimberly's dark eyes. A confusing reaction. New kids always consider us trouble at glance one, then do their best to avoid us as if we're carriers of the plague. I'm never bothered by it, but these three always feel rejected.

Shouldn't they *dread* meeting New Guy rather than hoping for the best? I never look forward to the future. I don't want to set myself up for disappointment.

See? This is one of the reasons I don't want to embrace my emotions. How do people navigate such a complicated maze?

Once we're inside, I split from the group with a wave. Our lockers are on opposite sides of the building.

Kimberly waves back, and Robb nods. He still won't meet my gaze.

Linnie calls, "See you at lunch, Jade." She never stops trying to include me.

A small ache erupts in my temples, and I cringe. The closer I get to my locker, the more intense the ache becomes. To be honest, my brain has gotten used to hurting from 7:30 to 8:30, during Mr. Parton's class.

Conditioning is real, no ifs, ands or buts about it.

At my locker, I empty my bag of every book but my mom's journal. For the next two weeks, I get to skip trig and spend the morning in Principal Hatcher's office.

According to Mr. Parton, who called my dad yesterday after school, detention wasn't enough of a punishment for me. They put their heads together and came up with this added "punishment."

My dad forced me to write an apology note for my behavior…only to toss it in the garbage after he'd read it.

> I'm sorry you play favorites, Mr. Parton, treat some students better than others. I'm sorry you see no value in people who are different than you.

"Anyone ever tell you that you have a major attitude problem?" Mercedes says as she sidles up to me.

"Almost everyone I meet. Thanks for noticing." I shut the locker and face her. The roses in her cheeks are the same shade as the roses printed on her dress. "May I suggest you take care of your business and I'll take care of mine?"

"I rest my case. At-ti-tude."

"What, you want to be a lawyer now?" When we were little, she wanted to be a princess. "Why does it matter, anyway? And why are you here, bugging me? I prefer the days we avoid each other."

She scowls at me. Voice whisper-soft, she says, "I saw you this morning, and I know you saw me."

"So?"

"So!" Her screech echoes through the hall.

People glance our way, and she withers, only to straighten her spine and glare at them. They quicken their pace, soon disappearing around a corner.

"If you tell anyone you saw me crying," she says, whispering again, "I'll… I'll…"

I roll my eyes. "You'll…you'll…what? Call me a bad name? Have your mom call my dad?" I pretend to shudder. "No, not that. Anything but that."

"You are *so* annoying. You accused Charlee of being a fraud. Hey, pot, have you met kettle?"

Is she serious? "I don't pretend to be something I'm not."

Her lips curl up in a grin completely devoid of humor. "You want everyone to think you don't care about anything or anyone—"

"I *don't* care," I interject.

"—but you forget our parents forced me to attend several family therapy sessions with you. According to Dr. Miller, the real Jade cares *too much*. About *everything*. With enough pressure, her armor *will* crack. Something we should avoid. We should coax her out instead. Ringing any bells?"

A cold sweat pops out on my forehead once again. "Don't push me, Mercedes."

"Don't antagonize me, Jade."

"Antagonize," I say. "That's a big word for such a tiny girl."

She offers me another grin—this one feral—before flouncing off. I trail after her; I don't know why. Or maybe I do? My hands are curled again. I just might punch her.

I turn the corner, only to lose sight of her and come upon Bobby Bay, her on-again/off-again boyfriend. Inhale, exhale. *Focus.* I bet Bobby dies of alcohol poisoning one day soon.

All right. I'm back to the old me. Mercedes doesn't matter. She means *nothing* to me.

My armor can't be cracked. I don't feel pressured about, well, anything.

Bobby is surrounded by other jocks on the football team. Some of those boys have been nice to my friends and me. Others have been as cruel as Mercedes and Charlee Ann.

"Heya, Jade. Wanna get laid by a real man?" Bobby leers at me in typical Bobby fashion. "Or are you still a lesbian?"

Or maybe someone stabs him.

Ever since I declined his offer of "pleasure beyond my wildest imagination," he's told everyone I must be gay. Because why else would I deny a stud like him? "No," I say, and tap my chin with a fingernail, pretending to ponder a conundrum. "Maybe I should be, since I still don't like dicks."

One boy laughs and slaps Bobby on the shoulder. Another boy snickers and elbows him in the stomach.

Bobby stops leering and starts glaring, a promise of retribution in his eyes. *Try. Please.*

I trek forward, turn another corner and enter a new hallway. Littering the walls are posters that read VOTE FOR MERCEDES, STUDENT BODY PRESIDENT. Her ultraperfect face smiles down at me.

She'll win, of course, and even more girls will try to emulate her. Sadly, no one will be the better for it.

Maybe I should run against her?

Nah. I'm just as bad as Mercedes. Love and nurture aren't in my wheelhouse.

Ready to get the day over with, I quicken my step, the loud *clump-clump* of my boots echoing despite the chatter around me. Kids purposely step aside to avoid me.

When I reach Principal Hatcher's office, her secretary waves me over. *She's* happy to see me at least.

"Jadey Jade Jade. Over here." Her name is Martha Stewart, I kid you not. She has curly gray hair, round cheeks, more freckles than Linnie and a plump figure. Basically, she's the living incarnation of Mrs. Claus, and I'm pretty sure she's immortal. "What am I going to do with you, my girl?"

"How about you bring me martinis while I read something inappropriate for school?" I say, easing into the chair next to her desk. I've never had a martini, but I like the idea of having one at school.

"Ha! Something like *1001 Ways to Die*?" She pats my hand. "I've always liked your sharp tongue. I've always liked you, period."

The lobby is big, separated from the hall of offices by a long yellow counter. There are three desks and a handful of chairs scattered about. Computers are up and running, other machines humming and beeping. In one of the offices in back, a phone is ringing. The walls are covered with red-and-blue banners, our school colors.

They read HOME OF THE FIGHTING TROJANS.

Kids from other schools often tease us about being named after condoms. They call us the Wad Squad and say we're "stiff competition," "all nuts," and tell us we should be careful so we don't blow our defensive line.

Our motto? We'll Go All the Way!

I skip my gaze over Mrs. Tsurugi's desk. The vice principal's assistant has yet to arrive. She's probably out in the halls tormenting— Whoa! My gaze zooms right back and snags on a boy who is sitting beside the desk. I don't recognize him. He must be the new kid Linnie mentioned.

She called him cute. She was wrong. Very, very wrong. He is really, *really* hot. Like, on-fire hot. I know this because I have eyes.

His hair is messy and dark, and his features appear chiseled from stone. Dark bronzed skin illuminates a heavy-lidded azure gaze. His shoulders are broad. A plain gray T-shirt hugs his biceps. His *bulging* biceps. Is he packing rocks under there?

He has so many muscles I bet he could survive an apocalypse. Or, you know, *anything*.

Between one second and the next, I'm exhibiting all the classic symptoms of a panic attack, or maybe a crush. My cheeks flush, my heart rate speeds up and my stomach churns.

Definitely a panic attack...even though I'm not usually—or ever—prone to bouts of worry.

I want to ignore him. I *should* ignore him. My brain doesn't get the memo. I gawk instead. He's a magnet for my gaze.

He's not just hot, I decide. He's beautiful in a raw, rough-and-tumble kind of way.

Bet he's a dumb jock. Does he play football? Basketball?

What are you doing? How many times have I complained about being judged for my looks? I shouldn't do the same thing to someone else. For all I know, this boy is sports inclined *and* whip smart.

He's definitely perceptive. As if sensing my scrutiny, he turns his head. Our gazes meet, and my heart rate accelerates once again. This time my palms begin to sweat.

His expression is somber…until he gives me a slow once-over. Then he grins, revealing straight white teeth, and my stomach churns harder.

I'm not sure what that ear-to-ear grin means. I have, like, zero experience with boys. Well, other than Robb, but he's a friend, and this guy isn't. Yet. Maybe he'd like to be?

I try to put myself in his place. A new kid in a new school after senior year has already kicked off. His entire life has probably been turned upside down and inside out. That's sad, right?

Besides, I need to treat him like I'd treat anyone else and prove I'm absolutely, positively *not* crushing.

"Who's the boy?" I ask Martha. I don't have to whisper. My screwed-up voice is low and raspy, always quiet.

She doesn't look up from her computer screen, her fingers pecking at her keyboard, but she grows stiff, tension radiating from her. Why? "He's new. A senior like you."

I wait for her to say more. Instead, she continues type, type, typing away.

Martha likes everyone, but she clearly has a problem with this boy. She must know something about him. Something she found in his file? "I'm going to talk with him," I say.

She stops at last, peering at me, her expression all *I am the wise wizard, and you are the scarecrow without a brain.*

For my ears alone, she says, "Do yourself a favor and avoid him."

"Why?"

She purses her lips as if she's just sucked on a lemon. "Because."

I wait for her to say more. She doesn't. "I'm going to talk with him," I repeat.

"He's a brawler, all right?" she rushes out. "He settles arguments with his fists."

My brow furrows. "Is that all?"

"All?" she squeaks. "Jade, he put a boy in the hospital."

"Which is where I'll put *him* if he makes a move against me." Amid her protests, I stand and close the distance. He watches me with a ruthless intensity that almost…unnerves me.

Shove, kick and bury emotion.

"Hello," I say, and ease into Mrs. Tsurugi's seat. "It's nice to meet you."

Brawler Boy blinks as if my boldness surprises him. "Hey." His voice is deep and strong, but also husky. He leans back in the chair, stretching out his jean-clad legs—his very long legs. The corners of his lips twitch, as if he's about to grin again, but a new one never blooms. "Nice to meet you, too. But why are you still whispering?"

"I'm not. Well, not on purpose." Out of habit, I rub the scars on my collarbone. "When I was a little girl, my vocal cords were permanently damaged."

All hint of amusement drains from him, and he shifts closer to me. "I'm sorry."

"Why? You asked a question, I answered."

The next look he gives me…it hovers somewhere between *She's a bug under a microscope* and *She's a blue-ribbon pie at the state fair.* Silence envelops us. When he rubs two fingers over the dark shadow of stubble on his jaw, I notice bruises on his knuckles.

What do boys and girls normally talk about? "So... what's your name?" My head tilts when I spot the edge of a tattoo peeking out from his shirtsleeve. The bottom of a heart, maybe. My first tattoo was a heart. One of my mother's drawings actually. Robb used one of the doodles in her journal as an outline.

"I'm Clarik."

Interesting. "Spelled *C-L-E-R-I-C*? As in, a religious leader?"

"Spelled *C-L-A-R-I-K*. As in, my grandmother's name was Claire, and my mother wanted to name me after her but she could think of no other way to masculinize it."

"I'm Jade."

"Jade, as in a combination of nephrite and jadeite, sometimes referred to as a symbol of heaven?"

He teases, but... "Yes. Jade, as in my dead mother's birthstone." I motion to the piece of paper folded in his hand. "Is that your class schedule?"

"Yes." He peers at me for a long while, the somberness back full force. Ignoring my question, he says, "I'm sorry about your mother."

"Why? You didn't kill her."

Blink, blink. "I'm rarely at a loss for words, but I have no idea how to respond to you right now."

An effect I have on everyone at some point or another. "You can start by telling me your class schedule. Who'd you get?"

First warning bell rings, and within seconds, the hallway clears of students. I don't have to look out the glass wall to know. Footsteps and chatter end. Lockers are no longer being slammed shut. Even the air around us changes, no longer clogged with clashing perfumes and colognes.

Clarik shrugs. "In order—Parton, Harper, Norfield, Reynolds, Frandemier and Busby."

"We have Parton and Norfield at the same time. Though I won't be attending Parton's class for the next two weeks. I'm being punished."

He leans back, anchoring his elbows on the top of his chair. "Any advice for me?"

I don't have to think long and hard about my answer. "Yes. Follow my lead and get in trouble so that you can miss as much of Parton's class as possible."

He chuckles, and the throaty sound washes over me. But as quickly as his amusement began, it fades, and he frowns. Then he scowls as if he's actually angry with me.

Why fight his laughter? Why blame me for it?

And he thinks *I'm* the odd one?

"Parton is an as—jerk, is he?" he finally asks.

"Asjerk?" I nod even as I wonder why he stopped himself from cursing. My ears are far from innocent. Maybe he's a closet gentleman and he considers me a lady. Totally plausible. Fiona would be over the moon. "Yes, yes, a thousand times yes—Parton is the biggest asjerk I've ever met."

"What'd you do to get exiled to the office?"

Besides doing what every self-help book I've ever read

advises and just being myself? "I offered him an unsolicited critique of his teaching skills."

His eyes twinkle as he says, "Feel free to give me an unsolicited critique *any*time."

"I don't know what that means."

He does that blinking thing and even laughs. His entire face lights up when he laughs.

Never, ever, never, *never* should he fight his laughter again.

"Clarik Iverson." Martha's voice reverberates through the room, and so does her disapproval. "Your guide is here."

A conflicting mix of disappointment and relief flashes over his rugged face, confusing me.

Martha says, "Principal Hatcher selected Mercedes because she lives in your neighborhood, so you be nice to her, you hear?"

Is she talking about *my* Mercedes? There are four at school.

Clarik stands and faces the girl who is waiting in the open doorway. I do the same. Yep. My Mercedes. If Clarik lives in her neighborhood, that means he lives in my neighborhood, too. Which isn't as much of a coincidence as it seems. Small school district, few neighborhoods.

Why wasn't *I* chosen as his guide? (1) I've been banned from Mr. Parton's classroom, which means (2) my morning is wide-open.

Doesn't take me long to puzzle out the answer. I mean, this isn't exactly a head-scratcher. Principal Hatcher doesn't want a member of the troublemaker clique to recruit anyone else.

In her pretty pink dress, Mercedes is as gorgeous as ever and sure to mesmerize. Her blond hair floats around her delicate shoulders, making her the picture of perfection and innocence.

Well. There goes any budding friendship Clarik and I may or may not have had. Mercedes will tell him to hate me, and he'll obey her because he'll be clouded by a fog of teen-boy lust.

Do you care?

No. No, of course not. Not really. Or at all. We're basically strangers. And it isn't like I took one look at him, fell in love, decided to marry him and have a million babies. I'm not that girl.

My attention returns to Clarik, who is looking at—No way. He's looking at me with what might be… affection? "It was nice meeting you, Jade."

Yeah, yeah, yeah. "Don't be too sure about that."

He smiles at me. "I'm already certain."

I can think of nothing to add, so I nod. For the first time in…ever? Someone has actually shocked me. He hung back to tell me goodbye rather than rushing off to meet Mercedes.

He might be a brawler, but he's also kind, and he's polite. I like him.

As he moves around the desk and heads for Mercedes, her eyes widen.

A pink flush stains her cheeks. "*You're* Clarik?"

"I am," he says.

I can almost *hear* her heartbeat, and it sounds a little

something like *Hubba, hubba. Hubba, hubba.* A word my stepmother uses to describe my dad. Great! Now I've grossed myself out.

"Well, slap my head and call me silly." Mercedes curls a silky lock around her finger, all coyness and charm. "I've got to be the luckiest girl here."

Ugh. Not the Southern accent. Her biggest tell. She's attracted to him, and Bobby is nothing but a memory.

She flashes me a *hands-off* glare before linking her arm with Clarik's. "Come on, cutie. We need to get you out of this office before you're contaminated by the trash."

The doors close behind them, cutting off his reply. Then they turn the corner, and suddenly they are out of view.

I drag my feet back to Martha's desk, wondering if Clarik will fall under Mercedes's spell like everyone else...if they'll start dating, becoming the new "it" couple...if I will be forced to watch them make out in the halls...

A tremor slides down my spine, and a slow burn spreads through my chest. My hands fist. Whoa. Hold up. I'm upset about a boy I just met dating a girl I don't like? That makes *zero* sense.

Martha pats the top of my hand. "You're better off, hon. That boy is pure trouble. He was kicked out of two schools for fighting. We're his last chance."

I can't believe I have to remind her of this, but here goes. "We don't know the whole story. The students could have provoked him."

"Do we *need* to know the whole story? Bottom line, he has a temper he can't control."

“Maybe he was protecting others from bullies. Maybe he stopped a crime from occurring.” Hey. It’s possible.

She twitters under her breath, and I think I detect the words “fool girls” and “bad boys,” before she sighs and type, type, types, ignoring me.

My curiosity about Clarik grows by leaps and bounds… until I bury it just like everything else, lock up my heart and return to my default setting.

Numb.

Chapter 3

You can't hide from pain.
One way or another, it always finds you.

—Miranda Leighton

Turns out, avoiding Clarik is the key to my continued calm. I make it through two classes without a hitch. Out of sight, out of mind. However, when I spot him at lunch, sitting next to Mercedes, I backslide. Anger sparks to life once again.

Inhale, exhale. Once I focus on my friends, the spark dies and all is well. With me at least. One of the boys Linnie slept with not too long ago snickers as he accidentally-on-purpose knocks over her tray, sending her running from the cafeteria, sobbing.

When I purposely-on-purpose knock over *his* tray, he actually fronts on me as if he's going to coldcock me. *Go ahead. Try.* I've taken self-defense classes. I can take a punch. Better yet, I can *throw* a punch.

A few years ago, my therapist recommended I sign up for some type of physical exercise that involved other people, possible new friends. My options were limited. Rock climbing, tandem biking, rowing or self-defense courses. I chose self-defense, and I'm quite good.

Robb and Kimberly step up to my side, acting as

backup. Robb eschews violence, but he will go to the mat for his girls. Kimberly will fight anyone, anytime, and doesn't even need a reason.

The boy fronts on my friends, too, only to pale and back away. Then he turns and runs, taking the same path as Linnie.

I turn, wondering what changed—and find Clarik. He's standing behind me.

So Linnie's former hookup wasn't afraid of my crew but nearly peed his pants at the sight of our new bruiser?

"You guys okay?" Clarik asks.

Robb stammers incoherently, his cheeks flushing. Finally he ducks his head and scampers away as if he's too flustered to deal. Kimberly flicks me an *I've got this* look before following him.

I so get his turmoil. My heart rate speeds up, making me wonder if I'm crushing again, or nervous. "We're, uh, fine. Thanks."

"Did I do something wrong?"

"Nope. He's shy, and you're cute, so..." I hike my shoulders in a shrug.

Clarik goes still. "You think I'm cute?"

"Yes, but only because I have eyes. And get real. Like you don't know every girl in this school has to wipe away drool whenever you walk by."

"Do you? I mean, you're a girl. And you go to this school. So..."

"Don't get too excited. I drool over leather-bound notebooks, too." Notebooks, journals and diaries with a cool design are my one obsession. "All right. Goodbye." I motor off without another word.

Out of sight, out of mind.

"That was brutal, man," Kimberly says when I catch up.

"Those eyes." Robb is wide-eyed and shell-shocked. "He looked at me with those eyes, and I forgot how to breathe."

"Trust me," I mutter. "I know the feeling."

We forgo lunch, using the time to track down and soothe Linnie. She's hiding in the band room, sitting in a shadowed corner, her knees drawn up to her chest. There are pink tear tracks on her cheeks.

"Why are people so cruel?" she says between ragged breaths. "What's wrong with me? Why does no one like me?"

"There is *nothing* wrong with you. And there are people who *love* you. I know, because I'm one of them. I will be here for you always." Robb eases beside her, takes her hand and kisses her knuckles. "Those boys…their rejection…it doesn't speak of *your* worth but *theirs.* And guess what? They aren't worth a moment of your time."

Kimberly sits on her other side. For once, the gruff, tough scrapper has a soft expression. "There are always going to be people who look at us and decide we're weird. As if weird is a bad thing! Average people have average lives. Extraordinary dreamers like us? We live, what? Say it with me. *Extraordinary* lives."

These two are dropping wisdom like it's hot, and pang after pang is cutting through my chest, cracking my armor. Different emotions attempt to break free of the hidden pile in my heart.

Robb catches my gaze and motions me over. "Come on, Jade. Get in on this."

I have to go. I have to go *now.*

I race from the room, his sadness boring holes in my back. I don't want to hurt him. I don't want to hurt any of my friends. But let's be real. I'm not needed, and they are better off without me. I tend to sprinkle a whole lot of awkward on any emotional situation.

Though I'm tempted to walk home early to avoid… well, everyone and everything, I stick it out for the day. I manage to steer clear of my friends, and I don't see Clarik again until our shared class. Good news! I barely react to his presence…or the fact that he smells like the sweetest summer rain.

He doesn't glance my way—before, during or after—and I'm glad. *Super*glad. Really.

As soon as the bell rings, he's out the door. On my way to detention, however, I run into my friends, and there's no avoiding them. They are camped out in front of my locker, discussing a rock concert they plan to attend over the weekend.

Last weekend they spent the night in a cemetery, taking and posting pictures. For the first time in…ever, I almost joined them for an after-school activity.

"You wanna go to the concert, Jade?" Linnie asks, sounding hopeful. She doesn't mention my lunchtime disappearance, but then she's gotten used to my swift getaways.

"Of course she doesn't," Kimberly grumbles at the same time I say, "No, thanks." Crowds and loud noises aren't my thing. I prefer quiet, peaceful nights.

Kimberly tosses her arms up. "Told you!"

Robb is quiet and doesn't even glance in my direction.

Pang. "I've got to get to detention," I say, storing my books and making my exit.

Detention takes place in an underclassman room, and there are only four other students present. I spend the allotted hour introspecting—a rare activity for me.

Will there come a point when Robb, Linnie and Kimberly wash their hands of me?

And why did Clarik not want to laugh this morning? Why did he tense up around me? That's odd, right? Unless he hates emotion, like me—which is totally possible and perhaps a means of controlling his temper.

But that raises another question. What do I make him feel? Besides amusement, I mean.

Argh! This has to stop.

After detention, I stalk outside, ready to walk home and shut myself in my room. The sun is bright—too bright—the air too hot for early November. Cotton-ball clouds fill a baby blue sky.

The parking lot should be empty, but cheerleaders and football players are climbing into their cars. Practice must have ended prematurely.

For the sake of time and energy, I avoid everyone... until a pearl-white Mercedes squeals to an abrupt stop in front of me. The girl Mercedes is perched behind the wheel. Yes, Mercedes drives a Mercedes. Yes, it's as cheesy and ridiculous as it sounds.

She rolls down the window and snaps, "You want a ride or what?"

So she can grill me about whether or not I told anyone I saw her crying? "I'd rather walk."

"Suit yourself." She's about to pull away when Bobby throws open the passenger door and slides inside the car.

He leans over to press a kiss into her cheek. "What's this I hear about you breaking up with me?" His tone softens, surprising me as he says, "You know we belong together, babe."

"Actually, I know I belong with a guy who adores me," she says in a singsong voice. "That's not you."

Has she finally wised up? Good for her. I don't like her—might even hate her if I bothered to feel anything—but I don't want anyone else messing with her. Her misery is *mine* to dish. "If you belong together," I say, "why can't you keep little Bobby in your pants, eh?"

A vein throbs in his forehead. "Stop trying to hurt Mercedes with your lies. She deserves better."

"She doesn't deserve the STD you'll surely give her." I bat my lashes innocently. "They don't call you Bay the Lay and Bob Has a Sore on His Corncob for nothing, *amirite*?"

I think that vein in his forehead bursts. His face turns beet red, and he reaches for the door handle as if he has every intention of crossing the distance and raging. *Bring it.*

Mercedes says, "Let's get out of here and talk in private." She flips me off and peels out.

Whatever. I resume my walk, sticking to the shadows as best I can, just in case Clarik lives in one of the houses I pass. I don't want to see him, because I do, in fact, want to see him.

At home, I'm able to relax my guard at last. I'm not the biggest fan of the interior, the walls and rugs a little too colorful for my taste—blue and pink here, yellow and green there—but I never complain. I'd hurt Fiona's feelings, and I do *not* want to hurt Fiona's feelings. She's a snot-crier. Her entire body heaves, her eyes swell and her skin turns red and blotchy. Tears rain down her cheeks, and her nose pours.

Apparently decorating is her "specialty," meaning she has taste and I don't. She stages homes for local real-estate agents. That's how she and my dad met, anyway. Dad was desperate to sell my childhood home, but the agent struggled to close a deal and called Fiona, who came over to assess the layout. She and my dad hit it off right away and married soon after.

I find Fiona in the kitchen, cooking dinner. Spotting me, she offers the semblance of a smile. "Hello, Jade."

"Hello." Anytime I wonder how and when she's going to die, I can't help but imagine my dad's reaction. Will he suffer a major breakdown or carry on as usual? With my mom and then Nadine, he had a few bad weeks but seemed to pick up the pieces quickly.

Steam rises from the chicken Fiona is shredding. I'm not sure what my dad sees in her. And I don't mean that in a cruel way. She's beautiful, and she's sweet. It's just… she looks nothing like my mother, who was short and curvy with pin-straight platinum-blond hair, just like mine. She looks nothing like Nadine, who could have passed for Mom's sister. Fiona is tall and slender with curly brown hair.

Well, usually slender. Right now she's six months pregnant and big as a house, and prettier because of it. She glows.

I sometimes wonder if my dad settled for her simply because she's the only person who could stand to be around me.

"How was your day?" she asks.

"Fine." When I say no more, disappointment flickers in her eyes. "What are you making?"

"Chicken and mushroom casserole."

My dad's favorite. My nightmare. Mushrooms are fungus, and I would rather eat toenails.

"Don't worry," she adds. "I'm making a second dish for you. Chicken casserole, no mushrooms."

Pang. Great! Now I have to be on guard at home, too? "I'm not really hungry," I say with more force than I intend.

"Oh," she says, once again projecting disappointment. "All right."

Pang, pang. Inhale, exhale.

Giggles the cat winds around her ankles and purrs. Fiona rescued him before she married my dad. The feline never giggles, but I have to admit he seems suspiciously gleeful anytime he pushes food or fine china off the countertops. Whenever I try to pet him, he claws my hand as if I'm attempting bloody murder.

I like him.

Fiona, I'm not so sure about. She's not a bad person. Actually, she's really nice. She's just…not my mom.

Gasping, she presses her hands against her rounded belly. "Your sister is kicking up a fuss."

When I first found out about the pregnancy, I experienced a blip of excitement. Before the accident, I'd wanted a sibling more than anything else in the world. Then I looked up infant mortality rates and found out they were shockingly high.

Fact is, everyone in the world is going to die at some point. No need to get attached.

"I'm going to change and go for a run," I mutter, and shut myself in my bedroom. A "paradise" Fiona decorated for me as a gift. Pink walls. White covers, floral sheets. A vanity stenciled with roses.

I drop my bag by the door and step into my closet where I change into a grunge tank and too-short shorts and pull on tennis shoes. Running helps me clear my head.

As I head to the front door, Fiona calls, "I know you're not hungry, but I'd like you to join us for dinner. Half an hour."

"No, thanks." I'm out the door before she can comment.

I run on the shoulder of the street, and I swear I smell the sweet scent of pumpkin and spice. Every lawn I encounter is manicured, despite the late season, every house in the neighborhood old but cared for.

Which house belongs to Clarik?

Ugh. Why am I still thinking about him?

Mercedes lives around the corner…there…in one of the bigger two-stories. She's standing in the driveway, Charlee Ann with her, the two yelling at each other.

"—can't have both boys," Charlee Ann is grumbling. "You have to pick so the rest of us can have a shot at the other one."

Mercedes spots me and narrows her eyes. "Run along, freak. You aren't wanted here. Or anywhere!"

Charlee Ann whips around to face me. Her eyes narrow, too. "Trying to get healthy so you'll live longer? How unfortunate for the rest of the world."

Whatever. I maintain a steady pace as I round the cul-de-sac.

The girls are long gone by the time I return, circling the entire neighborhood a second time. The sun is setting on the horizon, the sky ablaze with pink, purple and gold. I should probably return home and—

An old beat-up truck pulls up behind me and slows to a crawl, driving in the same direction I'm running. I slow, too, as the passenger-side window rolls down. Is some creep about to offer me a ride? *Go ahead. Go for it.* I'll punch him in the throat and break his voice box so he won't be offering anyone anything for a while.

Clarik!

Avoid! Avoid! Run faster. Tell him to get lost. Something!

Too late. He rests his elbow on the window ledge, and my heart actually skips a beat. Hmm. I must have overexerted myself. "Hey," he says.

"Hey." There's no playing cool in this situation. I'm currently drenched in sweat, and it's not exactly my best look or even a top one hundred contender.

"I never would have pegged the girl with bone tattoos as a runner."

He never even glanced in my direction during Norfield's class either, yet he noticed my tattoos. Besides an entire skeleton etched along my spine, I have individual bones scattered over my arm, like puzzle pieces, hidden inside other images. Doesn't take a genius to figure out why I chose them to forever decorate my skin; they're an extension of my "death obsession."

"I run every chance I get," I finally say. In more ways than one.

"I prefer a treadmill."

"Because you don't want other people ogling your body? Makes sense." I motion to his massive biceps with a tilt of my chin. "You also work with weights. Obvi."

His lips do that thing I'm coming to like, quirking up at the corners. Then they fall. *That*, I don't like. "Are you trying to tell me I'm deliciously strong and manly?"

"Strong and manly, yes," I answer. He's teasing me, but is he maybe…kind of…flirting with me, too? I decide to give teasing him back a shot. "I'm into dark things, but cannibalism isn't one of them. If your very large muscles are delicious, I'd rather not know."

He laughs outright, thrilling me. "Do you like very large muscles on your guys, Jade Leighton?"

He knows my last name even though I didn't tell him. My heart skips another beat. How odd. I'm too young for any kind of murmur or valve problems. Frowning, I press two fingers into the base of my neck, gauging my pulse.

Okay, I'm *definitely* suffering from tachycardia—a term I learned while studying other ways my mom could have died if she'd survived the crash.

My dad found my list one day and showed my therapist. Dr. Miller says it's one of the ways I self-soothe. My brain's way of saying to my heart: *We were going to lose Mom at some point, anyway, so why mourn the tragedy of her passing?*

"I don't have any guys," I say. "I don't date."

His dark brows knit together. "Don't date…as in never?"

"Exactly. Never."

"By choice? Or because boys are afraid of you?"

"Both?" I reply.

He motions to the smaller house ahead and says, "This is me."

I remain beside the truck as he pulls into the driveway and parks. Because leaving would be rude. We're in the middle of a conversation, and I have manners…when I choose to have manners.

A man hops off the porch and approaches, making me think he's been waiting for Clarik's return. He's tall, with dark hair and a barrel chest. His face is rough and weathered, and he's somehow familiar to me. Clarik's dad? He's wearing a ragged T-shirt and paint-stained jeans.

"Well, well. Who do we got here?" he asks, smiling at me. It's a kind smile, as if he means it with every fiber of his being and he's not just being polite.

"Uncle Tag, this is Jade." Clarik motions in my direction. "She goes to Hathaway."

We shake hands. His grip is firm, his palm calloused.

"Did I overhear you two planning a date?" Tag asks.

"No," Clarik says, the denial rushing from his mouth at warp speed.

Okay, all right. He *wasn't* flirting with me.

Tag frowns at him. "Stop being rude to our guest. You have no evening plans this weekend, boy. Go out, get to know each other better. You could use a friend."

"Uncle Tag, stop," Clarik grates, shifting from one

booted foot to the other. "Please. You're making Jade uncomfortable."

"No, he's not," I say. "And yes. I'll go out with you this weekend."

Tag beams at me, and if he were a teacher, I'm pretty sure I would have just earned an A on my test.

Clarik is the one to frown this time. He studies me, silent, the waning sunlight glittering in his electric blues. For a brief, stolen moment—a few seconds? an eternity?—I'm unable to breathe.

I should probably visit a clinic and get checked out.

"We'll go to dinner on Sunday," he finally says and looks away.

Just like that, breath fills my lungs again. And just like that, Clarik begins to grow tenser by the second. The same kind of tension I noticed while we were in the office. He doesn't want to go out with me, but he's too sweet to hurt my feelings.

I bet he's crushing on someone else, and yeah, okay, I don't have to dig through too many mental files to figure out the witch's name. I should back out, let him off the hook…but I'm going to proceed full steam ahead. One, I'll be doing him a huge favor by keeping him away from Mercedes and the heartache she will surely dish, and two, I'm so freaking curious about him. Once I've figured him out, my fascination with him will fade.

He'll thank me later, I'm sure of it.

Tag slaps him on the back. "Good, good. Glad that's settled. Now, did you pick up my Cheetos?"

"Yes, sir." Clarik reaches into the truck and withdraws two bags of White Cheddar Cheetos Puffs.

"Thank you kindly, Clarie. You're a good boy." Tag slaps him on the shoulder again before nodding at me. "It was a pleasure to meet you, Jade." He walks away then, leaving us alone.

Clarie? Should I leave, too? What's typical boy/girl just-planned nondate date protocol?

Expression unreadable, Clarik says, "Sorry about that. Look, I'm going to be brutally honest with you. I'm not interested in dating anyone right now."

Anyone, or just me? "Are you not into Goth girls? You prefer normal girls?"

"I don't care about the Goth thing. I just care about the girl inside." His head tilts to the side, his study of me intensifying, making me squirm. "What is Goth, anyway? To you, I mean."

He isn't the first person to ask. "A state of being, I guess. I tend to embrace what other people abhor, things labeled as *freakish*. I see beauty in darkness." *And in you. I see beauty in you.* What does that say about him, though? That there's darkness in *him*? "I understand and accept that I'm headed for the grave, that we're *all* headed for the grave, one way or another, one day or another. I'm not afraid."

No one has ever watched me as intensely as Clarik is now, as if he's taking in every microexpression and any secrets I might be hiding beyond my eyes. He proves it when he says, "You say you are unafraid of dying, and for yourself, yes, I buy it. But not for others. Your gaze shifted when you spoke of others dying."

He's perceptive, but I already knew that. If I let myself, I could worry 24/7 about how everyone close to me will die, and when.

"Anyway," he says, letting me off the hook. "Whatever you are, I like it. You're hot. Beyond hot. But, as I was saying, I'm not interested in dating anyone right now. My ex-girlfriend…she… It doesn't matter. If you and I go out, it'll be as friends, only friends. So if you'd rather not spend time with me, I'll understand and—"

"I still want to go, and I promise I won't make a pass at you," I interject. I'm not sure I know *how* to make a pass. But I do know his admission has added fuel to the fire of my curiosity. "How long did you and…whatever her name is…date?" And how long has he lived with his uncle? Why doesn't he live with his parents? And most important, does he truly think I'm hot?

One question at a time.

"Her name is Kendra, and we were together most of junior year."

Wow. Talk about a serious commitment, especially for people so young. "Are you not over her or something?"

An invisible curtain seems to fall over his features, hiding his expression. "That isn't really your business, is it?"

The harshness of his tone would have zipped the lips of a normal person. I've never claimed to be normal. "I'll take that as a *No, Jade, I sob into my pillow every night and pray she'll beg me to take her back*. So how long have you been single?"

His eyes narrow, his lashes nearly fusing together. "A couple of months." The words are ragged, shoved out from between clenched teeth.

Hmm. Kimberly claims it can takes years to get over

a long-term relationship. If someone starts dating too soon, they "rebound." A term I've never understood in relation to couples, not in the negative sense it's implied. In basketball, a ball that bounces back after striking a hard surface is a good thing, right? A second chance to make a shot.

"Why did you guys break up?" I ask. *And who ended things?*

He stuffs his hands in his pockets and rocks back on his heels. Between one blink and the next, he lets go of his irritation, a twinkle appearing in his eyes. That twinkle is different from the glimmer, merrier.

Man, his mood changes lightning fast. While I fight my emotions, he welcomes his with open arms.

"For a girl who supposedly doesn't care about anything or anyone, you sure do ask a lot of questions."

Thanks, Mercedes. Rather than confirm or deny it, I say, "Please tell me you aren't one of those people who believes everything everyone tells you, and that you have a few brain cells working independently of the rumor mill."

"I'm not a fan of the rumor mill or all of its many employees, but I'm not blind. Let's be real. At times there's something almost...robotic about you."

I shrug. "So? Robots are cool." Truth is, I'd rather be robotic than deal with my pain, even if happiness is the ultimate prize. Pain is awful. It's heavy and soul crushing. It's draining. It's a seemingly never-ending pit of despair. Why fall when you can coast?

"You proved my point for me," Clarik says. "I just insulted you, but you're not even close to offended."

"You want me to be offended?"

"Answering a question with another question. Now you're deflecting."

My eyes go wide. Deflecting. Psychology speak for *You put the focus back on me, yo.* Or something like that. "You've gone to therapy."

He stiffens, gives me a curt nod.

"So have I," I admit, and he relaxes.

He scrubs a hand down his beautiful face. Beautiful, arresting and unforgettable. Are his looks the reason I'm so fascinated by him? Crap. I can't be as shallow as Mercedes and Charlee Ann. I'd rather die.

"Would you like a bottle of water?" he asks, changing the subject *without* answering my original question about the breakup.

"No, thanks." I've taken up enough of his time. "I should probably head home before my battery dies."

He barks out one of those amazing laughs, and my breath hitches in my throat.

Okay, I really do need to head home or I might start twirling my hair Mercedes-style, might even ask if I can pet his chest. "See you around, *Clarie*."

His smile widens. "Right back at you, *Jadie*."

There's a twinge in my chest as I jog away. There's also a white-hot burn in my shaking thighs. I must have pushed myself too hard today and consumed too little fuel. Or Clarik struck again and somehow ruined my hard-won composure.

Maybe I should I cancel our nondate date, after all. And really, the scales are unbalanced. I'm curious. He's not. I'm eager. Well, as eager as I'm capable of being. He's not. I'm attracted to him. He's hung up on his ex.

There. I admitted it. I *am* attracted to Clarik Iverson. Besides being a hottie with a body, he's open and honest and blunt. He intrigues me.

Forget him. Focus. I try. I really do. Out of sight, out of mind, right?

Nope. Wrong. This time distance fails me.

Ugh. I think I need to immerse myself in everything Clarik Iverson. Find out what I can, while I can, and build up an immunity to him.

That's a thing. *Right?*

Or maybe it's just the worst idea I've ever had.

At home, my dad is in the living room, splayed in his recliner, watching TV. As soon as the door closes behind me, however, he lifts the remote to push Pause. Focusing on me, he says, "You made Fiona cry."

"Lately she's *always* crying." But okay, okay. I was a little curt with her when I rejected her casserole. I could have handled the situation better. "I should have been nicer to her."

I try to walk past him, but he jumps to his feet to block me. He's several inches taller than me, though not as tall as Clarik. He's muscular—he works out—but again, he's not as muscular as Clarik.

Um, maybe I should stop comparing the two? Gross.

Dad looks nothing like me. Over the years, his dark hair has thinned and grayed and his skin has deepened to a dusky bronze. I'm freckled, he isn't. Lines branch across his forehead, around his eyes and bracket his mouth. They aren't laugh lines—he rarely laughs. The sun has simply taken a toll. He's worked outside, in construction, ever since his senior year of high school.

In my mother's postwedding journal, she wrote about his dream of becoming a money manager slash accountant, said he liked to call himself a premillionaire. Then I came along and every bit of his college savings was poured into the care and feeding of baby Jade. Or the Poop Machine, as Mom affectionately called me.

Anger tightens Dad's features. "Don't you want to know *how* you made Fiona cry?"

"I know how," I tell him.

Dad ignores me, saying, "Despite being fatigued by work and the baby, she cooked us a delicious dinner. Made a casserole just for you. You told her you weren't hungry *after* she'd gone to so much trouble. Then you failed to return in time to eat with us."

"I'll eat now." Even though I'm not hungry. I live on protein shakes; they keep my energy up without upsetting a stomach that's never hungry. But if it will soothe Fiona, I'll shovel in a few bites of my "special" casserole.

He gives me a clipped shake of his head. "You were supposed to eat *with* us."

"I'll make breakfast. We can eat together then."

Deciding to double down on his anger, he roars, "Tomorrow doesn't fix today!"

His frustration is a pulse against my skin, but inside, my numbness holds steady. Here and now, I feel like the robot Clarik accused me of being.

Dad knows I'm the way I am on purpose, and the knowledge keeps his stress level on constant simmer.

"You probably want me to apologize to her, right?" I ask. "Well, I can't—"

"No. I don't want you to apologize. You wouldn't mean it. You wouldn't change." He wilts. "You'd only make things worse."

The numbness begins to melt. I graze my thumb over the broken-heart tattoo on my wrist, taking strength from the simple action. "If it makes you feel any better, I don't like hurting her. Or you."

"It doesn't." He sighs. "I should be used to this…to you. I shouldn't take your slights personally. But I'm not, and I do. I've tried to understand you, Jade. I've tried to sympathize with you, pamper you, scold you, scream at you, whisper at you, but nothing has worked. I can't reach you, and if I can't reach you, I can't help you."

"I don't want to be reached, Dad, and I don't need help. I don't want to change."

"I wish…" He heaves another sigh. "Never mind. It doesn't matter."

No need to finish his sentence. I already know what he intended to say. *I wish you were different, Jade.*

A new pang cuts through my chest, threatening to steal my next breath. "Why don't we just avoid each other for a few days?"

He flinches as if I punched him and says, "I'm your father. I'm not going to avoid you, even if you're ripping out my guts. All I want to do is love you, sweetheart. Why can't you see that?"

Pang. "Love is overrated." The people you love will die. It's a fact of life. The things you love will break, and the homes you love will be taken from you. Why put yourself through the heartache?

Plus I remember the hardships of my mom's ups and downs, how she could swing from the highest of highs to the lowest of lows.

Mom… *Pang, pang.* I know her secret hopes and dreams, deepest fears and hidden shames. I know she loved my dad and that love tore her apart. She thought my dad resented her, that he married her only because she was pregnant with me.

At least Fiona's pregnancy was planned. This baby is wanted. Whenever he sees Fiona, he wraps his arms around her and flattens his hands on her belly. Whenever the baby moves, he laughs and kisses Fiona's temple like *she's* doing something spectacular.

Before, the interactions elicited no reaction from me. Today? The memory alone makes my stomach clench as if I've been punched.

I've had enough emotional upheaval for one day.

"Do you want me to go back to therapy?" I ask. He let me stop last year because I wasn't making any progress. "Will that make you feel better?"

"I don't care about me feeling better. I care about *you* feeling better. I want you happy, like you were when you were a little girl. Remember how you used to laugh?"

I wish I could smile encouragingly at him now so he'll let me go, but I can't quite manage it; the action is foreign to me, like a language I've never learned. "That little girl died in the car crash, and the dead don't come back to life," I remind him. "I took her place. I'm here to stay."

His shoulders roll in. Ouch.

I step back, widening the distance between us. "Look, I really need to take a shower. And I'm tired. I think I'll go to bed early, okay?"

When I move around him this time, he lets me. His gaze bores two holes in my back. Fiona is down the hall, standing in the doorway of the master suite, her features pinched with worry.

"Jade," she says, reaching for me.

With my stomach growing more knotted by the second, I can't bring myself to deal with her even though I know I should. I enter my room, quietly shut the door and turn the lock.

I shower, change into a fresh tank and shorts. In an effort to keep my mind occupied, I read for several hours… before finally drifting off to sleep.

For the first time since the car accident that forever changed my life, I dream about my mother. We're sitting on swings in my backyard. My dad built a playground paradise for Ruby—the name he and Fiona picked out for my sister. Jade and Ruby. Precious gems, my "stone" is forever tarnished.

A thousand questions and statements rush through my mind, but the words that ultimately slip from my mouth? "I've read your journals. Well, two of them." I want her to know I held on to her in the only way I could.

Her smile reminds me of Robb's. All sadness, no good humor. "The darling man gave you the best of them, wanted you to remember the best of me. I wish he'd burned the others." Moonlight spills over her, creating a halo around her silvery-white hair. Her eyes are a startling shade of gold and mirrors of mine. Many of her freckles have faded, while I'm still covered in them.

"Burn them. Why?" I ask. I'd welcome a chance to learn even more about her.

"The pages are filled with darkness and pain, and you need no more of either, sweet Jade."

"I can handle it. Look at me. Darkness is kind of my thing."

She stops swaying to reach over and pat my knee. "There is the darkness you see, and then there is the darkness you feel. Suffering and pain. You aren't handling what you have now. Why would I willingly give you more?" Her gaze moves over my head, seeming to view far away. "If you do not handle your problems, they grow. If you do not appreciate and value the good things you have, you lose them."

"This is the philosophizing part of my dream, I guess."

"No, you don't. When you view your past, present and future through a dirty window, you can't see clearly. Perhaps it's time someone cleans the glass. Of course, someone will have to strip away your armor, too, and ensure you cannot hide."

"Okay, did you die and become the Riddler?" This is kind of ridiculous.

She slides from the swing to kneel in front of me and rest her hands on my knees. A startling fact crystalizes: in my dream, I can feel her. In my dream, she isn't a ghost. "You have become a cold shell of yourself, my darling. You have lost your zest for life. Your love for…everything. You no longer see beauty in anything. It's time to rise from the ashes—rise, rise, stronger than ever before."

Ugh. My subconscious is a bit of a (bad) poet and has joined my father's team. "I'm fine. I promise."

"Fine isn't good enough." Gold eyes beseech me. "You think your pain is hidden, but *you* are the one in hiding. The pain is going to find you, one way or another. Be ready. Fight it. Fight for better."

I trace a fingertip along the cool metal links that connect my swing to the upper bar. "I don't want better."

"You do, you just don't know it." Her grip tightens on my knees. "Yet."

I shake my head, locks of hair slapping my cheeks. "Sorry, Momma, but you don't know me. You've been gone a long time. I've grown. I've changed."

She smiles at me, but there's a tinge of sadness in this one. "I know you've become a bully."

What! Me? A bully? "No!"

"A bully hurts others and doesn't care enough to change. You hurt Robb today—twice. You hurt Fiona and your dad. You inadvertently insulted Clarik. You purposely insulted Mercedes. You didn't apologize to a single person."

"I'm not a bully," I grate. Bullies deliberately hurt people who are weaker.

"Besides," Mom adds, continuing as if I remained mute, "I don't need to know you to know the truth. Life doesn't hand out participant ribbons. Either you fight to live or you die. There's no middle ground."

"I'm fine," I insist. "I'm better than fine."

"Voltaire said it is difficult to free a fool from the chains she reveres. I say it is impossible," she mutters. "You are blinded by your own lies, but I'm going to shine light in your soul and chase the darkness away. One day—one day soon—you're going to *see*."

Unease prickles along my spine, and I gulp. "You're talking nonsense."

Her gaze flips up, meeting mine. Another sad smile curves the corners of her mouth. "Sleep now, baby girl. Sleep peacefully. Everything is about to change."

Chapter 4

Kindness gives to others.
Cruelty steals from your soul.

—*Miranda Leighton*

Each new day is an opportunity for tragedy.

The thought hits me as sunlight pushes through my curtains and fills my bedroom. I'm wide-awake and have been for hours. My eyes burn, and my temples ache. I recall the dream about my mom in Technicolor detail.

After her final words, I jolted upright with a gasp. Then I tossed and turned, my stomach twisting into a thousand knots. Even now, I'm certain she's wrong. I'm not a bully. I'm not a shell of myself—okay, maybe there's a slight possibility that I am *almost* a shell of myself, and that I'm hiding from my pain rather than hiding my pain. But I still find beauty in things. Even dark things. Especially dark things.

Hello, remember Clarik?

And yes, okay, I know I shouldn't care about the things my mom spouted. She was only a figment of my imagination. But I do care. Somewhere inside of me, there's a weak link, and I can't allow that part of me to flourish. I need to choke it out, or starve it. Something!

Determined, I stretch my arms overhead and climb

to unsteady legs. Lazing in bed and worrying isn't the answer.

Instead of going on my usual morning run and possibly bumping into Clarik—forget my immersion plan—I clean up and dress in my favorite shirt and jeans. Both garments are black and fit my state of mind. I plait my mass of hair and glance at my reflection.

What would Clarik think, if I were to bump into him?

Okay, there's no forgetting the plan.

I sit at my desk and look him up online. No matter how hard I search, I can't find a social media page for him. Interesting. Either he likes his privacy, or he's as unplugged as I am.

Maybe I'll ask Robb to do a little digging. He's a whiz with computers.

A knock sounds at my door. "Come in," I call.

My dad peeks his head inside the room. "I'm driving you to school this morning."

"Um, okay. Thanks?"

Irritation flashes in his eyes. "Get your stuff."

In the car, I expect some kind of lecture, but he doesn't speak a word. So weird! I spend the morning in the office, attend my next two classes, eat lunch with my friends, attend my *next* two classes and never catch sight of Clarik. Not until the last class of the day. He doesn't look at me, and like my dad, he doesn't speak to me.

After detention, I go running and pass his house once, twice. On the second trip, he's exiting his truck and catches a glimpse of me…

He doesn't smile or wave, just stomps into the house, leaving me baffled. And disappointed?

I run by his house the next day, and the next, but I don't see him again, and I'm pretty sure he's avoiding me. Maybe he's a total jerk, with no interest in me and he regrets our upcoming nondate date, or maybe he's as confused about me as I am about him.

He doesn't hang out with Mercedes either, even though she's available. Mercedes didn't take Bobby back after she broke up with him; I think she wants Clarik. I swear I catch her scanning the cafeteria with longing in her eyes. But she's as SOL as I am. He's stopped coming to the cafeteria. In class and every minute between, he keeps to himself. To my knowledge, he hasn't made friends with any of the cliques.

Maybe he's missing his buds at his old school and is afraid to make new ones, afraid he'll lose them, too.

No, that can't be it. He might keep to himself at sociable times, but he smiles and waves to everyone. Well, everyone except me. Not that he's mean to me, just dismissive. Despite his friendliness, he's developing a reputation as a boy with whom one does not screw. No one has to wonder how he feels about them. He says it, no matter how brutal.

By the time Sunday rolls around, I'm pretty sure acid has burned away my stomach lining. I don't know if my nondate date with Clarik is still on. If it is, I don't know what time he'll pick me up. I don't know his phone number, so I can't text and ask.

At noon, I shower, blow-dry my hair, apply a little makeup and zip myself in a black fit-and-flare dress. Just in case. And yes, my early-bird roots are showing. On my feet, I anchor my trusty combat boots in place.

My only accessory is a necklace with a tiny replica of a human skeleton dangling from the center.

A soft knock at my bedroom door sends a bolt of surprise through me, and my heart races. It's now 2:30. Clarik can't be here yet, can he? I rush to the door, turn the lock. Hinges squeak as the door opens…

Fiona stands before me, pretty in pink, her dark hair pulled back in a ponytail. "You have a visitor," she says with no small amount of shock.

No one ever comes over to visit me because I've issued zero invitations.

Today my mother's words choose that moment to play through my head. *If you do not appreciate and value the good things you have, you lose them.*

Whatever. Clarik is here, and my heart is now racing *faster.* I'm a little shocked myself. I mean, he actually came. Then Fiona steps aside, revealing Linnie.

"Surprise!" Linnie stretches out her arms, adorable in a black-and-white-striped shirt, short black skirt and ripped panty hose. Around her neck is a cameo choker. On her feet, black tennis shoes with red laces.

"Hi." I fight a wave of disappointment, wondering why she's here. She's never shown up like this. Something must be wrong. "What's going on?"

She soars past my stepmom and softly but firmly shuts the door. "Nothing, and yet everything."

"Maybe unpack that statement with a few facts?"

With a sigh, she throws herself across my unmade bed. "My parents have guests at the mausoleum, and I was ordered to stay in my room or leave. I knew I embarrassed them, but come on. This is ridiculous."

The mausoleum. Her palace of a home is complete with a tennis court, swimming pool, separate guesthouse—not a guest room, a guest*house*—a rose garden, a basketball court, and multiple marble waterfalls.

Her dad is a lawyer, and her mom, who comes from old money, runs a charity.

"Robb isn't answering his phone," she adds, "and Kimberly is still suffering from a hangover after last night's concert."

So I was third choice. I'm not hurt or even surprised. I have no right to be. "You're welcome to crash in my room as long as you want, but I might or might not have to leave at some point. I kinda sorta agreed to go on a nondate date with Clarik."

Linnie jolts upright. Golden sunlight pushes past the crack in my curtains to stream over her. "Clarik…as in the new guy Clarik?"

"The one and only."

"Wait. He asked you out? And I'm sorry! I'm sorry! I didn't mean to make you sound like dog food. My entire world just got overturned. You, the ice queen, are interested in a boy. And he's…well, he's nice…most of the time. I saw him carrying books for a special-needs kid. It was honestly the sweetest thing I've ever seen."

First I was compared to a robot, now an ice queen. I think I prefer being royalty.

"Nice boys can't be into me?" I ask.

"Well, I haven't noticed you two spending any time together. Or, you know, doing *anything* together."

I deflate as I say, "He didn't ask me out. His uncle did. Kind of. I accepted." I wave a hand through the air in lieu of offering an explanation. "I bet it's canceled. Clarik probably has other plans, but he can't tell me because he might or might not know where I live, and he definitely doesn't have my number."

"I'm sorry," she repeats. She falls back on the mattress and traces a heart on my pillow, saying, "Maybe we should go to Mercedes's party and get your mind off him. From what I've pieced together, her mom flew to Atlanta this morning to attend some kind of medical seminar and won't be back for two or three days."

Nadine is a general practitioner. Half the town sees her, but my family isn't among them.

"We're invited?" I ask, dubious.

"The entire school is invited."

"Mercedes and her ilk don't consider us part of the school, remember?" Unless she plans to strike at us in some way. "We're nothings. Nobodies."

Tears well in her eyes, and I immediately regret my words. Maybe I *am* a bully.

"Those kids are wrong, of course," I tell her. "We're the best of the lot. You especially."

After giving me a watery smile, she jumps up and throws her arms around me. She's…hugging me?

At first I stand perfectly still, my arms at my sides. But…

I don't like this. I don't like this *at all*. My chest is tightening. My breathing is jacked, my inhalations a little too quick and a lot too shallow. In a rush, I step back, out of her embrace.

Hurt crosses her expression, there and gone in a blink.

"I don't think I should go to the party," I say. "I should wait here. For Clarik. Just in case."

"He lives by you, yeah? Why don't we go to his house and ask him to join us?"

A crowd is not conducive to a proper interrogation—I mean conversation. "If you want to go, even though Mercedes might not even let you inside, let's sober up Kimberly so she can go with you."

Linnie's breath hitches. "You don't want to spend time with me. I should have known. I'm sorry. I shouldn't have come."

She steps toward the door, but I move into her path.

"Don't leave," I say, not liking the sudden paleness of her cheeks. I've seen that same shade of white in the mirror far too many times. "You're my friend, and I like hanging out with you." Too many times I've written in my journals about the importance of kindness, and yet I've shown very little to this girl—or anyone, really. I need to do better. I *will* do better.

"Sometimes I wish I could be more like you. Nothing bothers you, while *everything* bothers me."

"Some people say I'm hiding from the pain of my past," I mutter.

"Aren't we all?" Her shoulders roll in. "I can't go to the party with Kim. I stretched the truth, but only a little! She's got a hangover, yes, but she's also mad at me. Last night she caught me making out with her cousin."

"Why is she mad about that? I highly doubt *she* wants to sleep with him."

"Well…he sort of has…a girlfriend. A friend of Kim's," she admits, cheeks pink. "I should have slapped his face when he said he was falling for me, but I thought… hoped… Well, it doesn't matter now, does it?"

So he lied to her, telling her what she wanted to hear so that he could get off. Kimberly should be mad *at him*. "We all make mistakes. Kim knows it. She'll forgive you."

"Until then…let's get you ready for your maybe/maybe-not date that may or may not lead you to Mercedes's party." She takes my hand in hers, squeezes. "We have a million things to do to get you ready, and thanks to my dad's gold card, we're going to do them in style."

Dread flash-freezes the blood in my veins. "I can't think of a single thing I need to do."

"Hello. Your hair! Makeup! Clothes!" She waves a finger over me to indicate, well, all of me. "When's the last time you waxed?"

Uh, that would be *never.* "If I need a makeover to impress a boy, *I* will be unimpressed by *the boy.* So thank you for your offer, but I think I'm going to de—"

"Nope. Don't think." As she ushers me to the door, I realize that arguing with her will require more effort than I'm willing to give for something so minor. She loves to shop, so if this will make her happy…

"Fine. I'll go." I could use a distraction.

"All you need to do, Jade Leighton, is watch me work my magic."

Linnie's magic = torture.

Three hours later, she drives me home. I'm still in my dress because there was no way I was going to wear one of the miniskirts she picked out for me; the hem of each barely reached my panty line.

I want my goodie bits the way I want my pimples: concealed.

But to make Linnie happy, I let her choose my hairstyle. I now have bangs, cut by a razor so they wisp to the side, and I kind of actually…like them. A makeup specialist I want to introduce to Robb because I think they'd hit it off painted my face, giving me smoky eyes, longer and thicker lashes, "perma-flushed" cheeks and *I've got to be kissed now* glossy red lips.

I'm told I'm a mix of innocence and wantonness, and it's the perfect combination for snagging a boyfriend or making a guy regret letting me get away, whichever I prefer.

When she reaches my house, Linnie turns down the blare of music and slams on the brakes, nearly clipping the curb. "Clarik is going to die when he sees you."

"*If* he shows up," I mutter.

"If he doesn't, I'll spread a rumor that he once used an empty Doritos bag as a condom."

I almost—almost—smile. "I'm glad we're friends."

"Me, too." Leaning over, she air-kisses my cheek. "I'll see you tomorrow at school."

"You're not coming in? I thought we were going to ask Clarik to take us to Mercedes's party." At some point during our shopping extravaganza, I caved and agreed to her plan.

"Nah. Call me if you decide to go, though, and I'll meet you there. But there's no way I'm horning in on your date."

"It's not a—"

“Yeah, yeah. I know.”

Discarded cans of her favorite energy drink clink together as I exit the car. I trudge to my porch. The door is open, and I enter without a word. Amused voices pull me into the kitchen. My dad has his arms wrapped around Fiona, and he’s rubbing her belly.

Fiona spots me, and her jaw drops. “Jade! Oh, wow. You look amazing.”

“Thanks.” What else can I say, really?

She smiles and motions me over. “Come here. Feel. Ruby’s been kicking up a storm.”

I remain in place, my feet firmly planted on the floor. “No, thank you.” I’ve had enough emotional upheaval for one day.

Her smile fades.

My dad scowls at me. “Jade, your mother and sister deserve—”

“She’s not my mother.” The words rush from me, my tone sharper than usual.

“It’s okay. Really.” Fiona steps from my dad’s embrace, grabs a rag from the sink and begins to clean the already clean kitchen counter. “She doesn’t have to do anything she doesn’t want to do.”

Silent now, I head to my room to avoid my dad’s glare.

I spend the rest of the day watching the clock, watching and waiting…watching and waiting…kind of hating myself for being this girl. 5:04. I decide to change into a tank and jeans. 6:11. My dad knocks on the door to tell me dinner is ready, but I decline, just in case. 7:02. My life does not revolve around a boy, dang it! But come on! Will Clarik or won’t he?

I'm tempted to do as Linnie suggested and show up at his house. *Are we doing this or not?*

Then the clock strikes 7:23, and the doorbell rings. Breathless, I open my door in time to hear my dad say, "...to see Jade? Why?"

There's a tension-laden pause. Then, "I'm taking her to dinner."

Clarik's husky voice strokes me, and I gulp.

"Jade. To dinner," my dad says. "Anywhere else?"

"A welcome party. I'm new to the district."

Wait. So Mercedes is throwing the party in his honor? She wants him *bad*.

I'm stiff as a board as I shoot a quick text to Linnie, letting her know we will be attending, after all. My legs tremble as I make the small trek into the living room. Clarik looks me over the same way he did the day we met—and frowns. I'm not sure what to make of that, and I smooth sweaty palms down my sides.

I look him over, too, and my every pulse point flutters. He looks good. Really, really good. His dark hair is askew and yet the perfect frame for his face. His blue, blue eyes are positively electric. He's dressed casually in a T-shirt that reads ZOMBIES HATE FAST FOOD. The material hugs his shoulders and biceps. His jeans are faded and ripped, and his boots scuffed in several places. Leather cuffs circle his wrists, and several rings glint from his fingers.

He nods at me, his expression unreadable. "Hey, Jade."

My mouth goes dry. "Hey."

My dad spins around, his eyes wide. "You agreed to go to a party? With a boy?"

"Yes." Is he going to demand I stay home?

A grin suddenly brightens his features. He gives me a gentle push in Clarik's direction. "Go. Have fun. Stay out late. Do things you'll regret tomorrow."

I hear his unspoken words: *Be a normal kid for once.*

Fiona, who is standing by the coatrack, grins from ear to ear as well, and gives me a thumbs-up.

If I *were* normal, I'm pretty sure I would be humiliated right now.

Clarik opens the door and motions me out. He follows, close to my heels. The light from the porch chases away the evening darkness, providing a path to his truck.

Stray thought: I wonder how and when Clarik is going to die.

Ugh. I swallow a groan. If I start pondering all the ways he could kick the bucket, I'll get lost in my thoughts, lose track of my surroundings and spend what will probably be our only evening together in a fog. On the other hand…

No, no!

When we're seated inside, I notice he smells like vanilla cupcakes and lemonade, and my mouth waters for a taste. I've got a sweet tooth tonight. Noted.

"Your dad is…unique," Clarik says, easing the truck onto the road. "I halfway expected him to offer money for beer."

"Yeah, he wants me to be a normal kid," I admit. Truth is better than a lie, always. "Part of me was sure you wouldn't come. You've been avoiding me all week."

"Yes."

At least he didn't try to deny it. "Why?"

"I got to thinking. The only reason you'd agree to go out with me is if you want something more. A relationship," he adds, in case I'm an idiot and can't figure it out on my own. "I'm attracted to you, yes, but I'm never going to date you. If you're into a one-night stand, though, I'm your guy."

See? Brutally honest.

My stomach gives an unexpected twist. Am I the problem? Or is it his feelings for his ex? And why does it matter? I'm not interested in a relationship, either. "Do you one-night stand often?"

"Never have before," he says. Grumbles, really. "Okay, I don't want to talk about this."

"All right." I give him an out—for now—because too often I'm pushed to talk about things I don't want to talk about. "We'll be friends. Nothing more, nothing less. Okay? I won't develop feelings for you. Robot, remember? But I'm not on board for a bang and bail, either."

On the surface, a one-time thing might seem like my cup of tea. No attachment. We walk away before we can get serious and someone gets hurt. But I've seen the heartache Linnie deals with on a regular basis. I've witnessed her world crumble whenever an ex moves on to someone else.

Clarik nods. "I'm good with being your friend, Jade."

Good. That's good. "So...*friend*. Have you ever wondered how you're going to die?" The question escapes me before I can stop it, and I press my tongue to the roof of my mouth to stop myself from becoming a bigger tool and demanding he forget I asked.

Rather than freaking out the way Mercedes once

freaked out when I asked her the same question, he flicks me an amused glance. "I'm not sure how we segued into a conversation about death, but okay. I can roll. The answer is no. Have *you* wondered how you're going to die?"

"Not lately. But I used to—all the time."

"This is kind of...adorable."

Movements exaggerated, I grind my fists into my ears. "Please repeat what you just said. I'm certain I misheard. You did not just call *death thoughts* adorable."

"Adorably morbid, then. Fits the whole angel of death vibe you've got going on."

Angel of death? Who? What? *Me?*

Okay, yeah. The description fits.

"What was the top contender?" he asks.

"I always figured a car accident since the one that killed my mom failed to finish the job."

He reaches over to pat the top of my hand in a gesture of comfort. "I can't imagine the pain of losing a parent. I'm sorry."

Twist. Time to move on.

Before I can change the subject, however, he says, "Did you cry?"

"You mean did my mechanical tear ducts leak oil?" My tone is as dry as the desert. "The day of the accident, yes. Afterward? No."

He frowns at me. "You don't cry about a*nything*? Ever?"

"I guess nothing can compare to the trauma I experienced that day."

He opens his mouth only to snap it closed. "Okay, you told me how you think you'll die. Now tell me something you live for."

I've never actually entertained such a thought, and my mind blanks. "Let me get back to you on that. So, uh, where are you taking me for dinner?"

He doesn't comment about the topic switch, just goes along with it. "Uncle Tag has lived in this town all his life, right, and when I first arrived he took me to all his favorite places. Now I'm taking you to *my* favorite place. It's not much to look at, but the burgers are incredible." He turns a corner with ease. He's a good driver, completely at ease on the road, his hands steady on the wheel, his body relaxed. "By the way, you look beautiful."

Do not fluff your hair like an idiot. "Thank you."

"What? No denial? *What are you talking about, Clarik?*" he offers in a falsetto. *"I've never looked worse."*

I blink at him. "You would prefer I offer a denial, in essence calling you a liar?"

"No. Denial is what I'm used to receiving, that's all."

"From your ex-girlfriend?"

Car lights whiz past on the other side of the highway. "From *all* girls."

"Dude. That's because girls can't win. If she accepts a compliment, she's automatically considered a conceited witch. If she denies a compliment, she must have low self-esteem or she's playing coy. If she ignores a compliment because it makes her uncomfortable, she's got to be a total snob."

He opens his mouth, closes it. Opens, closes. "You're… right."

"Usually."

He snorts. "I'm going to ask you a question, okay, and I mean no insult."

Oookay.

"Why did you accept my uncle's invitation?"

Uh-oh. Suddenly I feel as if a spotlight is glaring on me. Why not lay it all out there? Besides, what's the worst that could happen? He laughs at me? So what?

"You said you're attracted to me, but… Well, I'm attracted to you, too, and I'd like not to be." There. Now he knows the truth, the full truth and nothing but the truth.

His attention whips to me, his hands jerking the wheel. The truck swerves, and he hurries to straighten it. "Let's see if I'm understanding you correctly." No longer does he sound amused or even friendly. "You think I'm hot, but you wish you *didn't* think I was hot."

In a nutshell. "Yes."

"So, what? Getting to know me will cure you of your attraction to me?"

The words are snarled, and I realize my mistake. I just insulted the crap out of him—out of his personality.

"I'm sorry," I say. "I didn't mean—"

"Forget it," he interjects, his tone as hard as a rock. "You don't have to worry. Nothing is going to happen between us. You're a bad bet. I've watched you. You like your friends, but you could walk away without missing a beat. If I fell for you… No. Just no."

Ouch. That *no* is final; there's zero doubt it in. And I can't argue with his logic. I *am* a bad bet. I *can* walk away. And I won't suddenly morph into a girl who's a great bet, who clings or cleaves or whatever it is he wants from a significant other, just to win him over. I'd rather play it safe. I *like* safe.

He pulls into a mom-and-pop drive-in burger joint I've never before noticed and parks at one of the only available slots.

"Just so you know," I say, "I told you my reason for accepting *at the time*. I've gotten to know you better already, and I like you *more*. But unlike other girls my age, I've never been attracted to anyone before. Not even movie stars or singers. Robots can't love," I add, trying my hand at teasing. "Why did *you* accept? And don't say you didn't want to hurt my feelings. You watched me, and I watched you."

Whoa. Back up. Realization strikes with all the finesse of a baseball bat. He watched me?

"You are as blunt as boxing gloves," I finish.

He shrugs, suddenly sheepish. "Let's just drop it, okay?"

If he thinks he can intrigue me with this mystery—Dang him, he's right. "Tell me," I insist. "I can take it."

He says, "I was curious about you…and I hoped to appease my curiosity so I could move on."

"The same reason as me, then. You seriously suck right now. And you are beyond lucky that I'm an unfeeling robot, or I'd smack you into next week."

He offers an invisible-hat tip, unrepentant but even more sheepish, and I roll my eyes.

"So tell me why you love this place," I say.

"I'll do better. I'll show you." He orders us both an onion burger and garlic fries and insists on paying. His way of making amends, I guess.

"Onions and garlic, huh?"

"Consider it friendship insurance."

I might as well stamp MOCK on my forehead as I say, "You need insurance against my irresistible appeal?"

"Nah. But I knew you'd need insurance against mine."

Ha! "Funny man."

I'm not superhungry—my stomach is a little too sensitive—but I'm curious about his favorite, and once the food arrives, I take a bite. Little moans slip past my lips as delicious flavors hit my tongue. Clarik smiles, and dang, it's a good look for him. He might have joked about his appeal, but I definitely need the insurance.

Not just for me, but for other girls at the party. That's right. I admit it. I don't want anyone else getting a shot with him.

"I think it's safe to say this is now one of my favorite places, too." I swallow another bite, and another and another. "I will absolutely be coming back."

We eat in silence for a bit, and it's nice, comfortable. Neither of us feels a pressing need to chatter about nothing simply to fill a void. Plus, the peace and quiet gives my curiosity time to grow.

"Tell me about you," I say. "How'd you end up at Hathaway High?"

"I was born in Florida and lived there for ten years. Then, one day out of the blue, my mom decided we needed to move to the other side of the country, so we set out for LA. But when we reached Oklahoma, the car broke down. She met and married my stepdad—*former* stepdad—soon after. I attended a couple different schools, but the most recent was Crossroads High, near Tuttle and Blanchard. Know it?"

Of course. "You guys kicked our butts in football last year."

He flashes me a toothy smile. "Yeah. I remember. I scored the winning touchdown."

"You're a jock, then," I say. My surprise is silly. The guy has muscles stacked upon muscles.

"I was. I got kicked off the team for fighting."

I like that he cops to the truth without prompting. "The day we met, you had bruises on your knuckles. Even if Mrs. Stewart hadn't mentioned your brawling history, I would have pegged you as a butt-stomper."

He gathers our trash and throws everything in the bin next to the truck. "I believe there's a right and wrong way to speak to a girl. Another guy disagreed."

"Is that why you moved here? To join our football team?"

"No. My mom and stepdad divorced, and she had to get a job for the first time in years. Despite the new income, we couldn't afford rent, so we moved in with my uncle."

We, he'd said. Not *her*. He takes coresponsibility for the bills. "Were you sad about the divorce? And what about your bio-dad? Is he in the picture?"

Those muscles I just admired? In an instant, they seem to turn to stone. "No. He's not."

I hit a nerve. Why?

He puts the truck in Reverse, backs out of the slot. "I thought we'd make an appearance at Mercedes's—"

"I know about the party," I interject. I notice he isn't curious enough about me to question me about my family life. "I overheard you talking with my dad."

"So you're on board?"

"Yes. Actually, we *have* to go. I told my friend Linnie we'd meet her there." A part of me enjoys the thought of ruining Mercedes's big night. There. There you go. Something I live for. She'll hate seeing me. Will hate seeing me with Clarik even more. I almost smile. Petty revenge should be beneath me. *Should.* "Have you met her? She's the redhead I hang with."

"Odd that you describe her hair color but not her relationship to you, eh?"

He... I... Argh! *Bad bet.*

"Nothing lasts," I tell him. "Eventually everyone dies. Love makes the loss hurt more."

As he merges into traffic, we lapse into silence. This one isn't as comfortable.

For a split second, I think I see my mother standing on the sidewalk, watching me as we drive past, her pale hair billowing in the wind. Impossible! And yet unease slithers around my neck and chokes me.

When I rotate in the seat to glance back, she's gone.

Chapter 5

Life is a labyrinth filled with obstacles,
tricks and traps, and other lost people.

—Miranda Leighton

"This isn't the way to Mercedes's house." We aren't headed back to our neighborhood but away from it.

"I'm told her father has a cabin in the woods," Clarik says.

Oh, yeah. That's right. "We called it the Hump Dump. Eddie, her dad, has a history of getting married and cheating on his wives. He uses the cabin as a love shack for his affairs."

I remember Eddie vividly. He sucks as much as Nadine, but to her credit, she did her best to shield her daughter from his parental incompetence. Never showing up when promised, forgetting birthdays, ignoring holidays and always apologizing.

He won't care if the place gets trashed. No, not true. He'll care, but he won't give Mercedes crap about it. Nadine would flip her ever-loving lid if one of her precious knickknacks got broken or a rug got stained.

"How do you know so much about Mercedes's dad?" Clarik asks.

"Her mom dated *my* dad for years. We were as close as

sisters. A few times Eddie took us both camping. Only he called it *glamping* since we stayed in the cabin."

"Wow. I never would have guessed you two used to get along."

By the time we get to the cabin, cars line both sides of the gravel road. Vehicles are positioned between thick oak trees and form a path to the only house on thirty acres of land. Kids from school are everywhere, interspersed with kids I've never seen. Some are drinking from beer bottles, some from red plastic cups. Some are puffing on cigarettes or weed, ribbons of smoke curling up, up, into the moonlight.

Clarik finds a place for his truck, emerges and strides around to open my door for me.

He's *definitely* a closet gentleman, and I like it.

Our shoulders bump as we head toward the cabin, and the unplanned contact jolts me, warm tingles riding the waves in my veins.

"Sorry," he mutters.

One day—one day soon—you're going to see. *Everything is about to change.*

Ignore dream Mom's warning. Focus. I need my wits.

On the porch, Mercedes and members of her group are huddled together. The core four. Bobby—are the two back together again?—Charlee Ann and the Wagner twins, Heaven and Nevaeh, whose hair I have always envied. Yes, even I suffer from the occasional case of the *I Wants.* Their black curls are full of personality while my colorless locks are board-straight and flat.

Mercedes spots Clarik and licks her lips as if he's dessert. Then her gaze moves to me, and for a moment, only a moment, she appears pleasantly surprised. I'm mistaken, surely. A second later, she's scowling and I'm relieved. Mercedes being happy to see me can mean only (1) the world is about to end, or (2) she's planned something evil à la *Carrie*.

Bobby winds his arm around her shoulders, but she shrugs him off. "Oh, goodie. It's Jade the Unlaid." In as deep and raspy a voice as he can manage, mimicking me, he says, "Look at me, everyone. I'm screwed up. I'm in an emotional prison, blah, blah."

Mercedes elbows his stomach, and he frowns at her, all *What'd I do?*

Tension rolls off Clarik in big, sweeping waves.

"Poor Bobby," I say. "He forgets that I witnessed him picking his nose and eating glue in elementary school and that I once caught him wetting himself at recess." One day, in junior high, I was sitting under the bleachers, hidden in shadows, and I saw his dad punch him in the gut. It wasn't a playful punch either; his dad gave the blow his all.

I did try to talk to Bobby the next day, and I even told our principal what I'd seen. Bobby told me I needed glasses, and the principal told me I shouldn't spread lies about people.

Bobby turns beet red and steps toward me, but Clarik bows up, pure aggression, his expression all *There is no line I will not cross*, and Bob the Cob backs down.

"Go on in, Jade," Heaven says.

The twins are actually pretty cool. They've never picked on the weak just for grins and giggles, and they've often mediated disagreements between classmates to prevent a fight from breaking out.

I reach for the door handle as Mercedes says in a stage whisper, "I'm sorry you got stuck driving Miss Crazy, Clarik. I'll make it up to you later."

In her mind, she's allowed to insult me, but Bobby isn't. I get it. Clarik doesn't. He goes rigid, as if he's been pushed to his breaking point.

I should zip my lips, let him think the worst of Mercedes and the best of me. But let's be honest. Like Mercedes, zipping my lips has never been my forte, and I'm absolutely willing to cut off my nose to spite my face.

In my best impersonation of her, I twitter, "Well, butter my butt and call me a biscuit. My name is Mercedes Turner, and I like long walks on the beach, cuddling in front of a warm fire and pretending I'm better than everyone else because deep down inside I know I'm just a waste of space." *Giggle, giggle.*

Mercedes pales, and more tension rolls off Clarik. I decide he's a modern-day Robin Hood. A defender of the weak, whoever the "weak" one happens to be.

Charlee Ann purses her lips as if she's just come across toxic waste. In her mind, she has. "You aren't wanted here, freak. Leave."

"She's my friend," Clarik says. "I don't like when my friends are insulted."

I reel, a little dizzy with realization. He admitted we're friends in a public place, even after I insulted Mercedes. He admitted we're friends in a public place without hesitation or shame. Is this heaven?

"Fine, fine. She can stay." Mercedes heaves an *I'm such a giver* sigh.

"Linnie, Kimberly and Robb are his friends, too," I say. His prefriends. He'll love them when he meets them, I'm sure of it.

"Whatever," she grumbles.

Bobby remains silent, glaring between Mercedes and Clarik.

Clarik reaches around me to open the front door, ever the gentleman, and ushers me into the living room.

The small space is overcrowded, different perfumes and colognes clashing in the air. Rock music pumps from a Bluetooth speaker, loud enough to irritate me but not loud enough to halt conversation. Furniture has been pushed aside to make room for dancing.

Anyone who spots Clarik shouts a happy greeting. He's been part of Hathaway High for a week, but everyone treats him as a long-lost loved one.

He nods in greeting before lowering his head to whisper straight into my ear. "I'm sorry. I brought you here, and they were rude."

Warm shivers cascade through me, and I gulp. Before I can respond—what the heck am I supposed to say?—soft arms and expensive perfume envelop me.

"You came!" Linnie squeals.

No time to stiffen. She lets me go a second later and sways on her feet. Her pupils nearly eclipse her irises as she focuses on Clarik. "And lookie look look at you. You're even hotter up close." She pinches his chin and gives his head a little shake. "Hot *and* a miracle worker.

No one else has ever gotten our Jade to leave her house on a Sunday. Or a Saturday. Or any weeknight."

I can't deny it. "Clarik, this is Linnie. Linnie, Clarik."

"Nice to meet you," he says with a genuine smile. It's nothing like the baring of teeth he gave to Bobby.

Her hand flutters to her chest, resting on her heart. "Did we just make a baby? I feel like we just made a baby."

Clarik is laughing as Robb sidles up to Linnie. Robb's gaze remains on the wood floor, his cheeks flushed. I suspect he'd rather be anywhere but here.

I do another round of introductions. "Clarik, this is Robb. Robb, Clarik."

"Nice to meet you, too," Clarik says.

"Um. Hi." Robb pulls at the collar of his shirt and clears his throat. He reaches out to shake Clarik's hand only to ball his own and drop his arm to his side. He's learned the hard way that some guys are threatened by physical contact with a gay male.

Pang.

Clarik reaches out, takes the hand Robb is no longer offering and shakes. Robb gasps, startled, and looks as if he's about to cry.

Pang, pang.

Ugh! I'm sick of those stupid pangs! What are these guys doing to me? Where is my cold detachment? I want it, *need* it. A stupid handshake shouldn't have the power to crack my hard-won armor. Nothing should!

"Gross. Who let the freaks in?" someone calls, and other kids laugh and snicker.

Clarik stiffens. I scan our surroundings. So many eyes

are on us now, watching our every move. So many ears, listening to our every word. I lift my chin, square my shoulders.

Two girls I don't know come over and, ignoring my friends, invite Clarik to swim with them in the pool out back. I'm surprised when he declines and the girls walk off, deflated.

Linnie and Robb gape at him. I play it cool. All right, fine. I'm gaping, too.

"What?" he asks me. "I came with you, therefore I stay with you."

I'm impressed, and okay, okay, I'm also a little irritated. I don't want him staying with me just because he's a gentleman. I want him to *want* to stay with me. Because we're friends…who will never date, who might or might not ever hang out again after tonight.

What am I going to do? Call and text him little anecdotes about my day?

I can see our future: I get to know him better, fall deeper into like with him and, yeah, okay, maybe I finally agree to a one-night stand. Afterward, if he still thinks I'm cool and wants to hang around me—and that's a big if—he'll reduce me to some kind of wingwoman so I can help him score *other* babes. No, thanks.

"Go," I tell him. Like a true friend, I wave him toward the path the girls took. "Have fun. With your clean-cut cuteness, you're cramping our style." Before he can respond, I turn to Robb and Linnie, cutting him from our group, and say, "Where's Kimberly? Is she here?" A clear dismissal of my nondate date.

"She's on her way," Robb says, speaking to me but casting Clarik a sympathetic glance.

There's a beat of silence, heavy and oppressive. Then Clarik mutters, "Bad bet," and strides away to join the swim team. I grimace.

"I bet one or both of the girls 'forgot' to bring a swimsuit," Linnie mutters before wagging a finger in my face. "Has lust rotted your brain? You just sent a grade A filet to a smorgasbord of hangry she-beasts. Why?"

I go with honesty. "I got a mental picture of our future, and it wasn't pretty. Better to end things now."

Robb peers straight into my eyes, unflinching, radiating unimaginable pain. Pain that calls to everything buried inside my heart.

I stumble back a step as if pushed. What horrors has this boy endured?

"You just cut him to the quick," he tells me, the words soft and quiet but lethal to my composure. "I know the feeling."

Ouch. And he isn't done. "I've loved you for years," he continues, "ever since seventh grade when you punched a boy who'd punched me, but there *is* such a thing as toxic love. I keep making excuses for your behavior. You're afraid to love back and get hurt, right? But there's only so much cold-shoulder a person can tolerate before they realize they're better off without you."

The urge to vomit overwhelms me.

You've become a bully.

Everything is about to change.

Maybe Robb would be better off without me. Maybe

all my friends would be better off without me. Might be time for me to jump ship and fly solo.

Every cell in my body rebels at the thought—which is the very reason I decide it has to be done. Tomorrow I will cut my friends loose.

A cold sweat pops up on my brow, and a lump grows in my throat.

Mercedes stops at my side and clasps my arm with a grip tight enough to bruise, and, oh, wow, I never thought I'd be glad to see her, but I'm desperate for a distraction.

"Excuse us. I'm going to borrow your soulless zombie friend for a sec." With a fake smile firmly in place, she draws me through the cabin and nods at guests.

We walk into a blocked-off hallway and enter a locked room. The room her father reserves for her, to be exact. She flips a switch and light spills from a crystal chandelier. A freaking chandelier the size of a grand piano. Only Mercedes would pick such a fancy light fixture. No, check that. Only Mercedes and Fiona. My stepmother would faint with delight. The bed, dresser and vanity are white while the covers, curtains and rug are pink; I'd bet every piece of furniture is a perfectly restored antique.

The door closes with an ominous *click*, and Mercedes rounds on me. "You shouldn't have come here."

"You invited the whole school, remember? And the guest of honor *personally* invited me," I add with a smirk. My words are a sword, and I am an excellent fencer.

She flinches, then parries. "As the host, I'm going to do you a favor and give you five minutes to leave. Without Clarik. If you stay, you'll be sorry—I'll make sure of it. I've wanted to make you cry *for years*, but I've always resisted. Today I've reached the end of my mercy."

Why today? And I don't have to wonder why she's wanted to make me cry. The desire is mutual. "What are you going to do? Insult me in front of everyone for the thousandth time?"

"I'm going to hurt you, and I don't care if I blow my chances with Clarik in the process."

So she *does* want him. If Clarik starts dating Mercedes…

Anger sparks. Huffing and puffing, I say, "What chances? Maybe you haven't noticed, but he couldn't get away from you fast enough outside."

"Oh, shut up," she says, her teeth gritted. "Also, you need to put your dad on a leash. Tell him to stay away from my mom."

"What are you talking about?"

"Either he came by the house bright and early this morning, or he snuck over sometime during the night and stayed. He doesn't know I watched him carry her bags to her car before hugging and kissing her goodbye."

If I'm an excellent fencer, she is a master. I feel an invisible blade cut through my stomach, acid leaking from the wound. "You're lying." Although, on my morning run, I *did* notice the absence of my dad's car in our driveway. But we returned at the same time, and he had a box of doughnuts in hand, so I assumed…

"Why would I lie?"

Easy. "To cause trouble. To hurt me. To amuse yourself. Take your pick."

"*Nothing* hurts you, remember?" She raises her chin.

"I used to like your dad and wish I could live with him instead of my mom." Her voice cracks, making me wonder just how badly she was hurt by our parents' breakup, but she rallies quickly. "I should have known he'd turn out to be a cheating jerk, just like every other male in the world."

"What kind of kiss was it?" I demand, suddenly understanding why today is the day she has no mercy to spare. Not that I believe she had any to begin with.

"A peck."

"So no tongue?" Even saying the words makes me shudder with revulsion.

"Yeah, but so what? If you knew anything about boys, you'd know tongue is for hello, not goodbye. Just tell him to stay away," she repeats. "And get the hell out of my cabin."

She storms off then, leaving me alone in the bedroom, the door open. I ease onto the edge of the bed, my mind whirling. My dad would not cheat on Fiona and risk a divorce before Ruby is even born.

Right? Right. But… People are flawed and constantly make mistakes. My dad is no exception. He was bound to let me down at some point or other.

Footsteps echo, drawing my attention. I cling to the distraction with a desperation that stuns me and glance up in time to see Clarik and Linnie stalk down the hall. As they pass, Clarik searches the room. His glance grazes me only to zoom back. He switches direction and, taking Linnie's hand to tug her alongside him, enters the bedroom.

I leap to my feet, my heart racing, my palms suddenly sweating.

"There you are," Linnie says. "We've been looking *everywhere*."

"Why?" I try not to stare at Clarik. His expression is cold as ice while he himself is hot as fire. He should look out of place amid the feminine furnishings, but he just looks sexy AF. "Did something happen?"

"Yes!" She sways slightly. "Mercedes dragged you away. I thought you were getting murdered, so I grabbed Clarik so we could save our damsel in distress." Leaning toward me, she places a hand at the side of her mouth and whisper-yells, "He's got muscles."

"I noticed," I mutter.

"You guys stay here." One step, two, she backs into the hall. "Talk to each other. Make up. I'm gonna go search for Robb. Someone called him an awful name, and he headed outside."

I want to beat "someone" into pulp. I also want Robb to stop caring what other people think. Only then will he find peace.

I hear Dr. Miller's voice in my head: *You truly believe* you *have found peace?*

Yes! Most times. Okay, sometimes. But sometimes is better than no time.

"We'll help—"

She cuts me off, saying, "I think he could use a break from you. He only agreed to come out with me tonight to get away from his parents. They told him to stop being gay or get out of their house."

Poor Robb. No wonder he looks so pained today. No wonder he called me on my crap.

He *will* be better off without me.

Linnie shuts the door, sealing Clarik and me inside. I expect him to bolt, but he prowls through the bedroom, looking everything over. Curious about Mercedes or curious in general?

I bite my tongue until I taste blood. "You're not wet. You didn't swim?"

"No." He offers no more. He reaches out to run a fingertip over a bejeweled picture frame of Mercedes and her dad, and his shirtsleeve lifts, revealing more of the tattoo on his biceps. Not a heart after all, but an elaborate cross with pointy ends. Thorny vines wrap around the center, with two roses in bloom. One rose is bloodred and the other is black and withered.

"Nice ink."

He pivots to face me, and he hasn't thawed a bit. "Do you have more than the ones on your arms?"

"I do. My back..." No one but my friends and my dad have seen them.

Before I can talk myself out of it, I turn and lift my shirt. He moves behind me and traces the different bones. His touch is warm and rough, and I shiver.

"The detail is stunning."

Do I detect a glimmer of warmth in his tone?

Thank you. I try to speak, but a lump clogs my throat. I shove my tank in place and whip around. As we stare at each other—his irises are so blue, so perfect—breathing is more difficult, because the air somehow is thicker. His vanilla scent envelops me, fogging my head. Heat radiates from him now, warming me inside and out.

I hate my reaction to him…because I love it.

Something I live for: his scent. Looking at him.

Here, now, I want to kiss him. My first. I want his lips on mine, his taste in my mouth. Managing to find my voice, I ask, "Do *you* have any other tattoos?"

"I do." He raises his shirt, revealing row after row of muscle and strength, and magnifying my body's reaction to him.

This boy doesn't have a six-pack; he has an eight-pack, and I'm suddenly, undeniably dying of thirst.

To my surprise, he *does* have a heart tattoo. A broken, bleeding heart etched over his breastbone. It isn't shaped like a traditional Valentine's Day heart but is an anatomically correct one. The image is gruesome, morbid, but somehow fitting.

I want to trace it, the way he traced mine—the very reason I glue my arms to my sides. "I… You are… What do they mean? The cross and the heart?"

He frowns at me. "You're the first person to ever ask."

"And that's a problem because…?"

"Do *your* tattoos mean anything?" he asks rather than answering my question.

"Of course." I trace my fingers over the broken heart. "This one represents my mother."

Those beautiful features soften as he points to the cross. "Fresh start." Then, pointing to the heart, he says, "Heartache can make you stronger."

I've never believed a fresh start is truly possible. Too many memories. If you cannot forget your past, you cannot help but drag it with you everywhere you go. But there's no way I'll share my assessment with Clarik.

My best guess is the heartache springs from his breakup.

We stare at each other for a long while, as if we're lost. Lost and never want to be found. The air grows even thicker, breathing even more difficult. I have one move—holding my breath as long as possible, refusing to inhale any more of that tantalizing vanilla scent.

A muscle jumps underneath his eye. Finally, he releases the hem of his shirt, the material falling, covering a chest I will forever see in my dreams.

"Do you think we'll remain friends after tonight?" I ask. I don't know why. "Talk and text and hang out?"

"No," he replies, as blunt as always. "I don't."

I shove my disappointment inside my heart and twist the lock. "Yeah," I say, my tone deadened. "I figured."

Bang, bang, bang. Following the loud, erratic knock, Linnie soars into the room. Her cheeks are pale, waxen, and she's trembling. "Jade, you need to leave. Leave now. You can crawl through the window."

I don't have to wonder what's going on. Mercedes has followed through with her threat.

Clarik steps in front of me, as if to shield me, and I'm taken aback. "What's going on?" he asks.

She wrings her hands together. "Well..."

I stalk down the hall, around a corner, and enter the living room, where the entire party has congregated. Almost everyone is holding a piece of paper. My hand trembles as I yank one out of some boy's clasp.

My name is doodled at the top, and a broken heart

that matches the one on my wrist decorates the margin. The text reads:

> I am a sea of nothingness. My life is a series of hurts—for others. Perhaps my dad would be better off without me.

This is a photocopied page from one of my journals. A passage I wrote while my dad and Nadine were dating. Mercedes must have kept it.

Mercedes, who wants to see me cry, who is angry about what might have happened between our parents and is lashing out at me. Who wants me to look like a fool in front of Clarik even if it blows her chances with him. Because she hates me more than she likes him.

At first I think I'm too shocked to react. We stare at each other, neither of us blinking. Like me, she's trembling. Her color is high, so high she looks sickly, but she doesn't back down. No, she winds up, bracing for a counterattack.

And I *will* attack. She's welcomed the entire school into our private war.

"You're right," Charlee Ann says and snickers. "We'd be better off without you."

Heaven and Nevaeh begin snatching papers. Heaven says, "Are you the one who did this, Charlee Ann?"

Nevaeh adds, "Because it's vile, even for you."

"Nothing to see here," Heaven tells the crowd as Charlee Ann sputters out a denial. "Go about your business."

If I am an angel of death, Clarik is an avenging angel. He works alongside the twins, a menacing presence no one dares question. Not even Bobby and his cohorts in crime.

Linnie, who found Robb as well as Kimberly, rallies around me with the others. Linnie and Robb try to hug me, but I shrug them off. Kimberly gets busy helping Clarik and the twins.

I stand there like an idiot, my ears ringing, my calm facade cracking. My tremors intensify. I'm the girl who thinks Robb should stop caring what other people think, yet here I am, feeling as if I'm a raw, open wound exposed to air for the first time.

This doesn't matter. These people do not matter. They mean nothing to me. Their opinion means *less* than nothing. I won't give Mercedes the satisfaction of watching me cry.

When Clarik gets an up-close-and-personal look at me, he abandons his efforts to destroy the evidence and barks an order to Robb. "Make sure Linnie and Kimberly get home safely." Then he takes my hand and ushers me out of the cabin, going straight to his truck.

I buckle up and slouch in my seat, the shoulder strap rubbing against my neck.

He stuffs the papers behind his seat and drives down the road. "I'm sorry."

"Not your fault," I mutter. "You did nothing wrong."

"I didn't apologize because I think I did something wrong, Jade. I apologized because I hate that something has hurt you."

"I'm not hurt."

He leaves that statement alone, saying, "The pages were from your diary, I'm guessing."

"It's from the summer before I started junior high, when my dad and Mercedes's mom were dating. Mercedes had access to my things." I thought I'd misplaced the diary, so she helped me search for it. Most likely she'd stolen it. And she'd kept it, all this time, waiting for the perfect time to strike. "We could have had our own bedrooms, but we decided to share one, because that's what sisters do."

"I had two stepbrothers, one older, one younger," he says, and I know he's doing his best to distract me. "I got along with the younger one at first, but never the older one. His dislike was contagious, I guess, because it wasn't long before the younger one began to avoid me, too."

"Were you sad? I bet you were sad. You're as far from a robot as a person can be."

His hands tighten on the steering wheel. "You're not a robot. You feel."

"Maybe. But I'm still a bad bet."

Silence overtakes us as his truck eats up the miles. It isn't long before he's parked at the side of my house. I unbuckle and open my door, certain I'll never see the inside of this truck again. I'll never go on another nondate date with Clarik, and that's okay. I'll be okay.

"Goodbye, Clarik."

A tension-laden pause. Then, "Goodbye, Jade."

My cheeks heat as I rush inside the house. My dad is in the living room, splayed on the couch and watching TV.

When he spots me, he jolts upright and frowns. His hair is messy, his shirt wrinkled and his sweatpants cut into shorts. "You're home early. Too early."

"Yes." I offer no more and move toward my room. I can't bring myself to look at him.

He pats the seat next to him. "Come here. Sit. Tell me about your evening."

Deep breath in…out… I close the distance and ease down. "What do you want to know?"

"Did you have fun?"

"Yes."

"What did you do?"

Had a little chat with Mercedes and found out you might or might not have hooked up with Nadine. And you? "Ate a burger, made an appearance at Clarik's welcome party and came home."

He heaves a weary sigh. He's disappointed. He's disappointed *in me.*

"Did you spend the night with Nadine Turner?" The words rush from my tongue before I can stop them.

"What? No!" He appears properly horrified.

Good, that's good. "Did you visit her bright and early this morning?"

Now he pinches the bridge of his nose. "Mercedes spotted me, I suppose."

Whack! A slap of shock, directly across my face. He did. He visited Nadine and kissed her goodbye. A sense of betrayal floods me. *Almost…can't…process.*

"Are you cheating on Fiona?" Does he hope to get back together with Nadine?

"No. Never. Yesterday Fiona had contractions. It's far too early, and I was worried. I wanted to speak with a doctor who wouldn't share my concerns with Fiona and freak her out. Nadine is my friend, so…" He shrugs.

"Since when are you two friends?"

"Since yesterday. Look, I wasn't around your mom much when she was pregnant with you, so I don't know what's normal and what isn't. Nadine assured me both Fiona and the baby are fine."

I'm not relieved, not even close. "Does Fiona know about the visit?"

His lips compress into a thin line. Yeah, I thought not.

I'm so over this night. *Everything is about to change.*

"If you can't talk to her about it, you probably shouldn't do it." I stand on unsteady legs and walk away.

There's a pause before he calls, "I love you, Jade." His voice is as hollow as mine.

Once I'm sealed inside my bedroom, I dress for a run rather than bed. I need to think, need to breathe. Giggles is perched on my bed. As I sneak out the window, unwilling to deal with my dad, he meows. Loudly. Sounding the alarm?

"Shh." I've done this a thousand times before. I'm sure I'll do it a thousand more.

I circle the neighborhood once…twice…five times, sticking to the sidewalks. My mind refuses to settle. Tomorrow I'll be breaking up with Robb, Linnie and Kimberly, as planned. I'll have to be direct and firm.

Linnie will probably cry. Kimberly will act like she doesn't care. Robb will definitely take it personally.

I suck.

I don't have to worry about cutting ties with Clarik. He'll go back to ignoring me, no doubt about it. Or maybe he'll nod a greeting every so often. What he won't do? Take a chance on a bad bet.

My dad… I don't know how to feel about him. He might not have cheated on Fiona, but he didn't do right by her, either.

"Why can't you stay away from me? Argh! Obsessed much?"

The familiar voice stops me in my tracks, and I come face-to-face with Mercedes. She left her own party? Why? Why would she do that?

She's in her front yard, sitting under a tree that towers next to the curb, mascara streaked down her cheeks. After pounding her fist into the ground a few times, dirt flying, she stands.

The sight of her tears only adds fuel to the fire of my rage.

I'm not ready to deal with her. I kick into a run, but she follows me.

"I hate you," she snarls.

"The feeling is mutual, I assure you," I snarl back. "What are you doing out here? No, you know what? It doesn't matter. I don't care. You do not want to be around me right now, Mercedes."

I turn the corner, and she follows.

"I told you to leave the party," she says between huffing breaths. "Why didn't you leave?"

"Are you trying to say what happened is *my fault*?" Rage, boiling over. I stop to glare at her. "How about this, then? Tomorrow I'm going to tell everyone about your bingeing and purging. I will give details. I haven't forgotten the way you used to hide junk food wrappers under our mattress and—"

Tremors sweep over her, and she crosses her arms over her middle. "N-no one will believe you."

Up ahead, headlights flash as a car turns the corner; those lights are closing in on us way too fast, as if there's a high-speed race in progress, and we are the finish line.

My heart jacks into a matching speed, and I move into a yard, next to Mercedes. Music is blasting. Laughter rings out, followed by a high-pitched, "Whoo-hoo!"

We're away from the road and should be safe, but they still seem to be barreling straight for us.

Tires squeal. Those lights! So bright! I grab Mercedes's arm and yank her out of the way. Together, we fall into a dewy flower bed—

Pain explodes through my head. For a moment, my vision goes black. So does my mind. Then stars wink into my line of sight, and my brain comes back online. The back of my skull must have banged into a rock. The pain shoots through the rest of my body, muscles clenching and knotting. My stomach threatens to rebel as the taste of old pennies coats my tongue.

A car door slams. Someone curses. I recognize his voice. Bobby Bay, no doubt about it. "They're dead. I think they're dead. What do we do?"

Other kids mutter replies, their panic making their words incoherent. Footsteps sound, followed by the roar of an engine and the squeal of tires.

The kids are driving away, leaving us to fend for ourselves? Great! This is the perfect end to my day, it really is.

Moaning, I sit up. My muscles and bones protest. My line of sight is hazy, but at least the world is coming back into view as I blink.

Mercedes rubs her chest and lumbers to her feet. "Stupid Bobby! I'm going to kill him."

"Why? Because he failed to kill *me*?"

"Jade—"

"Just…shut up." I'm tired and sore, and I'm done for the night. Done with *everything.*

"Thank you," she calls, her voice trembling. "For pulling me out of the way."

Whatever. I limp home, wincing with every step, and sneak through my window. Giggles is gone. I shower, pull on a tank top and clean underwear and crawl into bed. Despite my aches and pains, I drift into a fitful doze…

Once again, I dream of my mother. We're outside. I'm standing, but she's swinging on the swing set. I cross my arms and lean against the pole. The metal is cool against my skin, making me gasp. This feels so real. I can even smell burning wood, as if many of my neighbors are finally using their hearths.

"I made mistakes, but this is my chance to fix them," she says. "Don't worry. I'll make sure you have an ally."

My brow crinkles with confusion. "An ally for what?"

"I'm not going to let you destroy your life," she continues. "If you continue to hide from your pain, you will never live, never find happiness. I want you happy. So look at the world around you, my sweet. See how it has become a cold shell of itself. Without heart, it is twisted and wrong."

"What are you talking about, Mom?" The world around me is the same as always.

She flashes me a smile so sad that it makes my chest

hurt. “Remember that I love you. I love who you are—always have, always will. You don’t have to hide that girl away anymore, as if you are ashamed of her. It’s time you love her, too, and let her live.”

A second later, she’s gone.

Chapter 6

I can make it one minute…hour…day…week…year.
I can make it one step at a time.

—*Miranda Leighton*

I blink open my eyes, an intense flare of light causing them to sting and water as if I've been in a dark cave for years and have only just now awakened. There's a terrible taste in my mouth—I can imagine that tiny woodland creatures have crawled inside and died. What's wrong with me? Am I sick?

Wait. Mercedes…the near accident…slamming into the flower bed. At least I wasn't hit by the car. Then my mom appeared in my dreams and told me to love myself, to find happiness.

A knock sounds at my door—or is the knocking coming from inside my head? I groan as my temples throb.

"Jade," a deep voice calls.

My dad. I groan again. If I ignore him, he might go away, and I'll be able to sleep a little longer. I can—

"Jade, honey. Come on." No, he won't be going away. "We're going to eat breakfast like a real family."

"I'm not hungry," I grumble.

"You're never hungry. Get up, anyway."

Ugh. I'm not ready to face the day and say goodbye to

my friends…or endure teasing from other students about what I wrote as a newly minted teenager.

"Nadine is in the process of making pancakes for the rest of us. She's already whipped up your protein shake."

Nadine? He's seriously teasing me about spending time with her? And what does he mean, *the rest of us*?

Something's wrong. First, my dad is mega cheery. After last night he should be distant, even angry with me. Right? Second, he *wouldn't* tease me about Nadine with Fiona nearby.

I scramble from bed, my hair tumbling over my shoulders and into my eyes. A wave of dizziness makes me sway, and I rub my temples. My room—

Oh. My. *Goth.* My room has been transformed. My things are in boxes, and most of my furniture is gone. There isn't a vanity or a dresser. Just a bed and some boxes filled with my clothes. The walls are painted black with pinpricks of white—stars?—and the curtains that frame my window are black and ruffled, a perfect match to the comforter on the bed.

I like it, I like all of it, but nothing is mine, and it creeps me out. Did my dad and Fiona sneak into my room and redecorate while I slept? But…why?

Confusion mounts. The action must have dislodged a memory. I see my mother on the swing, smiling at me with a tinge of sadness.

Remember that I love you. I love who you are—always have, always will. You don't have to hide that girl away anymore as if you are ashamed of her. It's time you love her, too, and let her live.

It's time you love her…

It's. Time.

Everything is about to change.

Look at the world around you. See how it has become a cold shell of itself. Without heart, it is twisted and wrong.

I'm not going to let you destroy your life. If you continue to hide from your pain, you will never live, never find happiness. I want you happy.

Nauseous now, headache growing worse by the second, I yank on the first T-shirt and jeans I find. There's nothing odd about my clothes at least. That's a good sign, right?

I anchor my hair into a ponytail using a black scarf I never bought or received as a gift, because there isn't a rubber band anywhere. What else is different?

A quick search reveals my journals are gone. Mom's journals, too. Jaw clenched, I throw open my door, ready to wreak hell—and halt while gasping.

The hallway walls are painted black, and there are no pictures. This is… This is…

Argh! This is so *wrong.*

"Dad," I shout, launching forward—only to grind to a halt again. Nadine Turner *is* here, and she's bustling around the kitchen. But she's not the Nadine Turner I remember. Her once-sleek blond bob is now long, tangled and dyed black. Instead of yellow or red, her favorite colors, she's wearing black from head to toe. Even her lipstick is black.

My dad is sitting at the counter, watching her bustle here and there. Like Nadine, he's wearing black. He never wears black. I've always considered it a silent protest to my overuse of it. But…but…

"What is going on?" I demand. Even our dining room table is different. Before, it was round. Now it's square.

I want round!

Dad looks at me over his shoulder and grins. "Good morning, sleepyhead. You look beautiful, as usual." As he pushes a protein shake in my direction, his features carry a hint of wistfulness as well as an edge of sadness. "I wish your mom could see you. She'd be so proud."

Oookay. Does he have a fever? Food poisoning? A brain aneurysm?

Do *I*? My dad rarely compliments me—I'm too much of a disappointment, I suppose—and he never talks about my mom.

"I'm waiting for the punch line," I say.

His dark brows knit together, and he frowns. "I don't understand, honey. The punch line to what?"

"This." I spread my arms to indicate the entire house. "Are you guys playing a joke on me?" Or is this weird act some sort of punishment? No, surely not. My dad would never resort to such extreme measures. "Where is our table? The round one."

"You know we sold that table last year." He worries two fingers against the stubble on his jaw. "And a joke? About what?"

"Answering one of my questions with a question of your own is a good tactic, but it won't fly." My hands fist. "What's going on? Where's Fiona? Where's Giggles?"

He regards me for a long, silent moment, his frown deepening. "You're acting weird. I have no idea who Fiona is or what you've done with your giggles. Is that a new expression all the cool kids are saying?"

"Eat your breakfast, babe." Nadine slides a plate of pancakes across the counter before focusing on me—and smiling. She *never* smiles at me. "Is the protein shake the way you like it, freak?"

The affection in her tone suggestions "freak" is a term of endearment. *This. Is. Madness.* "What's she doing here, Dad?" Irritation and confusion continue to mount. I stomp my foot, feeling like the child I haven't been since my mother's death.

"That's no way to speak to your stepmother, Jade." He wags a finger in my direction. "Apologize."

My *what*? "She isn't my stepmother." The words wheeze from me.

Nadine grips the edge of the counter, her knuckles quickly bleaching of color. There's a silver bud in her eyebrow, and it glints in the light. Oh, sweet goodness. Her eyebrow is now pierced.

"I must have hurt your feelings," she says, "but I don't know how. Tell me and I'll fix it."

"Someone tell me what's going on before I *flip out*." Mercedes rounds the corner, her blue eyes wild. "Mom. What are we doing here? And why are you dressed like that?"

Both Nadine *and* Mercedes stayed the night here?

Nadine closes her eyes and draws in a deep breath as if she's praying for patience. "What's wrong with you girls today?" She scans her daughter's hot-pink sundress, the same one Mercedes wore last night. There are no grass stains to prove Bobby nearly killed us. "How many times do I have to tell you? You need to dress for the position you want, not the position you have. Go change your clothes. I'm sure Jade will let you borrow something appropriate."

"No way, no how." Mercedes slashes her hand through the air, clearly agitated. "Answer my questions. Tell me what's going on."

"Girls," my dad says on a sigh. "This isn't the way to speak to each other. Let's start the day with breakfast rather than attitude, all right?"

"You, be quiet." Mercedes turns her glare on me. "And you. You were supposed to tell him to stay away from my mother, not to get closer."

At least she—this—is normal, saving me from a total breakdown. But with a surge of relief comes a tide of fury. It burns inside me. Why is *she* the only one who understands that something strange is going on?

Scowling, I take a step toward her. "You better watch how you speak to me."

"She's right," Nadine says, shocking Mercedes. And me! "Freakling, you need to apologize to your stepdad and sister. Now."

Freakling? In unison, Mercedes and I snap, "We aren't sisters."

"I'm not apologizing to anyone," she adds.

A cell phone rings, and Nadine glances at the screen. With a curse, she snags the lab coat that is hanging on the hook beside the cabinets. "I've got to go. Don't wait up, babe. I'm working late tonight." She grabs her purse, saying, "Are you going to be able to handle our freaklings and this—whatever *this* is?"

"I certainly hope so." His fork clinks against his plate

as he leans back in his seat and stretches out his legs. "I'll keep you updated."

"You can tell me all about it when I get home." Unlike Fiona, who likes to kiss my dad every time she passes him, Nadine marches off, her high heels click-clacking against the floor tiles.

Hinges squeak as the front door opens and closes. A door closes. The roar of a car engine echoes from the walls.

Mercedes tosses her arms up. "Well? Someone tell me. What the hell is happening?"

"Dad," I say, ignoring her. "Why are my things in boxes? Where are Mom's journals? And why are you with that…that…harpy? Where's Fiona? And don't tell me you don't know who she is. She's your freaking wife."

He goes still and pale. "I honestly don't know who this Fiona person is. And who told you about your mother's journals?"

"Here's a better question," Mercedes interjects. "Why is *my mother* with *him*?"

I speak over her, saying, "Fiona is pregnant with your baby. My *real* sister. Ruby."

"Okay, enough." My dad stands, the motion jerky. "You two need to stop this. You hate each other, and that's fine, but it's past time you accepted the fact that I'm with Nadine and we're staying together. Also, I know you don't want to move out of the district, but it's happening. End of story." He dumps what remains of his pancakes in the trash and washes his plate at the sink. "We haven't gotten an offer on the house yet, but we will. Soon. I'm taking measures to—"

"Move?" I screech. Out of the district? Away from Linnie and Kimberly and Robb? A muscle constricts in my throat. Away from Clarik?

Planned to cut them out of my life, anyway. Why does this matter?

Inhale, exhale.

"No, no, no." Mercedes shakes her head, locks of hair slapping at her cheeks. "This isn't real. This isn't happening."

Ignore. "I'm seriously considering calling your supervisor and recommending drug testing, Dad." I rub my thumb over the broken-heart tattoo on my wrist. "And what do you mean, how do I even know about Mom's journals? You gave them to me on my sixteenth birthday."

"No, I didn't. I gave you a car." Features pinched, he says, "Grandma Beers has the journals, but I'm telling you, honey, you do *not* want to read them."

"I do." I haven't visited Grandma Beers in years. Or talked to her. She's a sweetheart, but she's old, and she's going to die sooner rather than later, and I don't like how tight my chest feels whenever we're together. "I will."

The color in his cheeks deepens as he grabs a set of keys from the hook and tosses them at me. "Go. This conversation is officially over. Drive your sister to school."

"Excuse me?" I grate. "You know I don't drive."

"Since when? And you're going to school. Don't even think about ditching again."

Again?

"Hello. Where's *my* car?" Mercedes demands.

Dad shakes his head at her. "You know your mom won't buy you a car until your grades improve."

She shrieks, "*What?* I'm making straight As. What more does she want?"

"Since when did your Ds become As?" he asks.

"Ds?" Her mouth opens and closes. She steps between us, looking from Dad to me, me to Dad, the wheels in her head clearly turning. "You're wrong. But then, it's clear you're missing a few screws."

"Go. *Now.* Don't forget to buy your tickets to Fright Night." He digs in his wallet and tosses us each a twenty-dollar bill.

"Fright Night?" we screech in unison.

"The costume party," he says. "The fund-raiser for a new dissection lab. Don't pretend you don't know."

Mercedes laughs, and the sound borders on hysteria. She snatches up the twenty. "Fright Night? Nope. I would *never* plan an event like that."

He rolls his eyes. "You didn't. Jade did."

What! What kind of bizarre upside-down world is this?

"You know what?" Dad says, and I can tell his temper is rising. "*I'll* go. All I wanted was a relaxing breakfast with my daughters before I had to spend eight hours under a sweltering sun. Instead, I'm actually looking forward to eight hours of peace."

Like Nadine, he stomps away. The door to his bedroom slams.

I set the car keys on the counter with forced calm. I'm not driving *anywhere.*

"Is this your idea of payback?" Mercedes demands. "Because you've gone too far."

"*I've* gone too far? *Me?*"

"Yes," she hisses. "You."

"Why don't you think before you speak? Or maybe your food-deprived brain no longer functions correctly. I haven't done anything. I haven't had time. And even if I *had* acted against you, neither of our parents would have played along." What's more, there's no way I could have painted all these walls so swiftly. They don't even smell of fresh paint.

"Whatever." She swipes up the keys, saying, "I'm leaving in five minutes, and I'm going to find out what's going on. You can come with, or you can stay here. For once, I'm the one who doesn't care."

We head to our bedrooms, and I realize she has the one next to mine. Ruby's nursery.

Pang.

Bury. Lock. In case Mercedes decides to leave without me, I hurriedly brush my teeth and pull on a pair of shoes. At least my headache is waning.

With three minutes to spare, I'm pacing in the living room, back and forth, back and forth, searching for calm but failing to find it. What am I going to do? How am I going to fix this, whatever *this* is?

Mercedes doesn't show up for another *ten* minutes, and she's still wearing the pink dress in protest.

Silent, we march outside. The morning air is fresh and warm, but my blood is chilled.

A car honks. A hearse—an actual, honest-to-goodness hearse—slows in front of my house. The passenger window rolls down, and I spy two girls from school. I've seen both girls around the halls, but neither has ever deigned to speak to me.

One girl has a black choker around her neck, faux fur draped over her shoulders and a black-and-white mesh top. The other girl looks like a 1950s pinup, rock-and-roll edition, with a sleeveless black-and-white polka-dot dress that reveals arms sleeved in colorful tattoos.

Have Linnie, Robb and Kimberly changed? What about Clarik?

One of the girls whistles. The other shouts, "Hey, Jade."

"Karly? McKayla?" Mercedes hurries toward them.

The girls peer at each other before bursting out laughing. The pinup says, "Aw. Look at the preppy, pretending she knows us." After blowing me a kiss, they speed away.

Oookay. This is new, too.

Mercedes's eyes are wide. "What just happened?"

"I have no idea," I reply softly.

We climb into the black Mustang parked in my driveway, Mercedes behind the wheel.

On the drive to school, three other cars honk at us. Two girls and one boy belt out friendly hellos to me. Only to me. Mercedes is flipped off, and it's...odd. Surreal.

When Mercedes parks in the school's lot, she scans the area, stunned. Every student...every *teacher*...is some type of Goth. And there are many, many types. Traditional, cyber, glam, baby doll, Victorian and more. Almost everyone is scowling, as if unhappy in their skin.

A common misconception: if you are part of the Goth subculture, you are always miserable.

"Hey, Jade!" someone calls. "I'm having a séance later. Will you come?"

This bizarro world must play to the stereotypes. Another common misconception is that all Goths are into black magic.

"No," I say, and moans of disappointment break out.

Look at the world around you. See how it has become a cold shell of itself. Without heart, it is twisted and wrong.

My mother's words drift through my mind, and icy foreboding chills the blood in my veins all over again. This is twisted and wrong.

If you do not appreciate and value the good things you have, you lose them.

It's time. Everything is about to change.

I want you happy.

Did my mother somehow *cause* this to happen?

A thousand denials rush through my head. Impossible! And ridiculous! But…

Maybe?

"I can't… I don't…" Mercedes struggles to find the right words. "Be honest with me, please. Are you paying these people to dress and act like this?"

"Are you?" I snap.

"No. Are *you*?" she asks again.

The vengeance side of me likes seeing her so confused and angry. "You would deserve it." This and more.

"Because if you are—"

"I'm not, okay. I'm not. Paying people to pretend to like me and hate you isn't my style. Especially when I planned to ditch my friends today and do the whole solitary thing. So trust me when I say this is my worst nightmare come to life."

She bangs her head against the steering wheel once, twice. "Okay. All right. Let's assume this *Freaky Friday* situation is real. In movies and books, the people who switched have to learn something. Let's figure out what we have to learn and report back to each other after school."

"Let me save you the trouble of digging. You need to learn a little something called compassion."

"And you need to learn how to live—love—like a real girl," she counters sharply.

We glare at each other as we emerge. I try to draw my numbness around me like a coat… And once again, I fail.

When Kimberly parks her Bronco a few spots down, I experience a wave of relief and decide I'm not going to ditch her or the others. Not now. I don't think I can do this on my own.

Kimberly emerges and I gawk. What the crap? She's wearing buttercup yellow, not a tattoo or piece of metal in sight.

Even still, I approach her. Her clothes do not matter, just the girl underneath them. "You won't believe—"

"Shut up, clone." She flips me off before shouldering past me to get to Mercedes. "Hey, lovely," she says to her sworn enemy. "I went by your house so you wouldn't have to ride with the stephorror, but you'd already gone." Her sandy-brown hair is combed away from her face and clipped with a glittery barrette in the shape of a flower. "Come on."

Mercedes looks just as flummoxed as I feel as Kimberly leads her away.

Don't appreciate…lose…

I pinch my arm, hard. Nope, I'm not dreaming. A blue sky and an ever-brightening sun still hang overhead. Cracked cement still acts as a foundation at my feet. Almost everyone at school is still Goth.

Mercedes was right about one thing. We need to assume this is real. Somehow, we've entered a creepy alternate universe, and we're trapped.

I blame Mom. Like the ghost of Jacob Marley in *A Christmas Carol*, she warned me what was to come. But she also said I'd have an ally. Mercedes is the only person who knows the whole world is messed up, but she is *not* an ally. Not even close.

Honk, honk, hoooonk. "I love you, Jade Leighton," a boy shouts, leaning out the passenger window of a passing sedan. "Will you go to homecoming dance with me? Please. With a cherry on top of me."

"This is not happening," I mutter. "Nope. Not happening."

I don't spare him a glance. If his feelings get hurt, so what? When I go back to the real world—I *will* go back to the real world—he won't remember this.

Heart tripping inside my chest, I sprint the rest of the way to school, determined to find Linnie, Robb and Clarik. They'll be the same as before. They'll like me. They must. Even if I don't like *myself* at the moment.

Have I ever?

Chapter 7

Fear is the enemy.
But how do you fight an enemy you can't see?

—Miranda Leighton

The tardy bell goes silent as I pass through the front doors. Front doors and a metal detector. An alarm blasts, but I ignore it, storming down a hall now cleared of students.

The security guard calls my name, which is odd. We've never met. He's a stranger to me.

If I continue walking away, I'm pretty sure he'll just chase me down. I'd rather not be singled out today of all days, so I backtrack, my stomach churning. At some point today, I'm going to barf. This is too much weird, too quickly.

He waves a scanner over me, and like the alarm, it goes off.

"It's the brow piercings," he finally says. His eyes—framed by thick black eyeliner—crinkle at the corners as he smiles and waves me on. "Sorry to keep you, but I had to check. You know the rules. I know a freakling like you wouldn't be packing heat. Go on. Get to class."

A freakling like me?

I remind myself to breathe. In and out, in and out.

"Um, thank you. I guess." I rush down the empty hallways. Forget the office. I'm going to Mr. Parton's class. That's where two of my four—I hope—remaining friends will be. Linnie and Clarik.

Walls, posters and banners whiz past me. When I come to one with Robb's picture, I skid to a stop.

Forever Missed.

Missed? What, did he move in this reality?

From the picture, his sad, dark eyes stare at me, beseeching me to help him. A look I've seen a thousand times before. But his hair is cut military short, and he's wearing a white button-down shirt, the wrinkles ironed out.

The letters *RIP* jump out at me, and I jolt. Rest in peace, as if he's…dead? Dead and gone? No, no, no. He *can't* be.

Tremors sweep through me as I turn my attention to another poster. The same image peers at me, begging for help. Only in this one, someone has drawn *X*s over Robb's eyes, blackened his teeth and etched skulls across his shirt. I struggle to breathe as I rip the image from the wall, then another and another.

Don't value what you have, lose it.

I can't… I don't…

I should have been nicer to him, should have showed him just how much he means—meant—to me. And I will! As soon as I wake up from this nightmare. *I'm learning, Mom. See!*

Everything will be okay. He's not really dead. He's *not.* This strange, horrible world is only temporary. Unless this was the path we were headed down in the real world? Had Robb planned to take his own life? What if my callous rejection—another one in a long string, and from someone who was supposed to love him—would have acted as the tipping point and sent him over the edge? Not that his decisions revolved around me, but cruelty is cruelty no matter how you slice it.

I change directions, rushing to the lobby. Martha is at her desk, but she's not the Martha I know and like. She's morphed into some sort of prom Goth, a sequined black dress hugging her ample curves. Her gray hair now boasts streaks of vibrant purple.

"What happened to Robb Martinez?" I demand.

She presses a hand over her heart. "Good gracious, Jade. You scared me half to death."

"Tell me," I shout. "Now." My breaths come fast and shallow, cold fingers of dread creeping down my spine.

"He killed himself." As calm as if we're discussing the weather, she gathers a stack of folders. "I hope you aren't blaming yourself. Mercedes and her flock might think your teasing led him to pull the trigger, but I promise you, everyone else knows better. You speak the truth, no matter how difficult. Now, if you'd like to schedule a session with the school counselor—"

"*My* teasing?" The entire awful world tilts, the ceiling trading places with the floor. Breath wheezes from me. My stomach roils, hard.

"Did no one tell you about his note?" she asks with a frown. "He said he had a mental picture of his future, thanks to you, and it wasn't pretty, that it would be better to end things now."

Those words…the same words I spoke at Mercedes's

party. About Clarik, not Robb! And yet so clearly I remember Robb's reaction to them. He'd peered at me with such hurt, as if I'd just upended his world.

I have to wonder again. Was he considering suicide, even then, and I missed the signs?

I never should have considered severing ties with my friends. They needed love and support, not more heartache. Heck, the same was true of everyone, I suppose. Even me. Even Mercedes.

"I should have been more careful with my words," I say softly. "I know that now. I'll guard my tongue."

"What are you talking about?" she asks.

One step, two, I back out of the lobby. Then I'm running...sprinting...my hair flying behind me. I reach Mr. Parton's class, and note the door is covered with red-and-black ribbons. Our new school colors? My hand freezes on the knob. What will I find inside?

Tremors growing worse, I open the door and step in. Mr. Parton stands at the head of the classroom. As soon as he spies me, he goes quiet. His thinning hair hasn't changed colors, but the strands are now long enough for a ponytail and—

My mouth flounders open and closed. No way I'm seeing what I think I'm seeing. *Blink, blink.* Nope, there's no change. Usually he sports a polyester suit and ugly tie. Today his T-shirt has a grunge-metal band logo, and his jeans are ripped.

"Welcome, Jade." His features light up with something akin to delight. "I'm glad you could make it. You always darken our day." He pushes his palms together, forming a steeple, and bows his head. "Come in, come in and have a seat. I'm about to start today's lesson."

Darken our day, he said, as if *he* finds beauty in darkness. *Twisted, wrong.* I laugh without humor, acid burning my throat as every eye finds me.

I scan the sea of familiar faces, but there's no sign of Linnie or Clarik. Maybe they're running late? Any second, they could fly through the door and demand to know what's going on. Together we'll figure out what I need to do to make things go back to normal.

I trip my way to one of two open desks, both of which are next to Charlee Ann, who is beaming at me. Along the way, a boy with thick silver chains wrapped around his neck winks at me.

"Hi, freak." A girl who's never spoken to me—only laughed at me—waves. A snake tattoo peeks from the collar of her black lace top. "Your party ruled the school last night!"

My party?

"Hey, you." Another girl waves. Hand-drawn teardrops decorate her cheeks. "Did you get my message? Want to do a taxidermy class tonight?"

"Or we could make a YouTube video about the best places to shop," another girl says.

A third girl sounds off. "Hey, where did you get those pants? Soooo *fright.*"

Fright?

Clattering voices blend together until I can no longer make out individual words. Everyone is peering at me as if I'm a shiny new car, paid in full, the keys already in the ignition. Everything inside me screams, *"This isn't happening!*" And yet the proof is sitting all around me, asking me to go hang out.

This kind of thing happens only in books and movies, never real life. Not *my* life.

"Jade?" Mr. Parton pads toward me, eyeing me with genuine concern. "Are you all right? Would you like to visit the nurse?"

Um, what would I even say to the nurse? Unless she has a magic wand to wake me from my nightmare, she's useless to me.

Another humorless laugh bubbles from me, tinged in budding hysteria. "I'm fine," I force myself to say. I'm not sure I'll ever be "fine" again.

The door opens and Linnie steps inside. Her gaze is downcast as she trudges over and sits at the desk next to mine. My heart pounds against my ribs, the bones threatening to crack. Like everyone else, she's different—familiar and yet *not*. Her strawberry locks are shorter, her black lipstick exchanged. Rather than a skintight dress, she's wearing a cotton T and capri pants.

She looks so…*innocent*, like she just came from a student council meeting, where she rallied to include an ice cream station in the cafeteria. Does she know people think my words led to Robb's death? Is she okay? Whether this world is legit or not, her pain is real.

Finally, she looks up. Looks at me. Looks away. I'm desperate to find an anchor in the midst of this craziness, but when I reach for her hands, she flinches as if I plan to smack her.

"Linnie," I whisper, my voice a little broken. "I'm your friend. I'm not going to hurt—"

“Leave me alone,” she snaps, so tense I fear she’ll shatter.

Everyone in the classroom watches us, fascinated. We might as well be standing center stage, illuminated by a spotlight.

I slink down in my chair. The truth might as well be claws sinking in and ripping me to shreds. This world is a cold shell of itself, a metaphor for the cold shell my mother thinks *I’ve* become. I have no friends here—no *real* friends—just as I thought I wanted. I’m alone. Robb is gone because my careless words stripped away his hope for a better life, and Linnie and Kimberly despise me. I’m enemy number one. The stepmother I never valued has been replaced with a stepmother I can’t stand, and the people who used to ignore me now worship me the way they once worshipped Mercedes.

What am I supposed to learn from their adoration? *Tell me and I’ll learn it, I swear!*

My mom called me a bully. At the time, I denied it. Well, I admit it. I *am* a bully. I hurt Robb, Linnie and Kimberly in ways I’ll forever regret. *Let me go back to real life now, and I’ll make it up to them. Please! I’ll even try to be happy.*

I wait, hopeful, but…nothing happens. My muscles bunch, preparing for flight. I don’t know where I can go, where I’ll be safe.

Mr. Parton begins his lecture, and I tune him out and focus on Linnie. If I can get her to remember me, to remember who she was—who she really is—I’ll have my ally. The ally I need more than air to breathe.

The Victorian Goth on her other side launches a spitball at her, and she winces. Several people snicker, but Linnie pretends they don't exist, even as a deeper red spills over her cheeks.

"I hear you like balls, so how about another?" Victorian mutters. She crumples up another paper and draws back her elbow, ready to launch.

"Stop," I snarl. These kids are Goth because it's cool, not for any other reason. They don't embrace what the mainstream world shuns—those who are different—or they would be nice to Linnie. "Leave her alone or I'll make you regret it. Understand?"

Victorian stills. Her horror-filled gaze widens, and she drops her hand onto her desk with a thump. "I'm so sorry, Jade. I didn't know we were supposed to leave the preppies alone today."

"Is something wrong?" Mr. Parton anchors his hands on his hips and glares at Linnie as if *she's* at fault for the disruption.

That hasn't changed. "She did nothing wrong."

Rather than berating me as usual, he jumps back into his lecture. Linnie pretends I no longer exist.

I have to reach her.

A finger lightly taps my arm. "Okay," Charlee Ann whispers. "You know I adore the crap out of you, right, but you are being seriously weird right now, and not in a good way."

I'm being weird? Me? Charlee Ann Richards just told me she adores the crap out of me! I'm no longer the mud caked on her three-hundred-dollar boots. And doesn't she just look sickeningly adorable? Black cobweb lace overlays her corset top. Red and black glitter surrounds her eyes, making her look like she's wearing a half mask.

I hate this. Defeat swamps me, and I drop my head into my upraised hands. *Can't deal.*

"Are you even listening to me?" She tosses a pencil at me. "Jade! For real already. The girl you just defended? She's your stepsister's favorite sidekick and a preppy to boot. They are no better than wild animals. As you like to tell me, you can't feed a wild animal without losing a finger."

Here, Linnie and Mercedes are best friends as well as pariahs, and I'm the current "it" girl, my word law.

"*Psst.* Jade. Pay attention to me before I have a meltdown."

"Just…leave Linnie alone, okay?" Frustration and anger boil inside me, destroying any semblance of numbness I had. Robotic? No longer! I feel, and there's no end in sight.

You think your pain is hidden, but you *are the one in hiding. The pain is going to find you, one way or another. Be ready. Fight it. Fight for better.*

I want you happy.

I jolt. Those words—*fight for better, I want you happy*—rattle around in my head. I can use my newfound popularity for good and make sure everyone in school likes Linnie and Kimberly. I can make their lives better. In turn, they'll be happy, which will make *me* happy. Or as close to happiness as someone like me can get. Surely some of the pain I harbor will fade. Things will go back to normal.

Robb will be alive. When I'm back in the real world,

I will remain friends with Robb, Linnie and Kimberly. In a few short hours, I've become intimately acquainted with loneliness, and I *hate* it.

"I don't want to fight with you," Charlee Ann whispers, dragging me out of my head.

"Girls." Mr. Parton offers us an apologetic smile. "I don't mind if you talk during class, but bring it down a notch. This is the second time I've been interrupted." He levels a pointed glare at Linnie, as if she's to blame for both instances.

"Sure thing, Mr. P." Charlee Ann flashes him a thumbs-up.

When he returns to his lecture, she leans closer to me. "If you want me to be nice to the preppies, pick one or two and I'll be nice," she says in a fierce but quiet voice. "But first, tell me why."

Here goes. My first move in the right direction. "Linnie and Kimberly are wonderful people. They have terrible pasts, and they have endured more abuses than you can even imagine. They deserve better than we've given them."

Her lips part. "Are you kidding me?"

"I never kid."

The person sitting behind me taps my shoulder, and dread fills me. What's next? I turn and find Bobby leering at me. His sandy-colored hair is so black it appears blue and, like Mr. Parton, his eyes are rimmed with black eyeliner.

"Mmm-mmm, you look good enough to eat." As his heavy-lidded gaze peruses me, he radiates the supreme confidence of a guy who believes every girl on the planet is hot for him. "We still on for this weekend?"

We're on for...never. "First, you shouldn't drink and drive. You could have killed someone." Namely Mercedes and me! "Second, unless we scheduled a boxing match, the answer is no."

He laughs as if I'm joking and reaches out to tuck a strand of hair behind my ear. I catch his wrist, push his hand away. Now he frowns.

When next he speaks, however, his voice dips low with suggestion and promise. "I know why you're mad. You think I forgot our anniversary. I didn't, I swear. I only pretended to forget so I could throw a party on Saturday."

I'm not going to pretend I like him. "Are we celebrating a year of loathing each other?"

The door bursts open and crashes against the wall, startling everyone in the room. Mercedes rushes inside, her gaze frantic, her expression wild, her hair now tangled around her shoulders.

"Miss Turner." Mr. Parton glares daggers at her. "You were transferred out of my class for a reason. You are to remain as far away from me as possible."

"Preppy alert," Bobby mutters.

"Anyone bring a tranq?" Charlee Ann quips. "Put the animal out of its misery, and save us from having to look at her. If she posts one more photo of her face, I'm going to barf."

Gales of laughter erupt.

"Charlee Ann?" Mercedes hurries toward the girl's desk. "How can you—"

"Ew." Charlee Ann shudders and tosses an eraser at

her. "The preppy is talking to me. Somebody make it stop. And leave. Definitely make it leave. It's stinking up the room."

"Please." Chalk white, she focuses on Bobby, who calls her a horrible name under his breath. "You have to remember me. You can't—"

"All right. That's enough." Mr. Parton storms to her side, grabs her arm. "First you disrupt my class, then you screech like a banshee. Go to the office, Miss Turner. Right now. I won't tolerate this kind of behavior."

I leap to my feet as she wrenches her arm from his grip.

"It's worse than we thought," she says to me, desperation drenching every word.

"I know." I lick my lips. "Mr. Parton," I say, "I'll make sure Mercedes goes to the office." I don't wait for his response, just drag my "stepsister" out of the room. Not that she puts up a fight.

Once the door closes behind us, she takes me by the shoulders and shakes me. "Tell me what to do. I don't know how to escape this hell. Everyone hates me. Me! People beg for my attention, and now I'm nothing, no one."

"I know," I repeat.

"You don't know *anything*. Someone actually threw gum in my hair!"

I quirk a brow at her. She threw gum in *my* hair a few weeks ago.

Withering, she presses her face against her upraised hands. "I'm sorry, okay?"

Yeah, right. Like she's ever been sorry about anything. "We'll find a way out." I can't believe anything less. I have to get back to Robb. For once, I'll accept his hug and tell him everything is going to be okay.

"Like you want to leave," she mutters. "You are everyone's everything here."

"I know," I reply a third time. "But I figured out my purpose. I'm going to use my power for good and make everyone like Linnie and Kimberly."

She snorts. "You think you're here to make an entire school fall into like with two Goth girls? Well, *former* Goth girls. That might be the dumbest thing you've ever said, and you've said some doozies."

"Then why are we here, huh? Tell me your best theory. Go ahead. I'm waiting… Still waiting…"

"We… I…"

"Yeah, that's what I thought. I should be able to get it done in a few days. Definitely by the end of the week," I say. "You never had any trouble getting people to do what you wanted."

"You know *nothing* about my life. But I guess you're about to." She tears a poster from the wall and shoves it at me. "Have you seen this?"

My knees almost buckle as I read. VOTE FOR JADE. CLASS PRESIDENT. My own face stares back at me as if I'm peering into a mirror. Same platinum hair and gold eyes. Same high cheekbones and freckles. Same blank expression.

I raise my chin. "This is more proof I'm supposed to lead everyone at school into a new era of tolerance."

She tosses the poster on the ground and stomps all over my face. "What am I supposed to do, huh? Cheer you… on…" Her voice trails off.

A boy—Clarik, I realize—turns the corner and strolls in our direction, his hands pushed into his pockets. A white T-shirt hugs his biceps, and ripped jeans cover his legs. He hasn't colored his hair either, the brown waves tumbling over his forehead and ears.

He looks exactly the same, as I hoped. He *must* be my ally!

My pulse trips into a wild rhythm. Mercedes instantly forgotten, I rush to Clarik and throw my arms around him. The first hug I've ever initiated. "I'm so glad you're here!"

He gives me a gentle push away from him, severing contact—rejecting me.

Horror, dejection and helplessness collide inside me, and it's like a sonic boom goes off, nearly drilling me to my knees. Is this how I made Robb and Linnie feel? My dad? Fiona?

He frowns down at me. "After what you did to Mercedes at the party," he says, "why would you ever think I'd be happy to see you?"

Chapter 8

True character is revealed during the worst moments of our lives.

—Miranda Leighton

I stagger back, the emotional deluge like acid in my veins. Clarik thinks *I* hurt *Mercedes.* He is not my ally. Not even close. I think… I think he's my enemy.

How is this supposed to help me get happy, Mother? Huh?

He's blaming me for a crime I didn't commit. Although…

I grind my back teeth. I told her I would tell the entire school about her eating disorder, and I meant it. I've only ever made promises, never threats. Judging by the way Clarik is looking at me right now, as if I'm a monster, I probably would have regretted it forever. Even though I would have been dishing Mercedes a taste of her own medicine, I would have *felt* like a monster.

You can't undo an action. Once it's done, it's done.

"That's another thing I meant to tell you," Mercedes says, her cheeks bright red. "Everyone thinks they read passages from my journal."

Deep breath in…out… "I didn't. I *wouldn't.*"

Ignoring me, Clarik studies Mercedes. "How are you doing today?"

"Horrible!" she cries. "This is the worst day of my life."

His arms wrap around her—he's *hugging* her? Longing pierces me, and though I shove and kick it, I can't seem to bury it. Suddenly I crave a hug with every fiber of my being. A hug that is freely given and means something to both the giver and receiver.

How many of those have I rejected from Linnie and Robb? Kimberly never tried. I always figured she was more like me than the others, but now I wonder if her rough, tough exterior is some kind of armor. Beneath her *I don't need anyone or anything* attitude, she could be crumbling.

I expect Mercedes to flip me off behind Clarik's back, but she's too busy clinging to him, as if she's finally found an anchor in a terrible storm.

"You like me," she says when they part. Her chin trembles as she dabs at her watery eyes. "I mean you don't hate me."

"Why would I hate you?" He gently chucks her on the chin. "If anyone gives you any trouble, let me know." His electric blues flick to me and narrow in warning. "I'll take care of it."

Calm. Steady. "I'm not going to hurt her. But…we are in the middle of a crisis, and I'm sure you're eager to get to class before Mr. Parton strokes out over your tardiness." I give Mercedes a little push away from Clarik. "Please excuse us."

"Yes," Mercedes says. "I need time with Jade."

Though reluctant, he nods at her. "I'll see you around."

I watch him saunter all the way to Mr. Parton's door,

and it's like an invisible cord connects my gaze to him. Maybe an invisible cord connects *his* gaze to *me*, as well. He glances over his shoulder to study me. He's frowning, but he's also thoughtful. Then he's gone, leaving me alone with my nightmare.

How can I miss him already?

I whirl on Mercedes. "You're going to tell him the truth. You're going to tell him that you hurt me, not the other way around. You're going to tell him *today*! You owe me."

"I owe you *nothing*," she says, even as her cheeks flush with what I assume is guilt.

"I saved you from being hit by a car, remember?"

"Anyway," she continues, "I'd have to explain our situation, and he will never believe me."

Dang her, she's right. "I've been thinking. I've had two dreams about my mother. Or what I thought were dreams. She said everything would change. I would see the shell of myself that I'd become, that I would have to fight for better, that she wants me happy and that I would have an ally."

Eyes nearly bugging out, she points to herself. "Ally. Me? And how did your dead mother put us in this...reverse reality?"

"I don't know, but nothing else makes sense."

"A ghost doesn't make sense."

"Does *anything*?"

"You didn't let me finish." Her shoulders roll in as she chews on her bottom lip. "A ghost doesn't make sense... and yet I kinda sorta maybe might have had a dream, too."

What? "Tell me. Tell me everything."

"There's not much to tell really. It was nighttime, and I was walking down a sidewalk, dragging a whole bunch of rocks that had been tied to my ankles. I passed a little girl who was crying. I asked her what was wrong, and she told me to go to hell, so I flipped her off and moved on. Your mom—"

"How do you know it was my mom?"

"I've seen pictures of her, okay? When our parents dated." A bitter note returns to her voice. "Miranda told me…" She presses her lips together.

"What?" I demand. "Just spit it out. She can't think any worse of you than I do."

Mercedes bristles. "She told me I'm self-absorbed, crave attention and put others down in order to build myself up, and that I'll be miserable until I learn to have empathy for others."

"So, basically she nailed it."

"I have faults, *just like anyone else*, but I also have good qualities."

I hope I'm not this deluded about myself.

"Look, I can't be stuck in this world. I just can't." Cursing, she slaps a hand against the bank of lockers. "Until your mom puts things back the way they were, I'm holing up in my bedroom. I don't care if I have to stay there for weeks, months—years, even. If I boycott her lesson, she can't teach, ergo she has no reason to persist."

I want to do the same, but problems are peeking from the mire of my thoughts like a Whac-A-Mole. The biggest one? "Time is going to pass regardless of what we do or do not accomplish. Doing nothing, hiding out, will *ensure* we're stuck here for years, maybe forever. We might as well—" ugh, I can't believe I'm going to say this and agree with my mother "—fight for better."

Perfect white teeth flash as Mercedes snarls at me. "I'm still going home. I'm not going to pretend everything's okay."

"Oh, yes, you are. Because if we ditch today, we'll be grounded, and if we're grounded, we won't be able to take a two-hour road trip to Grandma Beers's house—she lives in Tulsa—and read my mother's journals."

"And we want to read the journals because...?"

"Mom told me she made mistakes, and this was her chance to fix them. We need to find out what those mistakes were exactly. Knowledge is power. The more we know about the situation, the faster we'll succeed." Probably.

We have no other options.

"Fine," Mercedes says. "I'll go about my day as if I'm an actress on a bad soap opera. I'll even try to help you rehabilitate Lannie and Kasey."

"Linnie and Kimberly," I snarl. "They are perfect just the way they are."

"Whatever. But you...you need to get ready. The good opinion of others is like a drug. You're about to get a taste, and if you aren't careful, you might become addicted."

Pretending all is well proves more difficult than I imagined, and I'm not sure how I manage it. By lunch, however, my smile is brittle and my faux happiness is on the verge of total annihilation.

Girls ask me for fashion advice. "Do you like my hair?"

"Is my makeup too understated?"

"Should I pierce my eyebrow?"

These kids…they look to me for approval, the way they once looked to Mercedes, and it is a heavy burden to bear. Considering what my careless words did to Robb, I chose my responses carefully.

And yes, Mercedes was right. The good opinion of others *is* like a drug, especially during this trying time. I need support, and I get it.

However, every time Linnie and Kimberly see me, they call me a clone and a murderer, blaming me for Robb's suicide, and a little piece of me dies. Even still, I tell everyone I encounter how wonderful they are, and how we must be better, must do better, and treat them with kindness and respect.

As I tell the girl standing next to me in the lunch line about our new K and R policy, she nods, hanging on my every word. Last night she snickered at me, enjoying my humiliation as she read a passage from my journal. Today I'm a beloved rock star.

There's something so unsatisfying about it. Maybe because I know it isn't genuine.

I have no right to complain, though. Every time I buried an emotion, I hid my true self.

A boy with a Mohawk skateboards past us. "Hey, Jade. Watch this." He performs a jump and flips the board off a table. Before, teachers would have come running from the halls to stop him. Today teachers cheer him on alongside the students.

He looks to me, and I know. My reaction will determine whether his day is brightened or ruined.

"Good job," I tell him as I edge ever closer to the silverware, and he high-fives another kid.

Finally, I'm at the front of the line. The scent of over cooked meat and grease assails me, and I want to vomit as I collect my tray and move toward the tables. My gaze skids to my usual table in back. Linnie and Kimberly are there, alone, and they look so…traditional. But they don't look happy, not like before. Not that they were over-the-moon happy about anything then, what seems a lifetime ago.

Where is Mercedes?

"Jade! Over here," Charlee Ann calls from a table at my left.

Bobby is seated beside her. He pats the empty space on his other side with more force than necessary, making the action a command. The two smile at me, though Bobby's is brittle while Charlee Ann's appears sharp; they wave me over, just as I feared. Heaven and Nevaeh are there, too, busy talking among themselves.

Other jocks are there, as well. Not that they are jocks any longer. Word around the halls is sports are "out" and sitting in silence to contemplate the complexities of life and death is "in."

All around me, others call "Over here" and "Sit by me." Their voices blend together, becoming a high-pitched ring. Time slows to a torturous crawl. I have no real friends. No real ally. Mercedes is, and will always remain, an enemy. Too much has changed in too short a time. Not just around me, but *inside* me. So many emotions, trying to bubble up to the surface…

A wave of dizziness sweeps through me, and shallow

puffs of oxygen burn my lungs. But I'm not going to give in. I'm going to fight it. Fight for my friends. My true friends. I straighten my spine and close the distance, heading for Linnie and Kimberly's table.

I'll put action to my words.

When I place my tray beside Kimberly, she glances up, startled. Her jaw goes slack. Then her eyes narrow, and she nudges Linnie.

"Look who's decided to slum it," she says, her tone acerbic.

Linnie jolts to her feet. "Go back to your friends, and curse us with your black magic or whatever it is you do. Just stay away from us."

Another little piece of my heart dies, but I forge onward. "I want to talk with you, that's all."

"Leave us alone," Kimberly spits at me. "You've done enough."

"You like me, and I like you," I find myself saying in a rush, hoping against hope they'll remember me. "A lot. This is all a terrible misunderstanding. I'm doing everything in my power to make life better for you both. I would never do anything to hurt or—"

"*Never*, she says." Revulsion radiates from Linnie. "You pretended to be Robb's friend, too, but only in secret. And every time he reached out to you, you rejected him, just like his parents."

The truly sad thing? She's not describing something Mercedes did. I did this. Me. The real me.

Thanks, Mom. When she went total Riddler on me, she said she would clean a dirty window so that I could see my life clearly, that she would strip away my armor and take away my hiding places. The best way to strip away someone's armor? Hit it, again and again. At some point it *will* shatter. But why can't credit for this particular sin go to Mercedes since we've oh-so-clearly switched places?

The girls grab their trays and march out of the cafeteria without looking back to gauge my reaction, because they don't care. They hate me that much.

A new pang cuts through my chest, and suddenly every sob I've ever suppressed demands its due now, now, now. I press my lips together and somehow remain silent. But the action costs me. *Can't breathe…*

Sweat beads on my forehead. My world has been dumped upside down, cut up and glued back together with the pieces in the wrong place. I need to regroup.

I push to unsteady legs and stumble away, my tray in hand. Someone bumps into me, and I stumble. Sliced pears swish over the side of my tray.

"Watch ou—" I hear distantly. "Oh, hi, Jade. I'm so sorry. I should have looked where I was going. Fright shoes. Where'd you get them?"

"Jade?" someone else asks, voice filled with concern. "You okay?"

"Yo, Jade!" someone else calls as I dump my tray and run.

Chapter 9

*Today my therapist said people are like flowers.
Now I can't stop thinking about something that
happened to me as a little girl, when I helped
my mother plant a garden. We buried the seeds,
watered the soil and then we waited.
For weeks I would race outside to see if my flowers
had sprouted, and every day I would experience
disappointment when nothing happened.
But I couldn't see the struggle underneath the surface,
where roots were fighting to grow—to thrive.
Just because I couldn't see the change
didn't mean it wasn't happening. And finally,
one day, those flowers fought their way
aboveground and bloomed.*

—*Jade Leighton*,
one year ago

I make it to the parking lot before grinding to a halt. What am I doing? I can't leave. I told Mercedes we had to stay, and my reasons were valid.

Come on, come on. Find the beauty in the darkness.

I…can't. Bending over, my hands anchored on my knees, I try to breathe. Cold air envelops me, the heat wave seemingly over. The sky is dark gray, storm clouds ready to burst at the seams.

Footsteps hit my awareness. "A breakdown, Jade. Really?" Mercedes's voice cuts through my panic. "If you try to leave me here after convincing me to stay, I swear I'll kill you with a rusty spoon."

"Where have you been?" I don't bother looking up at her. When life throws a punch, some people go down easy. Others fight. Fight! I have to fight. I *will* fight. "Why weren't you in the cafeteria? I needed you." No, no, no. I did *not* just say I needed Mercedes Turner.

"Please. You don't need anyone or anything, ever."

I wish! "Where have you been?" I repeat.

"She was with me," a male voice says.

Clarik! Scuffed boots appear beside Mercedes's sandals. I straighten, my gaze zooming up, up, to meet his. Sunlight pays him proper homage, deepening the bronze hue of his skin. Those blue, blue eyes regard me without wavering.

One of his eyebrows arches under a fall of dark hair, his expression pure challenge.

As my pulse quickens, I press my tongue to the roof of my mouth. Clarik and Mercedes were—are—together?

"Do you two always fight like this?" he asks as he glances between us.

"Yes," we answer in unison.

"What—what are you guys doing out here?" I don't know what else to say. My mind has packed up and gone on vacation.

She flips her hair over her shoulder, as haughty as ever. "I *might* have had a *mini*meltdown when Charlee Ann and Bobby told me to… Well, it doesn't matter now." Tears well in her eyes, but she quickly blinks them away. "Of course, I didn't embarrass myself like you're doing. Look at you, all panicky and gross. At least I walked away with my dignity intact."

"Do you want your teeth intact, too?" I show her a fist I am more than happy to use.

Another hair flip, but this time there's a gleam of satisfaction in her eyes, as if she's happy I'm back in fighting form. Wait. She ribbed me to *help* me? Because if I'm angry, I'm not wallowing or dejected.

Well, crap.

"Why, Jade Montana Leighton," she says, exaggerating her Southern drawl. "Is that *anger* you're projecting at me now? It's as if you actually care about something."

"I *don't* care," I respond out of habit.

"I know! I've always known. You're a stone-cold—"

Clarik steps between us, becoming all that I can see, all that I want to see. "There's no need to fight. Jade, ignore her. You are as pretty as always."

Um, what happened to his disgust? "Th-thank you," I stammer. I should be happy he finds me attractive, but… He called me *beautiful* in the other reality. Pretty is kind of a downgrade.

"Quick question." He arches a brow at me. "Montana?"

Of course he would catch my middle name. "It's where my mom was born."

"Adorable."

Adorable again. One word, and yet it delivers a powerful punch of relief.

"Mercedes?" a soft voice calls from the door.

In unison, our group turns. I spot Linnie, and my heart squeezes in my chest. I take a step toward her, only to stop myself. She's waiting for her friend, and that is no longer me.

"Are they bothering you?" she asks. She looks ready to defend Mercedes to the death.

Mercedes sighs. "Your friends aren't as terrible as I thought," she tells me softly.

"They aren't terrible at all," I reply just as softly. "Did you tell Clarik about our switch?"

"No. Are you kidding? We tell *no one*, remember, or

we'll end up locked away in a padded room." Off she trots, joining Linnie and disappearing inside.

Clarik stuffs his hands in his pockets and studies my face. Whatever he sees—desperation, frustration, amusement, homicidal urges—softens him. "Do you want to risk death by rusty spoon and leave the campus for lunch?"

So much more than my murder is at stake. But…

He's the first good thing to happen to me all day, and I'm not ready to part with him. Just standing here with him somehow relaxes me. I'm no longer frazzled, and I don't feel pressured into acting like someone I'm not. I'm plain, ordinary Jade Leighton—a girl who wants to spend time with a boy. Nothing more, nothing less.

"You hate me," I remind him. "You think I posted passages from Mercedes's journal at that party. Why would you want to leave with me?"

"She told me you hurt people in a thousand different ways, but that isn't one of them. She also told me you're both going through something terrible, but she—and I quote—has it worse."

I'm going to kill *her* with a rusty spoon.

"Besides," he adds, "I was wrong to cast judgment earlier, and I'm sorry. I know there are always three sides to a story."

I think he's the first person to ever apologize to me and look like he means it with every fiber of his being.

Wait.

Back up. "Three sides?"

"Yours, theirs and the unbiased truth."

Dude. "That's kind of brilliant."

He unveils a little smile. "I read it on the internet."

Dude. He's got to be too good to be true. I pinch him. "Just making sure you're real."

He rolls his eyes. "Are we leaving or what?"

"We're leaving. Yes, please, and thank you," I say with a nod. Then I hesitate.

"Come on." When he turns and strides toward his truck, I fall into step beside him. "I'm curious. Are you and Mercedes friends or enemies? I honestly can't tell."

"Enemies." Right? But I don't want to discuss her. "Where are we going?"

"My favorite hamburger joint. I'm starved."

I'm not hungry, but I'd eat a seven-course feast if it meant I could spend time with him.

He opens the passenger door for me, and I slide into my seat. As I buckle up and settle in, I scrutinize every inch of the truck, looking for differences. Cracks snake through the dark leather, adding to the truck's charm. The floorboards are clean, no hint of clutter. The exact same. A good sign.

As he settles behind the wheel, the sound of his soft inhalations creates a soothing melody in my ears. And he smells good, even better than before. Like chocolate-covered almonds and cinnamon sticks.

"Wait," I say. "How are we going to leave campus without a pass?"

"No worries. I've got this." When he keys the ignition, classical music seeps from the speakers. Last time we were together in this truck, we talked and the radio remained off.

He turns a switch, and the music goes quiet. "Sorry." He eases the car into gear. "I know most of the world prefers heavy metal—"

"I enjoy classical music, too, but I never would have pegged you for a Beethoven fan."

He shrugs but offers no more. Oookay. This isn't something he wants to discuss. Got it.

A security guard wearing a black uniform waits at the edge of the parking lot, manning the booth attached to the gate, keeping students in and unnecessary visitors out. Without delay, he exits the booth and approaches the truck. The scruff of his goatee leads to a row of piercings down the center of his throat.

I recognize him and blink in surprise. This is Clarik's uncle Tag. No wonder I thought he was familiar the evening I met him.

His no-nonsense expression only hardens when he spots his nephew. He motions for Clarik to roll down the window, and says, "Where do you think you're going, boy?" His gaze shifts to me, and he frowns. "Hello, Miss Leighton."

"Um. Hi."

Clarik grips the wheel. "We're going to lunch."

Amid a tension-laden pause, I wonder if I should say something. Maybe I can talk Tag into letting us go since I'm the darling of the school and everything.

"You plan on coming back?" he asks with no prompting from me.

"We'll be back for next period," Clarik says. "You have my word."

Tag looks up at the sky as if he's praying for strength. "You're gonna be the death of me. You know that, don't you?"

"Yes." Clarik rests his elbow on the open window. "If not by accident, then by intense planning."

Some rusty, odd sound bursts from me, short and quick and anything but sweet. My eyes widen as I cover my mouth with my hand. Even Clarik's eyes widen as he focuses on me. I think… I think I just laughed.

He grins at me, slow and almost wicked, as if he likes what he heard *and* what he sees.

I frown. "I'm sorry. I don't know what came over me."

"Don't be sorry. Just do it again."

Tag looks at Clarik, then me, then Clarik again. "Fine. Go on, then, but you'd better not be late for your next class. And you'd better be careful with her. She needs to be returned in the same condition she left in, or it's my butt they'll flay."

"She will. You have my word."

As soon as the barrier lifts, Clarik speeds away.

I shift toward him while nibbling on my bottom lip. If this world is truly an opposite of the other—for the most part, anyway—then he took *Mercedes* on a nondate date yesterday. He thinks he told her about bits and pieces about his life. He might be attracted to her. *He better not be attracted to her.* He might consider *her* a bad bet.

Maybe I'm a *good* bet now.

I want to know more about his thoughts, his past—he is the perfect distraction from my problems—but I don't know the best way to go about this without seeming like a creeper who knows way too much about a complete stranger.

"Do you have girlfriend?" I finally ask. I already know the answer, but there's no other way to kick off a conversation about their relationship.

"Broke up with her not too long ago."

Okay. Now the floodgates have been opened. "What was she like? Why did you guys break up?" He wouldn't tell me before. Maybe he'll share this time.

He flicks me a guarded look. "I'll tell you, but I'll expect tit for tat."

He's curious about me, too? Warmth flutters in my torso. "Agreed."

"She was…sweet and almost painfully shy."

So nothing like me—boo. And nothing like Mercedes—yay. "Go on."

"We broke up because, apparently, I have a hero complex and tried to slay all her dragons."

Slay dragons… Does he mean the fights? Did his desire to throw down with other guys scare her?

I decide to ask. "You fought other guys on her behalf?"

"Brutally." The word whips from him, almost as if it's a warning.

I'm not afraid of him. I recognize his worth. He is a protector of the weak—he is rare and wonderful. Priceless.

He fiddles with knobs on the console. Cold air blows straight at me but warms quickly. Leaning my head against the window, I gaze out the foggy glass.

Cannot see clearly when looking through a dirty glass.

I wipe the fog away and spy tall green trees, with blackbirds flying overhead. Very pretty. What will I find if I wipe away the dirt on…what? My soul?

"All right. It's my turn," Clarik says, drawing my attention. "Are you dating Bobby Bay?"

"No. Gross. He is Mercedes's—" Nope. In this messed-up reality, they probably haven't dated. "No," I repeat. "We're not. Not now, not ever."

"You sure about that? He talks about you like you belong to him."

"When did you talk to him about me? What did he say exactly?"

"During third period. He said he noticed the way I watched you, and I had better keep my eyes off you or I'll lose them."

Bobby needs a crash course in basic human rights. "I don't belong to him. I don't belong to anyone."

"Good to know." As Clarik snakes around a corner, I tilt in his direction. The scent of chocolate intensifies.

"So…when did you watch me?" I press my hands together, forming a steeple in front of my mouth.

Suddenly sheepish, he says, "I have a confession. I moved into my uncle's house a few weeks ago, and I've seen you jog by the house almost every morning and evening. Saw you before I ever made it to school…maybe drooled a little."

Hello, shock and awe. Clarik Iverson drooled over me, and I'd had no idea. The corners of my mouth twitch, and it's another odd sensation that I've never experienced before.

Except…everything he's saying might be a lie. An illusion of the fake world.

"The first time I was struck by the total package. The hair." He pauses. "The body. Then I saw your eyes," he adds. "They were so…empty."

Or maybe these details *aren't* part of an illusion. Maybe they're true. Robots have empty eyes.

Empty. The word echoes in my head. No wonder he kept fighting his amusement the day we met. He didn't want to like me. "It made me a bad bet," I say, my tone hollow now.

"Yes." He casts me a curious glance. "When I was a kid, my mom would tell me how much I looked like my dad, and I wanted so badly to see him I would spend hours staring at myself in the mirror. Sometimes I'd even stare at my reflection in the window, hoping he'd drive up for one of his surprise visits. So often I saw that same emptiness in my eyes, because I knew he wasn't going to show up. I think that's why it sometimes hurt me to look at you."

Pang, pang. What a sad childhood he must have led, hoping and waiting for someone who would rarely show. At least I had closure. "Are my eyes empty today?"

"Today they are…wild. I like it." He drums his fingers over the steering wheel. "I had a hard time reconciling my desire to get to know you better with what I kept hearing about you. And that emptiness… I thought it would be better to keep my distance from you."

"I understand. You think I can easily walk away from my friends." Just like his father walked away from him. And hey, he wasn't wrong. I *did* plan to walk away.

"I'm sorry if I hurt your feelings by admitting—"

"Don't apologize. A hurtful truth is better than a pretty lie, always."

"If it helps, I don't think you're a bad bet anymore."

My pulse races, and I shiver. Something akin to hope blooms. "I noticed you, too, just so you know."

"Did you, now?" He casts me another glance, and this

time he is smiling. "So what's this I hear about you acting weird? Everyone is talking about the new Jade Leighton. How you lost your taste for blood sport or something."

"You wouldn't believe me if I told you."

"Try me."

I barely believe what happened, and I'm living through it. "Maybe I woke up living someone else's life."

His eyes shine with merriment as he says, "Fine. Don't tell me. I'll guess. You met a gorgeous boy, fell in love, and he melted the ice around your heart."

"You jest, but..." All of this began soon after I met him. "Do you have an after-school job?" I ask, changing the subject.

Silence. I think he's preparing to demand a more in-depth answer. Then he lifts his shoulders in a shrug, perhaps sensing the fragility of my calm. "No after-school job, but on weekends I restore cars, motorcycles, that sort of thing. What about you?"

"Nope, no job." Therapy used to take up too much of my time.

After a beat of silence, he says, "Last night I had a dream we were sitting in this truck, and you told me you wonder how and when people will die, yourself included."

First: he's dreaming about me! Second: bits and pieces of the real world must be seeping into the unreal one. This is good. Very, very good!

"Your dream got it right," I say. "I *do* think about death."

His brow furrows, but he says, "Have you wondered about *my* death?"

"No, but only because I thought you looked too strong to take out."

He raises an arm, flexes his biceps. "Yeah, you're probably right."

We reach our destination, and he eases the truck into an empty slot. "I hope you're as starved as I am."

No, but I'm going to eat, anyway, to keep up my strength. *Something* about me should be resilient while I'm fighting for better. "I'll have whatever you're having."

I unbuckle as he requests two cheeseburgers and two orders of fries. No onions and no garlic this time. Interesting. Does he not think we need friendship insurance in this reality?

"Oh, crap!" I dig in my pockets—my empty pockets. "I don't have any money."

"My treat," he says.

"No way." He works hard for his money, and I'm not going to mooch. "I'll pay you back tomorrow." Unless… "This isn't a date, is it?"

"Why, do you want it to be a date?"

"Oh, no, no, no, Clarie. You don't get to answer my question with a question. Don't wuss out on me now. Sack up and tell me the truth."

His eyes begin to shine again. "Let's call this a predate. I only just realized you aren't the person I thought you were. I need time to process."

"A predate. Yeah. I'm on board."

A car parks next to ours, and in back, a toddler draped in black happily waves her hands. Everyone around us is Goth, just like at school.

A cold shell. Mom wasn't wrong.

I don't want to be that way anymore.

We sit in silence until our food is delivered. My stomach is too knotted again, but I force myself to nibble on my burger.

"Come on," Clarik says. "You can do better than that."

With my gaze on his, I take an exaggerated bite. Bits of meat fall from the corners of my mouth and he laughs, and suddenly I want to laugh. Then the amazing flavors hit my tongue like they did on our nondate, and my eyes close as I savor. I even moan.

"Good, right?" he asks.

"*So* good." Somehow even better than yesterday.

He runs a fry along the seam of my lips. "Go on. Try this, too. The first taste is free..."

Another of those strange, rusty noises escapes me. Strange, yes, but more like a chuckle. "Are you my potato pusher now?"

"Yes, so do yourself a favor and eat it," he says, and I chomp off half the fry.

New flavors hit my tongue. Soon I'm devouring my food, scarfing down every crumb. When I finish, I moan for a different reason. I'm full for the first time in...ever.

"You are a maze of contradictions, Jade."

"A puzzle wrapped in an enigma, dipped in a mystery, and sprinkled with a paradox."

Deciding to take a risk, I dig out the phone I have so rarely used. "What's your number? You know, in case we decide to go on a date-date."

As he recites numbers—without hesitation, thank you very much—I type. "What's your number?" he asks then.

Relief washes through me, and I shoot him a text. Probably the lamest text in history.

Hi. This is Jade.

"Thanks." He smiles at me before glancing at the clock on the dash. "We better get back. If we're late, my uncle will use Mercedes's rusty spoon to murder *me*."

Dread crawls down my spine. "Yeah. We better get back." Back to school…back to finding a way to crawl out of my nightmare.

Chapter 10

Life is always throwing curveballs.
Just as soon as I duck one,
another ball is launched—right at my face.

—Miranda Beers

We return without incident and make it to class in time. He smiles at me the next time he sees me, but he doesn't try to speak to me again. He can't. After the final bell rings, Charlee Ann and the twins corner me.

I half listen to their chatter as I make my way to my locker.

"Do you want a ride home?" Charlee Ann asks.

A group of boys on skateboards fly past us. "No, thanks. I'm riding with…my stepsister." I'm pretty sure I'll never get used to referring to Mercedes as family.

Charlee Ann's shoulders slump with disappointment. "Okay. I guess I'll just see you tomorrow, then. Call me later, though. Love you."

I shrug, noncommittal. I haven't ever told Linnie, Kimberly and Robb that I love them, and I'm not going to start with Charlee Ann. "Later." I rush outside.

As planned, Mercedes drives me home. We discuss the day, and she tells me about a group of kids who started to insult her and the others but ended up walking away. Progress!

My dad's truck is parked in the driveway, alongside another car. One I recognize. Fiona is here. A spark of excitement flares, lighting a fire under my feet.

"Who's here?" Mercedes asks, staring at the car.

"My stepmom. Maybe things are going back to normal already." I dash out of the car and into the house.

Laughter draws me into the kitchen. My dad is standing behind the counter with a Goth Fiona sitting in front of it. She's wearing neck-to-toe black leather. The only splash of color comes from red crystals that dangle from her necklace. Her stomach is flat.

My blood flash-freezes. Things aren't going back to normal. Not even close.

Mercedes sidles up to me, taking in the scene.

Dad spots us before Fiona, and his amusement vanishes. A dark flush stains his cheeks. Guilt? "Girls. Hi. How was your day?"

"I've had better." Mercedes glances between the pair, her eyes narrowing. "Looks like I'm going to have a pretty crappy night, too."

Fiona hooks a tendril of hair behind her ear, and I almost—almost—walk over to hug her. Appreciate what you have or lose it.

"Um. Hi," I say.

"Hello," she responds with a kind grin. But then, she's always been kind to me, even on the days I was beyond rude to her.

"This is Fiona Hart." Dad motions to her, then frowns at me. "Hey. You mentioned a Fiona this morning. I hadn't met her yet, so I'm not sure how you knew we'd be using her to stage the house."

I shrug. My go-to response from now on.

"With her help," he says, "we're going to have an easier time selling."

"Sounds boring." Mercedes checks her cuticles. "Hey, I know! We'll let you guys get back to business, and we'll spend the night with Grandma...whatever. Right, Jade?"

"Grandma Beers. And yes. We're going to spend the night with her." I miss her. Despite my lack of encouragement, and her own crankiness, she sends me a card every year for my birthday.

Mercedes snickers. "Her last name is Beers? Seriously? How intoxicating."

Lord save me. "You're *so* original," I say, my tone drier than dirt. Countless times, my mom wrote about the idiots who made fun of her last name.

You're the only Beer I want to drink...

How about a white-hot Beer?

Let me look through your Beer goggles...

"After this morning's debacle," Dad says, "you guys need to spend the night in your rooms, thinking about ways to apologize to Nadine. Besides, Grandma lives two hours away."

Perform. Get this over with. "Yeah. He's right. Let's stay here, Mercedes. I'm eager to finish this morning's fight and tell you all the reasons I hate you."

Understanding dawns in her eyes. "Excellent. Because I'm pretty sure I have more reasons to hate you than you have—"

"Girls!" He scours a hand down his face. "Fine. Go to Tulsa."

Yeah. I thought so. "All right," I say, "but only because

you insist. You and your, uh, wife can enjoy a quiet night together." *Please, please let that wife be Fiona.*

I got a taste of life with Nadine this morning. I'm ready to appreciate what I had before the switch.

"Come on. Let's pack." Mercedes tugs me toward the hall.

I branch off into my bedroom, and she keeps going, heading into Ruby's room. (I'll never consider it Mercedes's room.) As I stuff clothes into a bag, my motions are clipped. Limited choices make the process quick, and yet Mercedes still manages to beat me back into the kitchen. She really *is* eager to go.

"Why the sudden interest in seeing your grandmother?" Dad asks.

Fiona pretends to focus on a folder filled with pictures and papers.

I shrug. Go-to response, remember? "Maybe I've learned the importance of family." He has no idea how true that statement is.

Everything from his expression to his posture softens. "You're right. Family is important. But aren't you supposed to be planning Fright Night?"

"Um..." Am I?

"She's decided to delegate," Mercedes says. "Because she deserves to live her life."

I catch a thread of bitterness in her tone. Does she sometimes feel as if *she* isn't really living?

"All right." He waves toward the door. "Go. Have fun. But you're going to have to leave Grandma's by 4:00 to get to school on time. And you will get to school on time, right?"

"Yes, sir." Mercedes needs no further prompting. "Thank you, Mr. Leighton." As she drags me out the door, I wave over my shoulder.

Less than a minute later, we're burning rubber out of the driveway. Mercedes fuming. "Your dad is married to my mom, and yet he was giggling with that…that—"

"Don't you dare call her a bad name." My nails dig into the passenger seat. "She's my stepmother. My *real* stepmother."

"Not today she's not."

Well. I can't argue with that. "Is your mom dating anyone in the real world?"

Some of her tension drains. "No one serious. Her overbearing personality sends most guys running for cover."

"Overbearing? You used to think she hung the moon."

"Please. The only thing she's ever hung is my sanity. She insults me daily. My hair. My weight. My future plans. Why would I ever be protective of her?"

I know all that, witnessed it firsthand, but I also assumed she valued her mother's opinion. Why else would she turn against me when our parents broke up?

"The apple doesn't fall far from the tree, eh?" I tell her. "*You* insult other kids daily."

"I do not!" She merges onto the highway with a little less finesse than usual, and slinks down in her seat. "I make suggestions for improvement."

"Isn't that the excuse your mother uses?"

"I… You…" She presses her lips together. One moment bleeds into another. Then, "The journals better get us on the right track," she grumbles. "If they don't…"

Yeah. If they don't, we're in serious trouble.

"I'm not sure how much more I can take." Her voice breaks at the edges, and tears stream down her cheeks, leaving dark smudges of mascara under her lashes. She put up a good front most of the day, but now her distress is eating her alive while feeding mine.

Honestly, I'm edging toward a breaking point as well, my one bright moment fading as realization sets in. In this reality, I'm not a bad bet to Clarik. There's hope for us, and I'm excited by the possibilities. Numb? Not even close. Empty? Hardly.

We could actually date; he's attracted to me, and intrigued by me, despite the awful things he's heard. But then what happens? I go back to the real world with real memories of our time together, only to get rejected by the real Clarik?

Is this what my mom wants? For us to become absolute wrecks in this world *and* the other?

Am I supposed to fight my pain and find happiness only to end up heartbroken?

And again, I have to wonder if the past he shared is an illusion.

"We will get through this," I finally say, my raspy voice hollow. "Whatever it takes."

"What if we *can't* get home?" There's a raw quality to her voice I've never heard from her before.

"We will." We have to. Not just for us, but for Robb. He deserves to live his life. And I owe him a million hugs.

"You say that so confidently." She sounds stronger at least. More like her normal self. "Be serious. Do you truly believe you'll read your mom's innermost thoughts, figure out her mistakes and find a way to get back to normal?"

I trace a finger across the dusty window, leaving a line. "Maybe." What other hope do we have?

A new well of tears glistens in her eyes. "And if not?"

"I don't know, okay? We'll take this one day at a time and worry about failure if, and only if, we do what we think is right but still remain in this messed-up world."

"In the meantime, I refuse to dress up as a Goth, just to show the world I'm not the freak in this relationship."

My teeth gnash with so much force I'm surprised I don't taste powdered enamel. "Stop calling me names, *preppy*. You've done it for years, and I'm sick of it."

"Aw, did I hurt your wittle feewings? Well, guess what? You hurt me, too, and I'm just returning the favor."

I sputter for a moment or twelve. "Returning the favor? What are you talking about?"

"Don't play ignorant. You know what you did."

"Obviously I *don't*. What I do know is this. Whatever you think I did, it is not—and will never be—a decent excuse for all the ways you've lashed out at me. And others!"

That only makes her madder. She jacks up the radio, effectively ending the conversation. Fine. Whatever. We've said all we need to say, anyway.

For the first time, however, I wonder if I've been the cause of our animosity all along. If, in my quest to remain alone and unaffected, I hurt her the way I've so often hurt Robb, Linnie and Kimberly.

I think back to the time our parents split, the last time she was ever nice to me. I remember how pale Mercedes was, how her chin trembled as she fought tears. I remember how calm I was.

"I'll come over every day," she'd told me between heaving breaths.

"No, thanks," I'd replied. I'd known her mother would protest. Mercedes might have visited at lot at first, but slowly those visits would have tapered until we no longer saw each other. Why prolong the inevitable? "I don't want to be your friend anymore."

I'd said goodbye then, and shut myself in my bedroom.

Cut and run. My specialty. Any regret or sorrow I'd felt, I'd buried.

In the present, my stomach sinks. I did hurt her. I hurt her badly, my apathy cutting like a knife. While she mourned the breakup of our family—and that was exactly what we were—I coldly, callously walked away, so she'd cut me back.

I'm a bad bet, just as Clarik said.

When we're a few miles away, I call Grandma Beers to let her know we're coming and we're close. By the time we park in her driveway, she's waiting in her doorway, grinning from ear to ear.

For a sixtysomething-year-old woman, she has very few wrinkles, but those she does have—laugh lines around her eyes and mouth—are deep. In the real world, she wore quintessential granny attire. An oversize floral print dress. In this fake one, she wears a skintight shirt and pants the color of tinfoil. Her makeup is hyperdone, with silver eye shadow, blush and lipstick. There are neon-green streaks in her once salt-and-pepper hair, and goggles perch on the crown of her head. But it is the grin that throws me the hardest.

"*That* is your grandmother?" Mercedes makes a sound that hovers somewhere between a groan and a laugh. "And I thought *mine* needed a makeover."

"This isn't the real Grandma Beers. Besides, what's on the outside doesn't matter." But, oh, wow, I sure do miss my muumuu-wearing granny. I didn't realize how much until this very moment, when the woman I know and love is gone—when it's too late to tell her.

No! As long as there's breath, there's hope. I won't go down easy. This isn't the end of my sweet grandma Beers.

"She's a cream puff, so you had better be on your best behavior." I exit the car and tentatively make my way to the porch. The headlights haven't shut off yet and illuminate my path, as well as the house. The small bungalow was once painted beige, but is now—what else?—black.

The temperature has dropped, and cold air brushes my face. It's almost as cold as the blood in my veins. I used to enjoy this time of night, when insects hummed lazily, shadows danced freely and stars winked from a perch of black velvet.

"Oh, my darkling," my grandma says. "I'm so happy to see you."

An invisible fist squeezes my heart. "I'm happy to see you, too."

She gives me the hug I need, wrapping her arms around me. I hug her back, clinging, probably squeezing a little too tight.

I'm forced to let her go when she steps back and says, "Who's your friend?"

"Mercedes Turner. She's my…stepsister."

Grandma brightens. "The infamous Mercedes. I've wanted to meet you." She draws the girl close for a hug. "You're as pretty as a picture."

"You have?" I expect Mercedes to protest. Instead, she returns the embrace with genuine enthusiasm, tears glistening in her eyes. "Well, of course you have. I'm wonderful."

"So is everyone you insult," I mutter.

She glares at me.

"No fighting. This is a combat-free zone." Grandma Beers lets her go and leads us inside the house…or maybe into a steampunk romance.

Edison light bulbs remain uncovered as they hang from every lamp, and every piece of furniture is either sleek-and-modern or a surprising mix of futuristic and antique. The shag carpet—the same neon green as her hair—has a pattern cut in the center, like the supposed alien symbols sometimes mowed into farm pastures.

"Sit, sit. I just made brownies. You'll love 'em." She winks at me. "I added a little bit of the hash for extra flavor."

What! I plop on the bright pink couch, and she pads into the kitchen as if she hasn't just rocked my world. She bakes sugar cookies, not pot brownies.

"I'll take two," Mercedes calls as she settles beside me. To me, she says softly, "This world is a garbage can, but your grandma is a treasure. When we divorce, I'm keeping her."

I'm keeping her, thank you. "We are *not* eating those

brownies. We have too much work to do, and we need a clear head."

She scowls at me. "Has anyone ever told you that you have a talent for ruining parties?"

I pop my jaw to stop myself from screeching like a banshee.

As she studies the room, she looks thoughtful. "I had no idea you Goths were so varied."

"Surprise. Even weirdoes like variety."

"I made a statement, not an insult," she grates. "Your reaction is stupid."

Ugh. She isn't wrong. "Sorry," I grumble. I'll do better.

A pause. Then she hesitantly asks, "What does it mean to be Goth? Again, I'm not meaning to be insulting. I'm curious."

I think she's trying to understand me, and it's...nice. "We see the world through a different lens, I guess. Darkness isn't something to fear. Differences aren't something to eschew, but to celebrate. The freaky things shunned by mainstream can be beautiful."

"Beautiful," she echoes. She nibbles on her bottom lip as she squirms. "I didn't tell you everything your mother said to me. I—according to her—need to be torn down so I'll understand the beauty of building someone up. I thought she was crazy. I thought I already knew. Then your grandma hugged me, told me she accepted me just as I am..." The tears return to her eyes.

"Yeah. I get it. I never wanted to let go of her, either."

She brushes an invisible piece of lint from her knee.

"Do you still wonder about how and when people are going to die?"

Uncomfortable with the current topic? Fine. I can roll. "Yes, but I'm going to stop. I realize it's become a precursor to pushing someone out of my life. Because if I don't care, I don't hurt when they leave me." I didn't intend to share so much with her or reveal the depths of my current vulnerability, but memories of our former friendship are messing me up.

We used to sit side by side all the time, lean into each other and talk about all our hopes and dreams.

"You're good at pushing people out of your life," she says softly.

"Yes. *Very* good."

"For years you've peered through me, as if I no longer exist in your precious universe. It makes me want to hurt you, to make you feel *something*."

"I get that, too."

A throat clears, and we both jump guiltily, as if we've been caught robbing a store at gunpoint. Grandma Beers is standing beside a partition that separates the living room from the kitchen, holding a tray. She glides to the coffee table and sets down the tray, which holds three glasses of orange juice, a bowl of pickles and a plate of brownies. Excuse me. *Hash* brownies.

"Go on," she says. "Eat. Everything is plant based, so it's good for you. Very nutritious."

Mercedes grabs two brownies, as planned.

Grandma smiles encouragingly. "So what brings you girls to my neck of the woods, considering no one has visited me…or called me…or written me…or texted me in years."

Guilt razes me. I open my mouth to respond, apologize, something, but my phone buzzes. My brow furrows. No one texts me, not even Linnie, Kimberly and Robb. They used to, but I never responded and they eventually gave up.

What a great friend I was, huh?

I check the screen to find a text from Clarik, and my heart flutters.

Hey, what are your plans this weekend?

Why? Does he want to hang out again? The flutters pick up speed, until the organ is hammering at my ribs.

"Well," Mercedes says, giving me a nudge, "Jade really, really wants to read her mother's journals. Right, Jade? Tell her."

"Yes." Trembling now, I store my phone in my pocket. I'll respond to him as soon as I'm alone and have figured out a halfway decent response.

I don't think *Dreaming of kissing you* will do me any favors.

When I glance up, I realize the color has drained from my grandmother's cheeks. "Why do you want to read the journals?" she asks.

"Because…just because." I won't lie, but I can't really tell her the truth, either. "I want to get to know Mom better."

"Jade, my darling." She sits in the chair across from the couch and peers at me with worried eyes. "What is this about? There's no reason to relive the past and taint the picturesque memory you have of her."

Picturesque? Not even close. "I know Mom wasn't perfect. And, Grandma? I'm not leaving until I've read those journals."

She closes her eyes, as if searching for calm, before facing me again. "Miranda wouldn't want you to know certain sides of her."

"I was five years old when she died, not five weeks. I remember her highs and lows. Besides, you're wrong about her. She's the one who sent us here."

Chapter 11

The tongue is a single muscle,
and yet it has the power to destroy a life.

—*Jade Leighton*

Grandma Beers laughs. "I think I've had one too many brownies. I know you didn't just say your mother—"

"Oh, yes, I did." I share a look with Mercedes, who shrugs, all *Do what you gotta do.* Then and there, I decide to tell Grandma Beers everything. If she thinks I'm crazy, she thinks I'm crazy.

As I spill the details, she listens raptly, interrupting every so often to ask a question. When I finish, her eyes are filled with tears.

"Do you believe us?" Mercedes asks, hopeful.

"Yes, of course. I've always known there are forces in this world that go beyond what we can see and hear."

That isn't the new Goth version of her talking. That's my real grandma Beers, who used to read me stories about heaven and hell, light versus dark.

"Your mother… I had no idea…should have seen the symptoms…" She wrings her hands. "Miranda had issues, Jade. Issues your father and I agreed to keep from you."

"I told you I remember Mom as she was. I haven't romanticized her." One day she would be euphoric, the world a playground, the next she would be down in the dumps.

"Yes, but you don't remember *everything*."

My chest clenches. Clenches so tight that the emotions I've hidden inside my heart begin to leak out. "All right. What did you guys keep from me?"

"Miranda...she...she suffered from depression. Actually, depression only scratches the surface." Grandma wrings her hands harder. "Back then, mental illness was taboo and treatment wasn't a viable option. Your mom... she tried..." She stands, squares her shoulders. "You need to hear this from Miranda, not me." Head high, she ushers us into a bedroom in back, where boxes are stacked next to the bed. Boxes filled with journals.

I wish he'd burned the others.

"Thank you." A lump grows in my throat as I trace my fingers over the corners of a box.

"I'll leave you alone." Mercedes is unusually subdued as she steps into the hall. "Take as long as you need."

The door closes, sealing me inside. I'm trembling as I sit on the bed, open a journal and dive headlong into an abyss...

One passage reads:

> I hate myself. And I hate my life. I feel as if I'm standing on top of a mountain screaming, screaming, *screaming*, but no one hears me. Why can't I be happy like everyone else? I don't even have a reason to be upset, or sad or tired. I'm so tired. My baby was supposed to make me better not worse, but I'm worse. Why am I worse?

Choking back bile, I run a trembling finger over the words. There's an invisible knife in my chest, and no matter how hard I tug, I can't remove it. The wound is soul-deep, more of my emotions leaking out. No, not leaking. Pouring. Pain and fear and anguish fill me, drowning *me.* My lungs constrict, and I wheeze. Hot tears streak down my cheeks.

On the bottom of the page, I read:

> Having her was a mistake. This world is a terrible place, and it will ruin her. I can't let it ruin her.

The words cause a flash of memory to take center stage in my mind. She's perched behind the wheel of a car, and I'm in the passenger seat. She looks over at me, her eyes wet and wild. There's black mascara streaked over her cheeks.

"I'll make things better for you, too, love," she says. "I promise."

Realization punches me, my brain rattling against my skull. My dad lied to me about the crash. Another car didn't hit us. My mother drove off the ledge, hoping to end her misery and stop me from being "ruined." She wanted to die.

She wanted *me* to die.

Death happens to all of us. No one gets out of this world alive. But death—cutting a life short—isn't the solution to a problem. Nor is hiding from my pain, and that's exactly what I've been doing.

Mom got that part right.

I've been a coward, so afraid of losing someone else,

of hurting again, hurting *more*, that I shut down. I didn't want to be happy; I survived when my mother did not, and part of me felt like I didn't *deserve* to be happy.

I sit on the bed all night, my mind in turmoil. I don't want to hurt anyone else. I don't want to hurt *myself* anymore. Happiness intrigues me. Why fight against it? Why not fight *for* it?

In the quiet, I think I hear a faded *beep, beep, beep.* The TV? I also detect a whispered conversation.

"—going to pull through this." I frown. That is my dad's voice. "I didn't know. I'm sorry. *I didn't know.*"

"How could you have known?" Fiona replies.

Are they here? "Dad," I call, but only silence greets me.

Their voices fade…but that infernal beeping continues. Suddenly the bed tilts—no, I'm falling, stretching out, a waft of sweet perfume teasing my nose. A waft I recognize. I roll to my side and…meet my mother's gaze. I'm too dazed to be surprised, too raw to react properly.

In her eyes I see shame and guilt. "I'm sorry," she says. "I hated for you to know, but you needed the truth. And this is my chance to make it up to you. I will *not* fail you."

"I'm not going to kill myself, if that's what you're thinking," I croak.

"Death comes in many forms, my love. The loss of a smile. The inability to laugh."

"I'll smile. I'll laugh." One day. Maybe. But not today. Not with her death—her suicide—fresh on my mind. My pain…it is visceral. I'm raw inside. Bleeding. "I'm ready to go back to the real world. Send us back. Please."

"No. Not yet. There's still more to do, more to learn."

The real reason she forced this change on Mercedes and me finally clicks, and I flinch. "I'm not here to help Linnie and Kimberly."

"That is just a bonus." Her image begins to fade. "Make things better for yourself, and you'll make things better for those around you."

I reach for her with a trembling hand, but she's gone. A sob bubbles up, but I swallow it back. No more tears. Not here, not now. What's done is done and can't be changed. I'll rage later, might even hate her. Here, now, I want only to forge ahead.

But how? How do I go on from here?

Sunlight pushes through the windows, and my awareness. A soft knock sounds at the door.

Mercedes peeks in, her eyes wide with curiosity but also concern. "Well?"

My eyes burn. From tears I desperately need to shed or fatigue? Probably both. With a grimace, I pull myself into an upright position.

"I spoke with her," I say. "Making life better for Linnie and Kimberly isn't our main objective. It's a bonus."

Practically vibrating with anticipation, she flies into the room and crouches in front of me. "And?"

"And she says we have to stay, that there's more to do, more to learn."

Her shoulders slump. "So, what *is* our main objective? What do we do now?"

"We go back to Oklahoma City. Go to class, as we promised my dad. Our objective is as simple as it is complicated. We have to stop hurting people—including ourselves."

★★★

By the time we're parked at school, my phone is filled with a thousand texts from Charlee Ann.

Where are you?

Are you mad at me?

I want to host a party this weekend. You'll come, right?

What are you going to wear?

There are messages from Bobby, too.

Why aren't you returning my calls?

I know we're off but there's nothing I want more than to be on.

You mean everything to me, baby.

In an effort to be more open and kind—or less hurtful—I tell Charlee Ann I'm not mad at her, and I'll think about the party. I tell Bobby we can be friends, nothing more.

Even my dad has messaged me.

Did you read the journals?

Are you all right?

Come straight home after school, okay?

I don't want him to worry all day, so I tell him I'm fine, and I will do as he requested.

And it's the truth. I'm totally fine—if "fine" means "a mess."

I also reply to Clarik and let him know I'm free, and I'd like to see him. No response comes, and I begin to understand why people stare at their phones so much. I will the stupid thing to chime.

"You ready to do this?" Mercedes asks.

"No, but I'm going to do it, anyway."

I open the car door, but she latches onto my wrist. "Smile at me," she commands.

"Excuse me?"

"Smile at me. Show me your 'kind face.'" She uses air quotes. "Because if you're going to stop hurting people, you've got to have the right look."

I force a smile.

She studies me for a moment and grimaces, then peers up at the sky. "How am I supposed to work with this, huh?"

"Dude. Ask yourself if you're off to a good start."

As I pull from her hold and march toward the building, she calls, "I'm off to a great start, thank you very much. I didn't flat-out say how ridiculous you look, now, did I?"

I fake-smile my way through Mr. Parton's class, just like I've seen Mercedes do pre–reality switch. Clarik is there, and we lock gazes multiple times, even smile at each other, but we don't have a chance to speak.

Dang him, why hasn't he responded to my text?

He's gone as soon as the bell rings, so I don't have a chance to ask.

On my way to my second class, I call out the most ludicrous greetings to people. Like "Hey, Karen! Are you working hard or hardly working today?" And "Good to see you, Deborah! Let's be sure to get our lunch on soon."

I'm nice to Charlee Ann and Bobby when we run into each other. Bobby takes it as a sign that I want to get back together, and I end up snapping at him. But that is my one and only slipup.

I receive multiple hate-glares from Linnie and Kimberly, but I keep my smile in place and wave.

On my way to my third class, I see a girl intentionally trip Mercedes. Everyone laughs, and I debate my options. Do I help her, perhaps hurting her, too, because she's supposed to be torn down before she can be built back up? Or do I walk away, hurting her another way by abandoning her yet again? By the time I decide to go with option one, she's already picked up her scattered books and rushed away.

By the time lunch rolls around, I feel strung out and as fragile as glass. This *cannot* be the path to happiness.

Also, I'm kind of in awe of Mercedes. She made it look so effortless.

The biggest perk? Being admired rather than reviled, and getting my admiration fix.

I wait at the cafeteria doors. When Mercedes arrives, I take her hand and lead her outside.

"Well?" I ask, letting the smile fade at long last as soon as we're holed up inside our car. Wow, my face hurts. "Are you playing well with the other children?"

"Yes! Even though they suck donkey balls," she grumbles.

With a groan, I scrub a hand down my face. "We're going to be here forever, aren't we?"

"Maybe not. I've been thinking. Maybe you need to have a heart-to-heart with your dad," she suggests. "That will make *him* happy, right? Since he's one of the most important people in your life…and your mom loved him…"

"I hate to say this but… I think you're right."

"Wait. What? I need you to say that again, only louder this time."

I roll my eyes. "We've got to be on the right track."

"Let's take it up a notch, though. Let's be *nicer.*"

Another groan escapes me.

Tap, tap, tap.

My head whips toward the window, and I gasp. Clarik is standing beside the car, holding three brown paper bags and smiling. *His* smile is genuine. Awareness makes my nerve endings tingle.

"What's he doing out here?" Mercedes asks.

Let's find out. The tingling gets worse—or better—as I lower the window, cool air gusting inside. "Hey."

Sunlight bathes him, painting a halo over his head. "Hey." He hands a brown paper bag to me, then to Mercedes. *Then* he climbs into the back of the car. He smells like strawberries and cream today. And—I sniff. The bag smells like turkey?

My mouth waters as I open the top. There's a sandwich and bag of chips inside.

The superhot guy brought us lunch. I mean *nice.* Supernice guy.

"I thought we could eat together." He opens his bag

and digs in. "And maybe you two could tell me why you're being so weird."

I share a look with Mercedes before unwrapping the sandwich and taking a bite. Not bad. Not as good as yesterday's hamburger, but still tasty.

"We accept the food and the company," I say, meeting his gaze in the rearview mirror. "But our weirdness isn't up for discussion."

The corners of his mouth curve into a grin as he nods. "Fair enough."

Mercedes stares at her food for a long while. As long as it takes me to eat half my sandwich, in fact. Her eyes are a little wild, her nostrils flaring as she breathes. She's ravenous, I know she is.

She holds her breath until her cheeks turn red. Fighting the craving? Fearful of Nadine's reaction if she gains a single pound?

Pang. I don't fight it, and I don't hide from it. It hurts me to see her like this. "I think I'm starting to like you, and it has nothing to do with your size."

She nibbles on her sandwich; it's not much, but it's something, and I'm proud of her. "This is good. Thank you."

"Welcome," Clarik says.

"It was a very kind thing to do." Deep in thought, she taps a manicured nail against her chin. "You gave me food, and it was kind. Gave. Giving. Kindness is giving."

As she babbles, I meet his gaze in the review mirror a second time. Those electric blues aren't watching her, but me—and they are blazing with heat. They burn through my armor. Shivers don't just overtake me; they overpower me.

"To me," he says, "kindness is treating people the way I want to be treated."

"So…like the queen of the world. Got it." When I open my mouth to reply, she reaches over to press a finger against my lips and quiet me. "Shh. I'm going to be kind to you, and *give* you a moment alone with Clarik, since you all but called eternal dibs on him. And look at me, learning my lessons, doing my part. Try to keep up."

I try to bite her finger, but she's too quick.

Laughing, she flies out of the car. The door slams shut with a thud that shakes the entire vehicle.

Heat spills over my cheeks, and I'm not sure why I'm embarrassed about her admission. Clarik and I have already admitted we're attracted to each other.

"One second." I exit the car, shut the door and call, "Mercedes." I fear she's going to go inside and make herself throw up.

Her step falters and she slowly pivots, clearly reluctant to face me. No hint of her amusement remains. "What?" she snaps.

"Beauty comes in every size, okay? I think you're hot, and if I were into girls I'd probably be all over you. It's just…being healthy matters most."

Twin circles of red paint her cheeks and it is then, that moment, I realize we are more alike than I ever thought possible. I have starved myself of emotion, and she has starved herself of food. We've been falling apart.

"Why do you even care?" she snaps now.

"I…don't know. I just kind of…do." She *is* my ally, no ifs, ands or buts about it, and I do care about her well-being.

Softening, she gives me an almost imperceptible nod

before resuming her trek into the school. Halfway there, she pauses to say over her shoulder, "And, Jade? Just so you know, nothing romantic can ever happen between us, so stop hinting."

"You are such a brat," I call.

I think I hear her giggle as she disappears beyond the doors.

I draw in a deep breath and slide into the car. Clarik is now behind the wheel.

Anticipation practically bubbles from him, as if he's been eager to get me alone. He wastes no time, saying, "Tell me something you live for."

So like the real world! Before, I didn't have an answer for him. Today I'm ready. "I live for…my first taste of happiness. What about you?"

He doesn't need to ponder. "My mom."

Before either of us can say anything else, the bell rings. We have five minutes to get to our next class. Well, crap.

He holds my gaze for several seconds, searching… searching… I'm not sure what he's hoping to find. Finally he says, "Come over to my house later? My mom has to work, and my uncle will be passed out on the couch. It'll just be you and me."

Spend time with him. Alone. In his home. I'm breathless with anticipation as I say, "Yes."

Chapter 12

Even the smallest light can be seen in the darkest night.

—Jade Leighton

I sail through the rest of the day, and my smile takes a lot less effort, even when I have to wait for Mercedes to complete detention.

"Thanks for that," she mutters on the ride home. "I had to go to delinquent central for being rude to Mr. Parton, a crime I didn't commit."

I'm not going to lie. Satisfaction fills me. "Did you enjoy the experience?" I ask, not even trying to hide my smugness. Perhaps I'm even bordering on happy.

"You know I didn't."

"Well, then. Congrats! Punishment for no reason is what truly sucks donkey balls. Maybe you can begin to understand how I felt when you let other students read my personal thoughts."

She *humphs* but doesn't speak for the rest of the drive.

At home, we find Dad, Nadine and Fiona in the kitchen. Fiona is directing a team of painters to color the walls dark gray while trying not to steal glances at my dad. Nadine is sitting at the counter, typing into a laptop as she goes over patient files. My dad is fetching bottled waters for the painters.

"Jade." Relief glitters in his eyes. He sets the remaining bottles on the counter and motions for me to follow him.

I cast Mercedes a glance before dragging my feet to the backyard. Like my mom, he sits on a swing. Apparently swing sets are the new black. I sit beside him.

"Are you okay?" he asks. "Truly?"

There are a thousand and one things I can say, but the first words to leave my mouth are, "She wanted me to die with her." *And now I'm supposed to believe she wants to help me.*

"Yes. After the accident, I found a note." He pushes out a weighty breath. "I'm so sorry, honey. I never wanted you to read her journals, but I couldn't bring myself to toss them. The truth shall set you free," he mutters.

The truth *hurts.* Talking about what I learned brings the pain right back to the surface. Air wheezes through my nose, but doesn't quite reach my lungs. It's too shallow. Acid swims inside my stomach as ice crystalizes in my veins. My ribs threaten to crack against the constant hammering of my heart. Pain swamps me, and I'm not sure I can overcome it.

"She loved you," he says, "but she was sick."

Part of me aches for her and the pain she struggled to overcome. Another part aches for me, for the little girl I was, and for my dad, who has carried this burden for years. This man has his faults, but he's my dad. He did what he felt was right.

I lean over and rest my head on his shoulder. He doesn't move, and I realize he's probably stunned. Even in this reality, I must have been as standoffish as ever. Plus, attitude is in. Then he winds his arms around my waist, holding me against him, and tears well in my eyes.

"What's this for?" he asks, his breath fanning through my hair.

"For you being you."

We stay like that for a long while. After kissing my forehead, he stands and draws me to my feet. "Come on. The painters are about to leave. You can go for your jog, clear your head, and I'll cook dinner. Sound good?"

"Sounds good."

He leads me into the kitchen, and the painters are already gone. So is Fiona. Nadine still sits at the counter, but she's focused on her daughter rather than her work.

"For goodness' sake, Mercedes, have a little pride in your appearance."

Mercedes's cheeks redden. She stalks off without glancing in my direction. A door slams.

"Nadine," my dad says on a sigh.

"I don't need another lecture about the way I treat my daughter. I'm honest with her because I love her." She returns to her files.

I run my tongue over my teeth, anger spilling from me. "You like honesty? Great. Here's a big dose of it, just for you." My dad squeezes my hand in warning, but my words are an unstoppable freight train. "The way you treat her is the way she treats others, so good job there. She's the most-hated girl at school, but she's pretty, so I guess that balances everything out, right? If you really loved your daughter, as you claim, you would build her up and not tear her down."

She lifts her chin and glares at my father. "Are you going to let her speak to me like that?"

I leave him to deal with his wife and knock on Mercedes's door.

"Go away," she shouts.

Fine. I shut myself in my room, anchor my hair in a ponytail, then exchange my clothes for a tank and shorts and my boots for running shoes. Clarik asked me to come by his house, but he never told me a time. I could text and ask him, but I'd rather see him.

I knock on Mercedes's door a second time and ask her if she'd like to join me. Got to practice this kindness thing, you know.

"Go away, Jade. I mean it."

"You'll feel better after—"

"Go. Away!" Something thumps against the door. A pillow, I'm guessing.

"Fine. Stew in solitary confinement."

As I exit the house, Dad and Nadine are still arguing. Outside, the sun is still shining, but the air is growing colder. In the distance, smoke wafts from a chimney, the scent of burning wood heavier with every breath I take.

I decide to jog around the neighborhood before seeing Clarik. I pass the lawn where I hit my head, when the car almost ran over Mercedes and me. My blood stains the rock by the flower bed, and the sight of it makes me dizzy. *Moving on.* I round the corner, Clarik's house coming into view. He's at the curb, putting the finishing touches on a brand-new mailbox.

He spots me and brightens, and the sight of his excitement causes a weight to lift from my shoulders. One I didn't know I'd been carrying around.

"Everything okay?" He pulls on the end of my pony tail, his gaze searching my face. "You look stressed."

"Be still my heart," I say, batting my lashes at him. I can't bring myself to paste on a smile. I just… I want to be myself with him. Let him get to know the real me, warts and all. "Exactly what every girl wants to hear from the guy she's—whatever."

He barks out a laugh. "Even stressed, you're the prettiest girl I've ever seen."

Pleasure heats my skin. "You told me to come over, so here I am."

He surprises me by taking my hand in his, linking our fingers, and the gesture is as comforting as a hug. "Let's go for a walk." He urges me forward, a comfortable stroll. "You can tell me why you didn't jog last night or this morning."

He watched for me? "Mercedes drove me to Tulsa to visit my grandmother." I lick my lips, suddenly nervous. Like tearing off a bandage, I admit the truth as fast as possible. "I learned some things about my mom. Terrible things about how she died. She killed herself and tried to kill me, too."

"I'm sorry. I wish you'd learned happy things." His grip tightens, his fingers seeming to flinch unconsciously. "Tell me something else you live for."

One of those lumps grows in my throat, this one barbed. "My unborn sister." *I will get you back, Ruby.* "And you?"

"My uncle."

A voice whispers behind us. "This is good. This is *very* good. She's making progress."

I twist around, but no one is there. Ugh. The stress of everything is clearly taking a toll.

"I told you how I never cry, right?" Wait. I'd told the old Clarik. "Since the age of five, I've cried only once. Last night. I've laughed only once. When I was with you."

"Do you *want* to cry and laugh again?"

"I kind of *do*." I'd fooled myself into believing I was content, but really I wasn't even close.

"Well, then. I can help you find your funny bone." He kicks out his leg, blocking my foot, causing me to launch forward. Our hands are still linked, and with a laugh of his own, he yanks me upright so that I crash into his chest, facing him.

One of those rusty, odd sounds bubbles up and slips from my mouth. This time, I recognize it for what it is. A laugh of my own. An actual laugh. This boy…

He's smiling as he wraps his arms around me and rests his hands on my lower back. His fingers toy with the waist of my shorts, tickling my skin under my shirt. "I've got the magic touch."

Curling my fingers into his shirt, I say, "All right. I told you a secret about me. Now it's your turn to tell me a secret about you."

"What do you want to know?"

So many things! I'm still a little fixated on his relationship with Kendra, so why not start there? "You were with your ex for a long time."

"That's true. I would even argue *too long*."

Well, that's good to hear. "So you don't miss her?"

"Not even a little." Gently, so gently, he brushes a lock of hair behind my ear. "But that isn't a secret."

Contact electrifies me, igniting a fire in my veins. "Tell me something you've never told anyone else, then."

A honk sounds as a car heads our way. Clarik leads me to the sidewalk, wraps his arms around me again and lets his fingers drape over the curve of my butt. The new position is superintimate, as strange as it is wonderful, and something I've never experienced.

"I've never met my biological father. He…" The muscles in his arms knot. "My mom got pregnant in college. He gave her money and told her to take care of the problem. She refused, and he dumped her. I think she hoped he'd fall in love with me after I was born, but no such luck."

Truth? Or illusion? Either way… "That blows chunks! And just so you know, he's missing out. Big-time." I rest my head against his chest and, in a mimicry of him, wrap my arms around his waist, holding him, offering comfort. "You are one of the best people I know."

You know what will make me happy? Dating this version of Clarik. Kissing him. Doing *more.* I want his arms around me, just like this, but I want his hands under my clothing.

If I'm going to deal with my pain, I want some pleasure on the side.

"Jade?" he says.

"Yes, Clarik."

"This position… I like it. I like it a lot. Which is why

things are going to get embarrassing if we don't separate ASAP."

He means… Oh my gosh! A gasp/laugh combination leaves me, and I straighten. His cheeks are a little pink, and it's freaking adorable.

"Want to go to Charlee Ann's party with me on Saturday?" he asks, bumping my shoulder.

My knees weaken, threatening to buckle. Clarik Iverson just asked me out on a date. A real one! My first. "What about your job?"

"I'm scheduled to work earlier in the day. The night is mine." He gives me an exaggerated eyebrow waggle. "Or should I say the night is *ours*."

I snort. "I want to spend more time with you, I do, but parties aren't my thing." I'm not sure I'll be able to pull off "kind" in a crowd, especially when the party is hosted by a girl I can't stand.

"No offense, Jaybird, but you've never been to a party with me. You don't know what you're missing."

Actually, I have *been to a party with you, Clarik.* But he's right about one thing. I will miss what he brings to the table.

Wait. Jaybird? How fricking adorable is that?

How can I resist this boy? Besides, what if the key to seeing my life clearly, to embracing my emotions, to finding my happiness, is doing things I wouldn't normally do?

"Okay. Yes," I say with a nod. "I will go to Charlee Ann's party with you."

"Thank you." He's smiling as he presses a swift kiss on my forehead.

His lips are soft and warm, and I miss them the second they're gone. Again he takes my hand, and we resume our walk.

"Let's have dinner at the drive-in before the party," I say. "It's *my* turn to buy *you* a meal." And not with my dad's money. Well, with my dad's money, but cash I'll earn by doing chores.

For the rest of the week, I will clean the entire house every evening, help cook dinner and wash all the dishes, really work for my allowance.

I expect a tendril of dread to snake through me, but all I feel is satisfaction.

"Deal," he says.

"One more thing." Releasing his hand, I jump in front of him. I flatten my palm against his chest to force him to stop. My nerves are razed, but I force myself to keep going. If my former numbness taught me anything, it's that there is no reward if there's no risk. "When the date is over, I'd really like it if you walked me to my door and…kissed me good-night. Just wanted you to know."

His smile returns, but it's slower to show itself this time, and far wickeder. "Consider yourself kissed at the door."

Chapter 13

In life, good and bad things are going to happen.
That's a fact.

—Jade Leighton

Each day is a new opportunity to go home, to our other reality.

Do we? No. And as the rest of the week drags by, I develop a routine. Wake up, jog with Clarik—he's always waiting on his porch, ready to join me.

He asks me to name something I live for. So far, I've added making up with Robb, Linnie and Kimberly to the list. Though I keep Robb's name to myself, considering what happened in this reality. Clarik's answers have included becoming a cop, making me laugh so hard I cry, and kissing me.

He has become my one bright light, and I can't get enough of him. I want more. I *need* it. I really, really like this version of Clarik.

After our jog, we go to school together. I avoid Charlee Ann and Bobby whenever possible, and catch a ride home with Clarik. He usually drops me off at my house; we change, then meet up again to go jogging. After I shower, I clean the house, cook dinner, do the dishes and go to sleep. Rinse and repeat.

My mom doesn't make another appearance.

I don't know how much longer I can be nice to everyone. Clarik and Mercedes are the only exceptions. I get to be myself around them.

Avoiding Charlee Ann and Bobby is tough. After Mr. Parton's class, Charlee Ann follows me around. Twice she's broken down and sobbed, wanting to know what she did to make me hate her. Let me count the ways. I assure her my feelings for her haven't changed. And Bobby keeps trying to corner me so we can discuss our "relationship."

Once, he grabs and shakes me, so I knee him in the balls. I've never been more grateful for the self-defense training Dr. Miller recommended. And Bobby is lucky. He'll be able to have his testicles surgically removed from his throat, no problem.

I don't mention the encounter to Clarik, knowing what will happen if I do. Bobby will die, and Clarik will go to prison for murder. No, thanks.

Turns out, I don't have to mention it for a fight to break out.

One morning Clarik is walking me to class, doing his best to make me laugh. He's always doing his best to make me laugh, something real-life Clarik wouldn't have done. Sometimes he succeeds. When he fails, I wonder if ever he'll get tired of having to work so hard and decide to wash his hands of me.

It's stressing me out. Basically I'm becoming one giant nerve ending. And now I'm rambling inside my head. Great!

Bobby rushes over, his friends lined up beside him. He's practically vibrating with rage.

"You need to stay away from my girl," he snarls, getting in Clarik's face.

"Your girl?" I say. "This is delving into stalker territory, Bobby."

Any other guy in the school would shrink back, desperate to escape the jock's fury. Not Clarik. He bows up, ready to throw down. "You don't want to fight me, Bay. Trust me on this. I will mop the floor with your blood."

"Guys." I try to step between them as panic flash-freezes the air in my lungs. "Don't do this. There's no need. Bobby, you should have stayed away. I'm not dating you, and you know it. Not now, not ever."

Nice isn't going to get me anywhere in this situation.

Clarik holds out his arm, keeping me back. "Perhaps he needs the information beaten into him."

"Bobby's gonna tear you a new one, Iverson," one of the jocks growls. The others cheer. Bobby continues to stand in place, inhaling and exhaling with force, his nostrils flaring.

A chanting crowd forms around us. "Fight, fight, fight." Cell phones are lifted and set to record.

"Go ahead," Clarik says and grins with ice-cold rage. "Throw the first punch. Then it's self-defense for me, and I can do all the damage I want."

"Go to class," I bellow. "Now."

For once in this reality, I'm ignored.

The bell rings, but all the students remain in place. Cheers grow louder, almost deafening. Then Principal

Hatcher comes storming down the hall, and everyone goes quiet.

"All right, that's enough. To your classrooms. Now." She claps her hands, indicating she means business. "In thirty seconds, anyone in this hallway will be suspended for a week."

There's a rush of footsteps as the hallway empties. Bobby stomps away.

Clarik frames my face with his big, beautiful hands. His skin is warm and calloused, and sends tingles racing through me. "If he gives you any trouble, tell me."

"Don't worry about me. I took self-defense lessons. I can handle a double-douche-canoe. If he gives *you* any trouble, tell *me*."

He gifts me with one of his perfect smiles, and it's white-hot.

I wrap my fingers around his wrists; the bones are so thick that the tips of my fingers aren't even close to touching. "Be careful, Clarie. I mean it. He's devious enough to ambush you."

We go our separate ways.

Later that day, I notice that Mercedes is avoiding me. I don't know why, or what I did wrong. I try to question her, but Linnie and Kimberly drag her away. That night—Friday—she stays the night with Linnie. Something I've never done. Envy pokes at me…

It's your own fault, and you know it.

At long last, Saturday arrives. Clarik is working till 6:00 and picking me up at 7:00. I spend the bulk of the day journaling and coming up with ways to get happy. Right now, though, everything revolves around the kiss

Clarik promised me, so I end up researching how to be an expert frencher.

By 6:45, I'm studying my reflection in the mirror, my heartbeat erratic, my palms sweaty. My dress is tight and black and overlaid with lace, and it perfectly conforms to my curves. The hem stops a few inches above my knees, revealing my fishnet stockings and tall boots. A necklace made of silver spikes completes the outfit.

"Dude. You look like a dominatrix." Mercedes stomps into my room and perches at the edge of my bed.

At the sight of her, excitement flares to life. What a difference a week makes. I guess she's grown on me. Like a fungus.

"We should exchange clothing," she says. Her canary-yellow sundress has a bow on the neckline, cinches at the waist, the skirt layered with ruffles.

"I'm going on a date with Clarik." How would he react to Preppy Jade? Honestly, I don't think he'd care one way or the other. To him, people are people, no matter what they wear. An admirable trait. "I'm comfortable in this dress." It's what I'm used to. "I would be a wreck of insecurity in yours."

"You're *always* confident," she grumbles. "It's not fair."

"Not confident," I say as I sit beside her. "Numb."

"But you're working on it, *right*?"

"Right. I hope to experience true happiness tonight." Before, when we first made the reality switch, I worried what would happen if I fell for Clarik, *then* returned to real life, where he considers me a bad bet, where he might not give me a second chance. I let the possibility get away from me for a while, but no longer.

I'm terrified of losing this version of him. But then, part of dealing with my pain is facing my fears.

Full steam ahead. No risk, no reward. I bump Mercedes's shoulder. "Why have you been avoiding me?"

She looks away. "Being around you is tough, okay? I think about all the ways I've hurt you, all the things I wish I could undo."

Hey, that's a start. "Would it make you feel better to know I no longer hate you? Now I only mildly dislike you."

The briefest smile appears. "Your friends…*my* friends. Linnie is basically an outcast in her own home—her parents act as if she's not there. Kimberly is constantly surrounded by creeps, and both girls are grief-stricken about Robb. Judging by everything they've said, he was an amazing guy."

Pang. "He was. He *is*."

"They go through so much crap at home. They didn't need me making everything worse at school. Now, I don't know how to help them, or how to build them up."

Pang, pang. "I had years to build them up and didn't. I only made things worse."

As for *my* new "friend"… Mercedes told me Charlee Ann's situation. Her parents have no boundaries for her. They lead busy lives, and don't really have time for her, don't really care what she does. That's got to hurt.

"Empathizing sucks," Mercedes grumbles.

Hear, hear. "It's good for us, though. I'm finally coming back to life."

"What's *that* like?"

"You've had your wisdom teeth pulled, right?" When

she nods, I say, "Remember how your mouth tingled and throbbed when the numbing shots wear off? That's how I've felt since the switch, every second of every day."

Her chin trembles, but she blinks her eyes and swallows, and her expression clears. "So. Is this your first date, ever?"

Officially? "Yes."

"Do you want my advice?"

"No. Absolutely not." I shake my head for emphasis.

"Too bad. Boys are not the be-all and end-all. Don't find your happiness in Clarik. He's human, and he's flawed. He's going to make mistakes. Find your happiness inside yourself."

That is the most profound thing she has ever said, and it's clear all this soul-searching has been good for her. "Speaking of boys, what's the deal with you and Bobby? Why'd you keep getting back together with him? By the way, I wanted to strangle him every time I heard he cheated on you."

"Thank you," she says, gifting me with a full smile. "Half the time, he was sweet and kind. I loved him then. The other half, he was cruel and hateful. That's when he would sleep with any girl he could get."

"You're worth so much more than half of a guy's affections."

"Am I, though?" With a heavy sigh, she falls back on the mattress. "This sucks. You're going on a date, and I'm stuck here like I'm toxic waste!"

"Pick up Linnie and Kimberly and meet me at Charlee Ann's party."

"No way. We weren't invited."

Oh, how the tides have turned. The old Jade would have gloated. This new Jade wants her ally at her side.

New Jade. The description fits. I *am* different. "Girl, our school might as well change its name to Leighton High. I *own* it. If I want you at a party, you get to go to a party."

"Power hasn't gone to your head *at all*." She thinks for a minute, heaves another sigh. "Yeah. Maybe I will."

A knock sounds at the front door, and I gulp. Once again, my heart speeds into overdrive and my palms begin to sweat.

"Jade," my dad calls. "A boy named Clarik is here."

"Coming." I grab my phone only to freeze in place, my feet as heavy as boulders.

"You've got this," Mercedes says. "You could spill pop all over him, leave the bathroom with toilet paper stuck to your shoe and talk for hours with spinach in your teeth, and he'd still like you. The way he looks at you…" She fans her cheeks.

The weight lifts, and I lean over to kiss her cheek. Part of being New Jade is being better about showing affection.

Her eyes widen as her hand flutters to her face, and I dash out the door. My dad looms in the entryway, his arms crossed over his chest. Clarik is a few feet away, taller, wider, his arms anchored behind his back.

Awareness punches me in the gut, stealing the air from my lungs. His dark hair is windblown and spiked. A black T-shirt hugs his muscular chest, and a pair of ripped jeans reveals different sections of his bronzed thighs.

Every horror I've endured in this fake world? Suddenly worth it.

"No drinking and driving," my dad says. "No *texting* and driving. No doing drugs of any kind."

"Daaa-aaad. You're ruining all our plans," I say with a pout. "If you tell me to leave my bag of cocaine here, I'm going to flip out."

His eyes narrow to tiny slits. "Ha ha. Very *not* funny." He pats the top of my head. "You better have fun, young lady, but not too much."

I join Clarik on the porch. He turns, quickly thrusting his arms in front of his body, so that my dad is never able to catch a glimpse of them. It's an odd move, awkward even.

At the truck, he opens my door and helps me in, moonlight glinting over fresh bruises on his knuckles. Ah. He got in a fight.

As I settle in my seat, he reaches out to toy with the ends of my hair. "You look… You *are* so beautiful."

Warmth suffuses my cheeks, and shivers rush down my spine. "Thank you. And you look…delicious. But I'm not going to let you distract me—yet. You got into a fight."

A blank mask shutters his expression, but he doesn't deny it. "I did."

When he offers no more details, I push. "With whom?"

"Doesn't matter." He pulls back, intending to escape to the driver's seat, but I latch onto his wrist, holding him in place. "You hungry?"

"It matters to me," I say, ignoring his question. "You matter."

"Do I?" He leans toward me, closer and closer, not stopping until our lips are only a whisper apart.

My cheeks heat another degree, making me feel feverish. Butterflies even take flight inside me. This is it. The moment I've been waiting for. My first kiss.

Except he simply brushes the tip of his nose against mine. "You were right. Bobby ambushed me. But he soon learned the error of his ways. When I fight, I do not lose. Ever."

Concern overshadows desire. "You're okay, though?"

"Better than." He reaches past me, and when he straightens, he's holding a bouquet of roses. There's one of every color. White, yellow. Pink, red. Blue and green. Orange and violet. "Your first date should be your best date."

Annnd desire overshadows concern. I think my bones are liquefying. "This," I say, "is something I'm living for."

He's grinning as he reaches past me again…and hands me a chocolate bar. "I asked Mercedes about your favorite dessert. She said you only drink protein shakes at home but checked the flavors you prefer and we deduced chocolate brownie is your favorite."

No one has ever gone to so much trouble just to make me happy. Trembling, I accept the candy bar, hug it to my chest, then lift the flowers to my nose and inhale deeply. The floral scent fogs my head, and my eyes begin to burn.

He ghosts two fingers along my jaw, and says, "You have no idea how many florists I had to visit before I found one who sells something other than black flowers."

"Thank you," I manage to croak. I wish I'd gotten

him something. Even a small token to let him know how much he's come to mean to me, how he's helped me in ways I never thought possible.

The most beautiful thing I've ever found in darkness—is Clarik. A bright light.

I don't think I'll ever go a day without thinking about him, and taking solace in the comfort he's given me. How am I supposed to give up this version of him?

Will he be the same in the real world?

As he climbs behind the wheel and we head off, a voice very much like Fiona's seeps from the radio. "I remember the day we met. You were so somber. You stared at me with those big eyes, never saying a word. I've tried to give you space, tried not to push, but I think I made a mistake. Maybe I should have crowded you, pushed as hard as possible."

As the woman speaks, I swear someone is stabbing my temples with a butter knife. I swallow a whimper, blink back tears. Inhale—*can't breathe, need to breathe.*

"You all right?" Clarik asks.

"Fine."

A man who sounds like my dad speaks next. "What can I do? How can I reach her?"

My temples throb even harder as he cries. Sobs, really. Big, choking sounds. Poor guy. The pain in his tone… it's sharp enough to cut glass and mirrors the pain I'm currently fighting—inside and out.

Clarik fiddles with the radio, and a soft, romantic song replaces the talk show. Bit by bit, the pain ebbs, and I'm able to breathe again.

"You're not fine." Reaching over, he takes my hand, squeezes. "Are you nervous?"

"As a heart attack." Attack…yes! I think I just had a panic attack.

He snorts. "The saying is as *serious* as a heart attack."

"See! Nerves have fried my brain cells."

In a move straight out of books and movies, he brings my hand to his mouth to kiss my knuckles. "I promise not to bite…unless you ask me nicely."

Chapter 14

No girl has ever been happier than me.
Oh, what a glorious day.

—*Miranda Beers*

Clarik doesn't take me to our favorite drive-in for our first official date. He takes me to an Italian restaurant, where every person on staff and every patron is Goth. The walls are black. The only light source is a single candle in the center of each table, as well as a French wrought-iron chandelier that is attached to the ceiling with chains. Very medieval torture chamber meets Gothic romance.

The sight no longer shocks me.

"I know you had your heart set on a burger," he says, holding out my chair, "but since you insisted on paying, I decided we should eat something fancier."

As if! "I know you, Clarie. You're going to fight me for the check."

He's smiling as he claims the chair across from me. "This is true. But I'm not sure how I feel about being so predictable."

"Predictability isn't something you have to worry about." He has a thousand different layers, and every time I peel one away, a new one takes its place.

We chatter about our day until the waiter takes our order. As we wait for our food to arrive, and even as we eat it, the conversation grows more personal.

"It's your hundredth birthday," Clarik says. "Where do you see yourself?"

"Oh, man. I've never looked ahead to the future." But it's past time I do so. "Maybe I'll become a forensic anthropologist and study bones. I'll probably Golden Girl it with Linnie, Kimberly and Robb, and I'll definitely have a ton of cats. I'll be happy." I hope. "You?"

Thankfully he doesn't remind me of Robb's death. "I will have a dog. Or four. Dogs and cats *can* get along, you know. I'll also have a smokin' hot hundred-year-old babe in bed with me, and I will be satisfied I've done everything on my bucket list."

Dude. I think I'm jealous of the hundred-year-old babe. "Let's hear some of those to-dos."

"Travel the world. Freeze Mentos into ice cubes and put them in someone's soda, then laugh until I cry when the cubes explode. Mail out Hogwarts rejection letters to all my friends, then tell them all I got in. Throw a party with fake alcohol to see how many people get 'wasted.' Put vanilla pudding in a mayo jar and eat it in public."

"So you're a jokester." *That* I didn't know about him. "All right. Here's a question for you. If you were a superhero, what would everyone call you?"

He doesn't hesitate. "Thunderbolt. I strike fast, and I strike hard."

I laugh, the sound no longer quite so rusty. "Before, I think I would have been Miss Roboto. She can't feel, but she can kill. Now? I'd probably be something lame like Madam Makeout. All I think about anymore is kissing you."

Those blue eyes twinkle. "I'm going to leave that statement alone—for now—or I will kiss you right here and now. So. What about your supervillain name?"

Kiss me right here and now! "Probably something like… Dreaded Bringer of Dark."

"*Nice.* I'd be something like Beast Unstoppable."

Unstoppable. Yes. The description fits him well.

Thoughtful, he takes a drink of his sweet tea. "What's the stupidest thing you've ever spent money on?"

A painful memory surfaces, and I say, "You first."

"When I was little, I paid my cousin three dollars—my entire savings—to teach me how to use the toaster."

Another laugh escapes me, but I sober quickly. Here goes. "I bought a cup of water from a girl in elementary school. Cost me one dime. I thought she was selling it so she could buy a bag of popcorn. Turns out she just wanted to watch me drink toilet water."

Candlelight flickers over his chiseled features, twining with shadows. "If you're trying to talk me out of kissing you later, you're failing."

He still plans to kiss me!

I need a distraction before I slide right out of my seat. "You mentioned becoming a cop." I dip a breadstick in Alfredo sauce. I'm full, but the flavors are amazing, and the way Clarik watches me eat…even more so. I think I could eat until I burst, as long as his gaze stayed on me. "That will be your job. What will be your hobbies?"

"I like working with my hands. Restoring old cars. Making furniture."

"You make furniture? Because I could use a new kitchen table. A round one." And I like the thought of sitting and eating at a Clarik original.

He wiggles his brows at me. "How about a bed?"

I throw a piece of breadstick at him, and he chuckles.

"I actually excel at tables," he says. "And chairs. And dressers. Anything my mom wants, really. She's my favorite person in the world, and I like making her happy."

And I like him. A lot. What I feel for him I've never felt for anyone else. Part of me wants to put up walls and protect myself from future hurts—Old Jade at work again. New Jade feels and deals.

Happy, Mom?

"You are a good son," I say.

"She's a good mom."

When we finish our dinner, we head to Charlee Ann's party. Music blares from open windows, and kids stumble in and out the front door. Some even congregate around the porch, laughing and drinking beer. Boys and girls have already coupled-off, several of those pairs making out on blankets that are draped over the ground throughout the front lawn.

Are Charlee Ann's parties always like this?

"Stay on the lookout for Mercedes, Linnie and Kimberly," I say. "They might be crashing."

"Will do." With his arm draped around my waist, holding me close, Clarik ushers me inside the house. The living room is crammed with bodies, creating a sea of halter tops, short pleated skirts and piercings.

Voices call out greetings.

"Look, Jade's here!" This, from Heaven.

"Hi, Jade. Sweet! Are you officially with Clarik?" Nevaeh asks.

A girl I don't know says, "Does that mean Bobby is available?"

Everyone has to shout over the music, and I pretend I can't hear. The *thump, thump* of bass causes a slight vibration to glide down my spine as kids dance with wild abandon. Smiles abound. Hands wander. Some of the attendees are even pushing through the crowd, playing tag.

"You want something to drink?" Clarik speaks directly into my ear, warm breath fanning the lobe.

Shivers cascade through me. "No, thank you." Buzzed, there's no telling what I'd blurt out. "Unless you're offering water?"

"From the kitchen or bathroom?" he asks, then laughs. "Too soon?"

Funny guy! He leads me into the kitchen. Amid cheers and whistles, a group of boys dance atop the table.

"Take it off!" Charlee Ann shouts with glee.

One of the boys swings his hips as he tugs off his shirt. When his eyes meet mine, he grins and tosses the garment at me.

Clarik releases me long enough to toss the shirt in the garbage, and he's no longer smiling. Jealous? Why does the thought thrill me?

An equally shirtless Bobby stands in the corner. He's trying to walk away, but a girl is pulling on the waist of his pants. Finally, he gives in and stands still, even leaning into her… I catch sight of Mercedes, and my hackles rise. No, no, no! She needs someone who treats her right. Bobby isn't that someone. Why can't she see it? I mean, he just tried to leave her side because he doesn't want to be seen with her.

Although I suppose I can guess. She wants to recapture something of her real life, when things made more sense.

She bats her lashes up at him and twirls a strand of hair as she speaks and he laughs. Then he spots me and loses all hint of amusement. He jumps away from her as if she pushed him. Doesn't take a genius to guess why. He's embarrassed to be seen with her.

Okay. He's not *any* girl's someone.

Chalk white, she runs off, tears glistening in her eyes. Whether she likes him or not, rejection hurts. When she passes me, I snag her wrist, but she wrenches free. Bobby, the tool, doesn't go after her, but remains focused on me. One of his eyes is black and blue, and there's a knot on his jaw.

Clarik did good.

In the living room, several boys chortle and call someone a preppy. I don't have to wonder who that someone is. I turn, seeing former football players escort Mercedes, Linnie and Kimberly to the door. Former, because football isn't "fright" anymore. All three girls are now soaked with beer.

Someone turns down the music. Someone else slurs, "You don't belong here."

Clarik stiffens, menace radiating from him.

"Yes, I do belong here." Mercedes's tortured gaze darts around the room and finally clashes with mine. "I do!" The words are a statement as much as an accusation.

"Stop." I race forward, jumping in front of the door

to block her progress. "What is *wrong* with you people? Are you monsters? Because that is how you're acting."

For once in this world, my word isn't law.

"Out of the way, Jade," a boy says. "We're taking out the trash."

"The girls are staying." I stand to my full height, my shoulders squared. "*You* are going."

Clarik takes a post at my side. Intractable. Unmovable. "Get your hands off the girls. *Now.*"

If I thought he radiated menace before, well, I was wrong. Very wrong. *This* is menace in its purest form. There's no doubt in my mind he will kill, if necessary, to protect the innocent.

The girls are released at last, and the guys scramble away, perhaps hoping to hide in the kitchen. Wise move.

Mercedes smooths quaking hands down her dress. Though she's staring out at the attendees, she speaks softly, for my ears alone. "I'm not going to say thank you."

"I'm sure the world would end if you did." My tone is just as soft. "Just do yourself a favor and remember what you told me about boys."

"He told me I'm the most beautiful girl he's ever seen." She sniffles. "I thought he was remembering me, and it just… It felt good to be wanted again, even if by a jerk."

He was using her. How can she not see the truth?

Looking through a dirty window…

"You deserve better," I tell her.

"I know."

Linnie and Kimberly watch the byplay warily, as if I'm the wild animal I supposedly accused them of being, and they're on safari. *Don't get too close, and don't offer food. You'll get bit.*

Across the distance, Charlee Ann and Bobby are watching, too. Only they aren't wary. They are as furious as Mercedes, their eyes narrowed, their lips compressed into thin lines.

"Want us to take you home?" I ask Mercedes.

She thinks for a minute, shakes her head. "No. We're not going to be chased away as if we've done something wrong."

Gotta admire her ovaries of steel. She's covered in beer but determined to show the world she's a force to be reckoned with.

"All right, then." I take Clarik's hand and squeeze. "We'll stay, too."

He squeezes back. And for the rest of the night, we remain on the sidelines, guarding the girls, all *Make a move against them, see what happens.* They dance and laugh and no one disturbs them or calls them ugly names.

No one embraces their presence either, but hey, progress is progress. One baby step at a time.

Part of me envies the bond that has developed between the three girls. The way they hold hands and give each other spontaneous hugs. Why didn't I appreciate my friends when I had the chance?

You lose what you do not value.

In real life—IRL—I'm going to do so much better. In every way, shape and form, I'm going to show these girls, and Robb, how much they mean to me.

What will I show Clarik?

"I should have taken you to a movie," he says. Once

again, he's whispering in my ear, making me shiver. "Sorry the date has morphed into a—"

"Oh, no. Don't you dare apologize. I'm glad we're here, doing what we're doing. Without us, there's no telling what would have happened to the girls."

Leaning down, he brushes his nose against me. Like before, I thrill.

"Clarie," I say.

"Yes, Jaybird."

I begin to vomit words. "I know we haven't talked about this, and it's far too soon for me to bring it up, but what the heck, I'm going to do it anyway because I need to know, so okay, here goes…are we exclusive while we figure this thing out? Or will we be exclusive in the future, maybe, or never, and don't worry—there's no wrong answer, except for anything but option A."

Electric blues gleam with an intensity that leaves me breathless. "I want to be exclusive while we figure this out. I hate the idea of sharing you with another guy."

Melting… Wait. I'm smiling! Miracle of miracles, the corners of my mouth are actually lifted.

Clarik goes still, as still as a statue. "You. Are. Exquisite."

There's a curl of heat low in my gut. "Thank you."

We lean into each other, closer… A tap on my shoulder makes me gasp.

"Hate to break up such an embarrassing moment," Mercedes says, "but we're ready to leave."

I jolt, facing her, my cheeks warming further. If we're leaving, that means I have T minus fifteen minutes—give or take a minute or two—until kiss time. Is my breath fresh? Maybe I should ask Clarik to wait at the door of my house while I go inside to brush my teeth.

"Right," I reply. "Let's go."

Hand in hand, we walk the girls to Mercedes's car. Or rather, my birthday car.

Linnie studies me before she claims a seat in back. "Thank you." Her tone is as gentle as her precious heart.

I will do anything for you, anytime. "You're welcome," I say, not wanting to freak her out.

Kimberly acknowledges my presence with a nod, and Mercedes pauses before climbing behind the wheel.

Gaze steady on mine, she says, "Fine. I'm going to do it. I'm going to utter those two little words. *Thank* and *you.* And, Jade? I'm sorry for before. For every time I've hurt you." She's inside, the door slammed closed, before I have a chance to respond.

Not that I would have known what to tell her. Shock has fried my brain.

As the car speeds away, Clarik cups my nape. "You ready to go home?"

"Yes." *No. Maybe. Possibly.*

"You're nervous again."

"Yes," I repeat. "I think I just want to get our first kiss over with. I'll be better next time." Surely.

He leads me to his truck…where he swings me around, pressing me against the door. I gasp. Cool metal at my back, hot boy at my front. "Over with, huh?"

I peer up at Clarik, my heart thudding against my ribs, the rest of the world forgotten. We are the only two people alive, this stolen moment the only thing that matters.

"You know I've never been kissed," I croak. "I could totally suck."

His pupils flare while his eyelids grow heavy. "I really hope that you do."

His tone is a sex purr, and threatens to undo what remains of my calm. "Why?"

He flashes a quick smile, then once again brushes his nose against mine. "I'll show you when I get you home."

And deal with these nerves the entire drive? No! I grip his shirt and pull him closer. "Kiss me now. Over with, remember?"

He searches my face. Whatever he sees, he likes. His hands settle on my waist, and he lowers his head. Slowly. Torturously. My racing heart stops thudding and starts hammering. *Bang, bang, bang.* But he doesn't kiss me.

"What do you like about me?" he asks.

Ugh! No more talkie talk. But even still, I say, "You first. What do *you* like about *me*?"

"You once told me I couldn't answer your question with a question, and yet you've done it to me twice now."

"Do as I say, not as I do. So?"

He looks ready to smile again. "You look fragile and yet you can be as tough as nails. You aren't afraid of the dark. You'll rush into a burning building if it means saving someone who can't save themselves. Anytime I make you smile, I feel like I'm king of the world."

Oh. My. Wow.

I grip his shirt tighter. "You look as mean as a rattler but you can be as sweet as sugar. You aren't afraid to step into the dark right at my side, or rush anywhere to save anyone. And when you make me laugh, I feel like I'm a queen who has seduced a king."

The smile breaks free, but the rest of him is tense, and growing tenser by the second. A good tense, as if desire is filling him and any moment now he'll burst apart at the seams. Then the smile is gone completely, and his eyes are crackling with flame.

My light.

"I live for...you," he says, and the admission rocks my world.

I'm still reeling, careening, as he presses his lips against mine. They are incredibly soft and wonderfully sweet, like the beginning of a dream, when I hover in a magical place between awareness and sleep.

His hands slid up, up my torso, over my shoulders, and tangle in my hair. My knees grow weak, threatening to buckle. My blood doesn't just heat this time—it sings with sensation. I *feel*. Pleasure, amazement. Desire. Urgency.

"Clarik." The second I utter his name, breathless, the tone of the kiss changes. From sweet and exploratory to wild and fierce. All-consuming.

He angles my head the way he wants it and licks my lips, coaxing them to part. Then, oh, then, his tongue sweeps inside, claiming me with startling intensity.

My thoughts fog as never before, my stomach flip-flops and my skin burns with heat. My knees stop threatening, and start acting, buckling under my weight. No need to worry. Clarik catches me, his fingers back on my waist, hoisting me up. He's strong, even stronger than I thought.

His body presses flush against mine as he uses the truck to anchor me in place, allowing his hands to wander…

Down my sides, around, before flattening on the back of my thighs. With a little maneuvering, he ensures my legs wrap around him.

The new position heightens every sensation.

Then he sucks on my tongue.

I jolt, my nails sinking into his scalp. The pleasure! Mind-blowing. Earth-shattering. I cling to him, desperate to get closer…closer… I need to be closer to him. Now. Tomorrow. *Please, please, please don't let our time together end.*

A noise startles us both—laughing kids—and we break apart. We're panting. The kids stumble past us, having no idea we're hidden in the shadows, no idea what we've just done.

Even when they're gone, we remain in place, my back still pressed against the truck, legs wrapped around Clarik's waist. How am I supposed to walk after this?

Finally, he breaks the silence. "That was…"

I run his bottom lip between my teeth. "If you say anything less than divine, I'll bite off your tongue the next time it's in my mouth."

"Just as long as there *is* a next time, eh?" He grins. "To be honest, our first kiss was absolutely, one hundred percent…divine."

I pluck at the collar of his shirt, then play with the ends of his hair. "The best kiss of your life?" Nothing could possibly be better…right?

Oh, crap. What if it wasn't the best? I shouldn't have asked. I shouldn't have—

"Without question," he says, and I nearly faint from relief. He presses his forehead to mine, tension suddenly radiating from him. "This feels like a dream. I don't want to wake up."

"Then don't. Stay with me." *Forever.*

No, no, not forever. One day, I'll have to give him up and…and…my heart shudders.

"There are things you don't know about me," he says.

"Such as?"

"I've been…arrested twice."

I don't have to guess why. "For fighting."

"Yes. Girls were hurt, and I reacted." He searches my gaze, his breath fanning my face. "Does knowing I've been behind bars scare you or make you want to run away from me?"

"No." Linnie was once arrested for shoplifting. The richest girl in school filched a cheap pair of earrings. Not because she liked them, but because she was angry with her parents and hoped to get their attention. And Kimberly was arrested for public intoxication.

People sometimes do stupid things. That doesn't always make them inherently bad, just human.

"Here's the thing," he adds. "I *liked* making those abusers hurt right back. It was wrong, and I maybe should have responded in a healthier way, but I can't go back."

With my forehead still pressed against his, my fingers now sliding through his silky dark hair, I say, "You're right. It probably wasn't a healthy way to respond, but I'm the queen of bad decisions. What I'm not? Your judge. I know you will never harm me."

"I… Thank you."

A sharp ache blooms in my chest, and it's followed by a very strong urge to cry. I don't want to cry. Not here, not now. I don't want to spoil this beautiful moment. We are sharing with each other, caring *for* each other, and offering comfort.

He pecks my forehead and steps back, forcing my legs to lower so that I'm standing.

"We'd better go," he says. "You have a curfew, I'm sure, and once again I have a condition that makes me unsuitable for the public."

I'm not yet operating at optimal conditions, and concern overwhelms me. "Are you sick?"

"You're really going to make me say it." He nibbles on my ear and whispers, "It's called a hard-on, Jaybird, and it flares up every time I see you."

As I blush and try my best to look anywhere but down, he laughs outright.

"Come on." He leads me to the passenger side of the vehicle and helps me settle in, his knuckles brushing my thighs as he buckles me up and winks at me.

And it is then, that very moment, that second, that I fall head over heels in love with Clarik Iverson.

Has love changed me? Am I happy? Have I fought my pain—my past, my demons? Is this a better life? Can I win Clarik in the real world? Will he give me a chance?

The questions plague me all night long, and I toss and turn. Any moment, I could wake up back in real life, even though I haven't done everything my mother wanted. Maybe she isn't in control, though. Maybe it's always been me. Maybe *I'm* responsible.

Why haven't I returned, then?

Whispers penetrate my awareness, even though no one is nearby, and no radio is on. My dad begs me to wake up, wake up, *wake up*, and talk to him, please. Fiona chatters on and on about her pregnancy. Ruby is kicking up a storm, and might just be a soccer player in the making. Grandma Beers tells me about the brownies she can't wait to bake me—no mention of hash—and Mercedes admits she misses me. She even apologizes for sharing my journal entries.

Linnie, Kimberly and even Robb tell me stories about their days. I'm most shocked to hear Clarik's voice, too. He replays his first thoughts about me, and our first interaction, how kind I am, and how pretty, and how much he wants the chance to get to know me better. How he will do anything to see me smile.

Part of me wonders if I'm hearing into the other reality, if the walls between the two are crumbling.

When I lumber from bed, I find a message from Clarik on my phone.

Miss you already. Later, gator. (I swear that isn't as cheesy as it sounds. When I lived in Florida, a gator was our mascot.)

I text back: So you're a gator, and I'm a jaybird?

Clarik: Jaybirds make tasty treats. VERY tasty...

I'm smiling as I brush my teeth. Smiling as I shower and dress. Smiling as I realize, yes, I am happy.

I lose that smile when I hear my dad and Nadine fighting about everything and nothing.

I'm happy, but they are not. I'm happy, while Robb is dead and Ruby is nonexistent.

Maybe I'm not so happy, after all.

I coast through the next school week, spending more time with Clarik, Mercedes and her crew. Linnie and Kimberly have stopped freezing me out. They don't look or speak to me, but they don't run from me, either. Baby steps.

However, Charlee Ann and Bobby no longer want anything to do with me. Apparently they've started dating, making Charlee Ann the queen of school rather than my lady-in-waiting.

Heavy is the head that wears the crown.

My crown is now tarnished. Charlee Ann decided I wasn't worth the effort the day she scolded me about my behavior at the party and my response came in the form of a question. "Why are you Goth?"

She'd sputtered for a minute. "Because...just because."

Cold shell. I'm no longer adored by everyone at every time, and to be honest, I miss it more than I expected.

"Hey, Fright Night is tomorrow. Are you going?" Mercedes asks me Friday at lunch.

We're sitting at a table in the back. The "reject" table.

"Tickets are sold out," I say. Everyone is excited about the costume party Charlee Ann had to organize in my place, since I bailed on the planning committee. Guilt razes me. She's not my favorite person, but I shouldn't have left her in the lurch. "I forgot to get one."

"I got us tickets." Clarik is at my side and kisses my temple.

I squirm in my seat. He's almost too good to be true.

"I got you guys tickets," Mercedes tells Linnie and Kimberly.

"You are the sweetest," Linnie says, throwing her arms around my stepsister.

Mercedes accepts the hug and returns it, causing my chest to ache.

Kimberly pats her on the shoulder, and Mercedes blows her a kiss.

They are bonded now. Bonded in a way they've never been with me. Because I wouldn't let them in.

Just think. I could have had this camaraderie with them all along.

After school, Clarik drops me off at home. "See you in a bit."

Mercedes comes into my bedroom, watching as I change into my running clothes and shoes. "Do you ever wonder if we're stuck in a dream?" she asks, sitting at the edge of my bed.

"I wonder if we'll ever get home." If part of me now wants to stay… There are bad things here, but there are good things, too. "We've done everything I thought we needed to do. Dude. You've been nice to *everyone*." What's more, nothing has seemed fake.

She blooms, as if she's a flower I just watered. "In the beginning, I would look at people and remind myself that we all have our internal scars. I can't see them but that doesn't mean they aren't there, and I shouldn't add to them. Now it's second nature. I can't stop…even though I really want to. Life would be easier."

"*I'm* learning easier isn't always better." I sit beside her, pat her knee. "I'm proud of you."

"I'm proud of you, too. I've noticed the glitter of happiness in your eyes. And the smiles! It's weird to see you wear one, but a smile is much better than the panic I've glimpsed."

"I don't want to lose Clarik," I admit. "What if he doesn't want to take a chance on me when we get home? What if he's not the same Clarik I've come to know and love?"

"Of course he'll take a chance on you. You're smart, pretty and halfway decent. And yeah, okay, he might have fought it, but he still wanted to be with you. Everyone could see it. But whether or not he'll be different…that, I don't know."

"Wait, wait, wait. Let's backtrack. Did you just *compliment* me?"

"Don't go getting a big head. I said *halfway* decent. You've still got a lot of growing to do." She bumps my shoulder with her own. "But we can't stay here. You know that, right?"

Pang. "I do." I kiss her cheek and stand. Giving and receiving affection is getting easier for me, just like sharing and caring. "I'm going for a run. And I think… I think I'm going to tell Clarik about the parallel world." I'm going to open up and reveal my fears.

I'm going to take a chance.

"If we want different results," I say, "we have to do something different."

"Agreed. Maybe I'll tell Linnie and Kimberly, too. If we end up in a padded room, we'll deal." She throws a pillow at me, saying, "Now go. Get out of here before you chicken out. Don't trip and fall and break your leg while you're jogging. Or do."

"Yeah, yeah. I'll miss you, too."

We share a smile before I head out. Dad and Nadine haven't made it home from work, allowing me to make my way to Clarik's house without further ado.

No one answers the door, but I hear hammering in back. The gate is unlocked. An invitation if ever I received one. "Hello?"

"Back here," Clarik calls.

I quicken my step to find him inside a detached garage he's turned into a workshop. He's shirtless, his jeans hanging low on his waist. Sweat beads on his bronzed skin, sluicing down rope after rope of muscle.

"Wow. You weren't exaggerating. You're—" *a banquet of sexy* "—really good at this."

"I had a few more touches to add and thought I'd be done by the time you got here." He's seated in front of a round table, carving ivy along the edges.

"Is this for your mom?" I ask.

There's a slight pause. "This kitchen table is for a gorgeous girl who claims she desperately needs one."

What! He's building the table for *me*? Is this boy even real?

No! No, he's not.

He sets the chisel on a long, retractable table, the metal clanging against other tools, some I can't even identify, stands and reaches out to nudge my jaw closed. "Don't even think about saying no."

"Please. The only words you're going to hear from me are *work faster*."

He chuckles and pulls me close for a hug. "You like it?"

"I love it. Thank you."

In the back of my mind, I think I hear my dad whisper, "Come home, Jade. Come home to us. Please."

Clearly, I'm going crazy. But that's okay. I have Clarik.

I cling to him, praying I never have to let go, and say, "There's something I have to tell you."

Chapter 15

Your choices, your consequences.

—Jude Leighton

He stiffens, but says, "All right. I'm listening."

"You'll think I'm crazy," I reply.

"Jaybird, I *already* think you're crazy. Which isn't an insult. We're all crazy in one way or another."

"Yes. Okay. I'll tell you. Just give me a minute or twenty to think about the right way to do it." I release him at last and pace in front of him, back and forth, back and forth. Maybe he'll believe me, maybe he won't.

"What's going on, Jade?" Concern drips from each word. "I can take it, whatever it is."

Words I have spoken myself. Forget finding the right way to do this. There isn't a right way. There's only the truth.

I draw in a deep breath, hold it…hold…and then I do it. As I exhale, I tell him everything. The appearance of my mom in my dreams. Her warning. The way the entire world turned Goth overnight, except Mercedes, my unwilling ally.

He listens, never once interrupting me. His expression darkens, and a familiar tension radiates from him.

When I finish, he doesn't immediately respond. Birds chirp, and a car putters down the road.

Finally, Clarik takes my hand and squeezes. "I believe you."

Wait. "What?" He does? "But…but *why*?"

"I've had dreams about you," he admits. "About some of the very things you just told me. About our lives before, and this world gone wrong. Everything you told me helped me make sense of everything I've seen in my head."

I'm about to tell him he couldn't possibly have dreamed about the real world, since he himself isn't real, only to remember I'm living the impossible myself.

Somehow, my mom paved the way for my big reveal, saving me from any skepticism.

"Thank you." Filled with relief, I throw myself into his arms. He falls backward, until we are sprawled on the ground, laughing. "Thank you, thank you, a thousand times thank you."

He rolls me to my back, his muscled weight pinning me down, thrilling me. A dark lock of hair tumbles over his forehead. I'm trembling, almost giddy as I reach up to brush it away.

"If we go back to the real world, will I remember our time together?" he asks.

"I don't know. Maybe you'll dream about it again." A girl can hope.

"Will we be this good together, though? I don't want to lose what we have. It's selfish of me, I know, but you are the favorite part of my day, every day."

His gaze… He has enraptured me. I can't look away.

"You're the favorite part of my day, too. You don't know it, but you've helped me pick up the pieces of my broken heart and weld them back together. Losing what we have will shatter it all over again, but staying here would be selfish of *me*. I'd be hurting my dad and stepmom—my real stepmom. My sister who hasn't yet been born. Robb. Mercedes."

"Jade," he rasps.

"Whatever happens, it'll be okay," I tell him, praying I'm right. "Just…kiss me so I can brand myself on your soul and you *can't* forget me."

The next morning, Mercedes and Nadine go shopping for tonight's Fright Night, and I go to the school to help Charlee Ann set up. Heaven and Nevaeh are there, too.

The twins are happy to see me. Charlee Ann, not so much. But she doesn't ask me to leave, either.

"I'm sorry I dumped all the planning on you," I tell her. I should have gotten my butt in gear, should have created a garden party, with paper lanterns and silk flowers, full of color, just as Mercedes originally planned. "I'm sorry I've been so rude and dismissive toward you."

Charlee Ann shrugs and doesn't acknowledge me again until right at 4:00 when we finish hanging decorations and setting up tables. Only three hours, and Clarik will pick me up.

"Thanks for all your help, guys." She nods in my direction at least.

I do as Mercedes has learned to do, and remind myself that Charlee Ann is human and flawed with a past I know nothing about. *Hurts* I know nothing about.

I give her a hug she doesn't return, and she reminds me of Old Jade. She's rigid and unwelcoming and can't get away from me fast enough. This is a dose of my own medicine, and it leaves a foul taste in my mouth. My friends deserved so much better.

"I'll see you tonight," I say, and she won't meet my eyes. *Her* eyes are watery.

I give her another hug before walking home, where I shower and blow-dry my hair. Then I do something I've never done before. I curl the strands. I have to borrow Mercedes's curling iron, and watch a million YouTube videos, but I do a pretty good job, if I do say so myself.

I also borrow one of Mercedes's outfits. A light pink fit-and-flare dress with bows and ruffles and a pretty lace trim.

Here's the thing.

So many times I've said the outside doesn't matter, that we must love people for who they are, not what they look like. It's past time I acted like I believe my words.

Once, Light Night would have been my Fright Night. Today? Fright Night is my Light Night.

My bedroom door suddenly swings open. "Be honest," Mercedes says. "How terrible do I look?"

My mouth falls open as I take in her appearance. "Are you wearing *black leather*?" A corset top with black crystals and satin ribbons perfectly complements a pair of black leather pants.

Her cheeks redden, the color spreading over her exposed collarbone. "Yeah. So?" Defiant, she lifts her chin. Thick black eyeliner rims her eyes, not the subdued brown she usually prefers. She's taken "smoky eye" to a whole new level, and even traded pink lipstick for black.

"You look beautiful," I say. "But..."

"But?"

"Tell me why you're dressed like that."

"Mom asked me to give it a try, okay? And when I finally agreed, she looked at me as if I'm worthy of her love for the first time in my life."

"You shouldn't have to earn her love, Mercedes."

"You and I both know *should* and *shouldn't* have no bearing on reality."

She's not wrong. "Have Kimberly and Linnie seen you?"

"Yes, and they didn't like it." With a huff, she sits on the edge of my bed. The leather squeaks as it rubs together, heralding the return of her blush.

"You have to do what's right for you."

"Maybe I'll stay home," she grumbles.

"Please. You know you want to go."

"Maybe." She sticks out her tongue. "But if I do, it's not because you're the boss of me."

"I know." I meet her gaze in the mirror, a wave of affection washing through me. "It's because I'm your friend."

We share a tremulous smile, and it's as real and genuine as the bond between us. And there *is* a bond between us.

"When we get back to the real world, I'm throwing a party. Oh!" She claps her hands with relish. "It will be the biggest party Hathaway High has ever seen." She pauses, then adds hesitantly, her eyes now downcast, "You'll come, won't you? Kimberly, Linnie and Robb, too."

"Of course I'll come. But are you sure you want to do that? No one will understand your newfound friendliness. Trust me. You might even lose Charlee Ann's friendship."

Up goes her chin. "Friends have your back through thick and thin. I wouldn't have made it through this without Linnie and Kimberly. They're wonderful people, and they deserve my best. Besides, I've seen firsthand the baggage they carry. I'm not going to add to their load ever again. I'll be a soothing balm rather than a thorn."

Even though I've been along for the ride, the change in her is startling. And absolutely beautiful. I hope the same can be said of *my* transformation.

"I'm pretty sure I know the answer to this, but I'd like to hear it from you," I say. "Why did you hate me after our parents split?"

She plucks at a thread in my comforter. "When my mother told me we were moving out, I cried. I threatened to run away, and begged to stay with you. The thought of being without you…broke me. Then it came time to leave, and you said you didn't want to be my friend anymore. You walked away, as if I meant *nothing* to you. Afterward I just… I wanted to hurt you as badly as you hurt me."

I close the distance, sit beside her and take her hand in mine. "I'm sorry. Back then—until this whole reality switch—I became my coldest, my numbest, whenever something major happened to me. I see now that it was a defense mechanism I developed after my mom died. I couldn't deal with the pain, so I simply shut down."

And I can't do that anymore.

I need to face my pain once and for all. I've gone head-to-head with a wave of it here and there, but never have I strapped on a pair of boxing gloves and actively gone to battle against pain and fear.

Fight the pain, win the joy. And I'm so ready for my joy. Tonight, after the party, I'm going to do it. I'm going to war.

Tomorrow, I go home. I know it with every fiber of my being.

"I understand that," Mercedes says. "*Now.* I've learned a lot about you these past few weeks. You're a good person, Jade, and *I'm* sorry for the way I've treated you."

"So I'm forgiven?"

"You are. I hope I am, too?"

"Absolutely."

Outside the room, a door slams.

"You think I haven't noticed the way you look at our *decorator*?" Nadine shouts.

"I would never cheat on you, Nadine."

Great. Our parents are caught up in another screaming match.

"Ugh." Mercedes stands. "I'm going to Linnie's. She texted to tell me Kimberly is already there. I'll see you at Fright Night." To avoid our parents, she climbs out my window.

Lucky girl. I finish primping and though I want to sneak out the window as well, I go through the kitchen. My dad is there, slapping together a sandwich, Nadine out of sight.

I move to his side and rest my head on his shoulder. "I love you, Dad."

Misery pours from him, but he says, "I love you, too, honey."

Standing on my tiptoes, I kiss his cheek. "I'm going to Fright Night with Clarik. Don't wait up, okay?"

"Have fun."

"I will. This time, I will." I know Clarik is supposed to pick me up, but I don't want to wait to see him. If this is our last night together…

I'm going to cherish every second.

"And, Dad," I say. "I have a feeling tomorrow is going to be a much better day for you."

My pace swift, I dart out the door and through the neighborhood. The night is cold, brutally so now that the heat wave has ended, and I wish I'd grabbed a coat. Goose bumps break out over every inch of visible skin. Tree limbs dance and whistle.

Behind me, lights flash. Kids laugh, and a car engine purrs. I whip around, my heart racing, part of me expecting another near-collision, as if I've finally come full circle. No, no, my heart isn't just racing, it is pounding, pounding so hard, agonizing me.

"She's crashing," I hear someone shout. And yet, no one is nearby.

The headlights are so bright I'm momentarily blinded…then the car passes me without incident, and my heartbeat calms. I breathe a sigh of relief.

Beyond ready to see Clarik, I quicken my pace. By the time I reach his door, I'm shivering, my teeth chattering. He appears a few seconds later, surprised to see me.

"Jaybird. Did you walk in the cold?" His gaze slides to

the driveway, where only his truck is parked. "I thought I was picking you up."

I'm going to miss that nickname. Will he use it in the real world? "You were, but I wanted to see you, so…" I spread my arms. "Here I am."

He reaches out, takes my hand and pulls me inside the house. "Come in. Warm up." Then his gaze roves over me and heats. "You look… Wow. Like a tasty treat I'm going to devour."

The cold air is forgotten as I drink him in. He is gorgeous in a white button-down and black slacks. And his house—

I gasp. This is the first time I've been inside. His home is mine, preswitch. Same layout. Same colorful walls, same "country chic" furnishings. Only these furnishings Clarik built for his mom.

Considering everything about the switch has meant something, I can only assume this is supposed to be an example of symbolism. That Clarik has become my home.

With the interior, there are only two differences that I can see. The beam anchored to the living room wall has pictures of Clarik and his mom rather than me and mine, and there is a grand piano in the corner by the window.

"What?" he asks.

"I just… I love your home, that's all." I miss it.

"Thank you. Did I mention I love your dress?"

"It might have come up."

"It wasn't the only thing," he mutters.

Oh, no, he didn't! I snort-laugh. "Who knew I would look good in lace and ruffles and *pink*." I'm out of my element, and not too long ago, I thought I would be too uncomfortable to function in this type of clothing. Wrong! My clothes do not define me. However, they help me express myself when I cannot find the words.

"My mom is still at work," he says, "and my uncle is out on a date."

We're alone, perhaps for the final time. A sense of urgency overtakes me, sprinkled with a bit of sadness, but I beat the feelings back. I'm going to savor this night and enjoy every second as if it is my last...because it just might be.

"I'll give you the penny tour." He leads me to his bedroom, which is very different from mine. No pink frills for him. A small bed with dark blue covers occupies the far wall. There's a desk, a computer and lots of workout equipment I don't recognize. The bookshelf is filled with books about carpentry, but also fiction. His tastes span the gamut, everything from horror by Amy Lukavics, postapocalyptic tales by Kresley Cole, to steampunk by Kady Cross.

"Don't freak out, but..." He walks to the desk and lifts the picture frame. "You're my girlfriend, and I like to look at you."

My bones do that melting thing as I study the picture inside. It's of me. One someone took while I was unaware. We're at a party, and I'm tucked against his side, gazing up at him with a half smile on my face.

"Why would I freak out?" I ask.

"Thought you might think I'm moving too fast."

"We're way past too fast, Clarie." And life can be short. We must enjoy what we have, while we have it.

He gives me a swift kiss before taking me into the kitchen. Like the living room, it's a replica of my old one. Stainless-steel appliances, a pink-veined marble counter. A refrigerator with a single magnet in the center, which has the number to my dad's favorite pizza place.

"What do you think?" he asks.

"I love it," I reply honestly.

We return to the living room. I'm drawn to the piano, the only real difference in the two homes. I try to imagine him sitting on the bench, his fingers racing over the keys, but can't quite manage it.

"Do you play?" I ask.

"I do."

"Play something for me, then." I press my palms together, forming a steeple. "Please."

After a prolonged hesitation, he settles on the piano bench. He flicks me a glance, saying, "If this doesn't prove how much I like you, nothing will," before focusing on the keys.

His nervousness is endearing. He's usually so strong and confident about...well, everything.

Then music fills the room, and I close my eyes, losing track of my thoughts. The notes are tender and beautiful and they lift me up, up, as if my spirit is actually rising from my body. I'm positively giddy. But my body holds on tight, unwilling to relinquish any part of me. When the pace slows, the melody deepening, I'm wrenched into a thousand places of heartbreak. The kind I've not let myself feel. Deep and world-changing. The kind that leaves scars.

How is this possible? How is he doing this?

Does he play in real life?

I would blame black magic, as Mercedes once accused me of wielding, but there's nothing evil or wicked here. Only light, shining so brightly, chasing away darkness.

If my reality hadn't shifted, I would have remained on the same, terrible road. Fighting my feelings, determined to remain numb. I would have missed the opportunity to get to know Clarik—and myself.

I remember how stubborn I was in that other life, so determined to hold on to *nothing*. I never let myself enjoy my days, or the people populating them, and eventually I *would* have forgotten about Clarik and my friends, never understanding the treasure I was giving up.

Now I realize. I don't know what's going to happen when I return to real life. Don't know if anyone else will remember what happened. I still don't know if real-life Clarik will want anything to do with me, or if our relationship will be this good, but at least I'm equipped to fight for better.

Whatever happens, I'm not letting this part of him go. I'll hold him close in my heart, always.

He doesn't sing, and yet deep in my soul, a voice whispers. My mother's voice. *You've come so far, my love. You see clearly now. You understand. You're doing what I never had the strength to do. You're winning.*

When the song ends, quiet descends. The only sound to be heard is the rasp of our uneven breathing.

My eyes slowly open. Clarik is peering at me with uncertainty. For the first time in our acquaintance, he appears vulnerable.

"That was absolutely beautiful," I tell him.

"Thank you."

He stands as I close the distance. I run my fingers through his silky hair, and he kisses my temple. His lips linger over my skin, his warm breath a gentle caress.

"I'll finish dressing so we can head out," he says. "Unless you want to stay here?"

"I would love to stay, I really would." I want to stay and never leave. "You have no idea how much—"

"Oh, I think I have an inkling." His dry tone makes me laugh, and I'm happy to note the sound no longer has any hint of rust.

Look at me. Happy! "But I need to be at the party. For my girls."

"I understand." Electric blues glitter with adoration, and it's far more addicting than any I got at school. "Give me two minutes."

After one more kiss to my forehead…then one on the tip of my nose…then one on my lips, as if he can't bear to leave me, my fingers fisting the collar of his shirt, holding him in place…he rushes off, leaving me desperate and aching.

In need of a distraction, I walk around the living room again. The pictures of him and his mother are precious. In each one, they're both smiling ear to ear. Their love for each other is palpable.

"I'm ready." His voice comes from behind me.

I turn and smile at him, drinking him in once again, feeling as if I'm soaring and crashing at the same time. He's changed out of the button-down and slacks. Now he's wearing a pink T-shirt to match my dress, and his customary ripped jeans tucked into combat boots.

Awareness locks me in place, crackles in the air.

"I want to kiss you again," he rasps. "*Need* to kiss you."

Breathing becomes more difficult. So does speech, but I manage to whisper, "Yes. Please."

He stalks toward me, sensual in a way I never imagined possible. His steps match the beats of my heart. Quick. Almost frantic. Our lips meet in a wild rush. My arms wind around him, because not holding him isn't an option. The scent of him fills my nose—home, he even smells like home tonight. His tongue tangles with mine, claiming me. Possessing me. A hot, wet pursuit.

On the walk over here, there was no hint of a storm. Now I would swear I hear thunder, as if the sky itself is clapping for us.

I sizzle from the inside out, burning, burning from head to toe. My hands slide up, up his muscled stomach, his pecs, and comb through his hair. *His* hands flatten on my lower back; he urges me forward until there is nothing but a wisp of air separating us.

This kiss is everything. Life and death rolled into one glorious blaze. It somehow makes up for every time I've been called a freak, every boy who has ever found me lacking...every horror I've endured in my short lifetime.

But everything with a beginning has an end. He cups my face and gently pulls my lower lip through his teeth. Slowly, with regret, he lifts his head.

I gaze up at him with heavy-lidded eyes, and I'm panting a little. His lips are wet, swollen and a darker shade of pink than before. I'm sure mine bear a striking resemblance.

"This is it, isn't it?" he asks, his voice rough, broken. "Our last night together."

He senses it, too, then. "You're not going to forget me," I remind him. "I'm branded here." I tap his temple.

"And here," he says, and taps his chest.

Chapter 16

I read somewhere that fear is an enemy
at your back with a knife at your throat.
My enemy decided to bring a machete.

—Jade Leighton

We walk into the building hand in hand, and it is a bittersweet moment. The beginning of the end…or the end of the beginning. Only time will tell.

Clarik tries to give our tickets to the welcome committee, but they are too busy gawking at me to notice. Finally, I place the tickets on the table and draw my boyfriend into the gym.

If Halloween and Victorian Goth had a baby, and that baby grew up, married *The Phantom of the Opera*, and those two had a baby, *that* baby would be the gym at Hathaway High.

Black lace hangs from the ceiling to create canopied circles. A half-moon of dark purple settees occupies the area in front of a life-size gilt mirror and crow-shaped candelabras. Red velvet is draped over the snack table, where finger foods are, in fact, shaped like human fingers. A "skeleton" is spread over a second table, a crimson stream of juice pouring from its mouth into a punch bowl. To top everything off, a creepy version of a waltz plays in the background.

"You did this?" Clarik asks.

"I helped Charlee Ann set up, that's all. She did the planning while I figured out my life."

"Well, then, I'm officially impressed with both of you."

"You mean you were only unofficially impressed with me before?"

"Exactly."

The party is already in full swing, music blasting as dancers go wild. Many of the attendees cast me glances, all *What is she wearing?* Even the teachers stare at me as if I've grown two heads. I lift my chin another notch. I'm different once again. So what? I'm still me, and I'm proud of me, whether I'm wearing pink or black.

Charlee Ann pushes through the masses to approach me, horror contorting her features. The leather dress she's sporting is similar to the one I wore to school about a month ago, before my realities switched, only she has cut out two swatches of material. One from her chest, revealing the wealth of her cleavage, and one from her midsection. On her feet are five-inch stilettos. Her hair, now dyed multiple shades of blue, is piled in ringlets atop her head.

"I thought you were getting back on track," she says.

"I was. I am. This is me, a girl who will always be a little bit different from the norm. It's okay if you don't like me," I tell her. "I've learned to like myself. And let's be honest, some people clash. That's just the way it is. I hope it's me, and not my clothes, that makes the decision for you."

She looks between Clarik and me, anger darkening her eyes. "Why can't you see? Clothes are a reflection of who we are inside. They *are* a part of you. And you, not me, are the one who is throwing everything away as if it means nothing. Status. Friendship. Love."

"Status is nothing. To me at least. But friendship and love have come to mean everything. And yes, I admit it took me a while to learn the difference between those three things, but now that I have… I've honestly never been happier. I truly hope you can say the same, Charlee Ann. I do."

She opens her mouth, then snaps it closed before marching away. Her loss. I lead Clarik to the dance floor. Despite the frantic beat of the music, he wraps his arms around me, holding me close, and I rest my cheek on his shoulder.

"I love you," he whispers into my ear, his hold on me tightening.

"I love you, too," I whisper back. It's such a perfect moment, but it's also bittersweet. Even if he gives me a second chance when I return to real life, he won't remember this. He won't look at me with the adoration I've come to crave.

But that's okay. This, too, is a shell of itself. It's twisted and wrong, because it isn't real.

It isn't real—but it can be. I can win his heart, and offer my own. I will give it my all, nothing held back, unafraid of rejection or loss.

I could lose him at any time. He could die in a car crash, or a disease could take him. Anyone I love could die today, tomorrow, next year. *I* could die. Let's face it, the grim reaper has never been picky, or punctual or interested in what does or doesn't work for us.

But when I die, I don't want all my regrets flashing before my eyes. What I could have done. What I should have done. The experiences I could have had, the lives I could have touched.

I want to die knowing I lived every second to the fullest. Zero regrets. I want to have dreams, and plan ahead and anticipate and embrace the highs and lows, always, always, *always* fighting for better.

Mercedes shows up a short time later, flanked by Linnie and Kimberly, who are wearing black to support their friend. All three girls are smiling, and it's contagious. They even dance around Clarik and me, and we can't help but flail alongside them. More and more kids join us.

Mercedes takes my hand and twirls me. "Are you happy?"

"I'm happy. And you?"

"I'm getting there."

"You aren't so bad, Leighton," Kimberly says.

Linnie gives me a thumbs-up and I beam. "I hope you come back to us."

The words stop me in my tracks. "Come back to you?" Is she remembering?

Her brow furrows, and she gives a little laugh. "I just said I agreed with Kim."

Oh. Well, that's something at least.

We part ways when a ravenous Clarik ushers me to the buffet table. We fill our plates and claim a table in back, where we devour every crumb. We talk and laugh and just enjoy each other…until I notice a commotion in front of the locker room doors. Bobby and friends are laughing as they pass around a black corset top and leather pants.

A chord of familiarity strikes me like a whip. I've seen those clothes—on Mercedes.

Where is she? Dread wrings the air out of my lungs. Sweat beads on my back as I search the gym for any sign of my stepsister, finding none.

"Something's wrong." I'm already moving forward. Clarik remains on my heels.

Other kids have sectioned off. No sign of Linnie or Kimberly, either. Whispers—rumors—are spreading like wildfire, and soon assailing my ears. I pick up words I never ever want to hear again, and my teeth grind.

"—ahead. Take a peek. She's in the bathroom now." Bobby points to the doorway to the lockers.

She. Meaning Mercedes?

Are Linnie and Kimberly with her, perhaps just as vulnerable? I look around and still find no sign of them.

That's it. I've had enough. "You are rotten to the core, Bobby Bay." I stalk over and rip the clothing away from the boys, one piece after the other, and the laughter dies a savage death.

Bobby narrows his gaze on me. "You don't want to do this, Jade. Go away."

"Or what?" Clarik is a tower of menace and rage behind me.

The picture of stubbornness, Bobby stands his ground. "Or Jade will get the same treatment as her stepsister, that's what."

I look over my shoulder, my gaze pleading with Clarik

to help me help Mercedes before things get out of control. "Guard the locker entrance. Don't let anyone through."

He gives me a curt nod, and I rush off, pushing past the boys. No one tries to stop me. I race down a narrow corridor and into the girls' locker room. I search every stall, but there's no sign of her. Did she find a spare set of clothing and leave?

A cruel burst of laughter echoes from the other side of the wall…

My eyes widen. The *boys'* locker room.

I dash back into the hall and turn the corner, then fly into the boys' room. And there she is, pressed into the far wall, next to the hand dryer, her quivering hands covering her breasts as tears spill from her eyes and splash onto the floor.

Humiliation radiates from her, her sobs quiet and yet devastating. I know she's scared, can guess she wants to scream for help, but also doesn't want anyone else to see her like this.

Two boys stand a few feet away, both in profile to me. One boy is leering while the other cups his junk and makes lewd suggestions.

This is not okay. This is *never* okay.

I suddenly and totally get why Clarik enjoyed hurting other people's abusers. I'm not going to waste time with conversation. Surprise is my friend. So, I use it.

Without making a sound, I attack full force, nothing held back.

Step one. I close the distance. Step two. I bang Leer with my shoulder, tossing the clothes I'm holding at his face, and kick Lewd in the side, causing him to fly into the nearest stall. He isn't able to catch himself, so the toilet stops him. The rim slams into his knees and they buckle. I follow him in, ensuring his forehead slams into the porcelain lid on the way down.

Lights out. Just…like…that. Lewd slinks to the floor, his eyes closed, his body motionless. How'd he like it if I stripped him, took pictures and showed everyone, huh?

Leer regains his bearings and raises his fists, ready for a fight. Before he has a chance to raise another block, I *jab, jab* his nose. Cartilage snaps, and blood pours down his chin. Howling, he drops to his knees.

My instructor's voice rises inside my mind. *Never let your emotions direct your actions.*

That has never before been a problem. Here and now, rage is flooding me. How *dare* these idiots treat another human being like this? How *dare* they violate her privacy and threaten her?

I kick Leer while he's down. His head snaps to the side and he crash-lands—on his face.

"You like to hurt people who can't defend themselves, huh? Well, today, so do I." I close the distance once again, menace accompanying every step.

Today my superhero name is Angel of Vengeance.

"Please…no…stop." Leer crab-walks back, trying to escape me, but he leaves himself wide-open to another attack. His most vulnerable body part is, well, vulnerable. I take advantage, the way he took advantage of Mercedes's situation, and kick him between the legs. Another howl. His entire body jerks from the intense shot of pain.

"S-stop."

"I'll stop when you carry the same internal scars you've

given her." I position myself at the side of his head, lift my foot…and stomp. The tread of my shoe slams into his nose.

He jerks again, then collapses, as motionless as his friend. Blood pours from his broken nose.

"Jade."

A whisper. *Mercedes's* whisper, ragged and broken.

Boys forgotten, I gather the clothes I threw at Leer and rush to her side. She's taken cover inside a stall now and doesn't seem to react to my presence, even though she summoned me. She is looking somewhere far, far away, and her tears have stopped falling. I think part of her mind has checked out.

Slowly, not wanting to startle her, I crouch in front of her. "I'm going to dress you, okay?"

Still no reaction. As gently as possible, I wrap the corset around her middle, move behind her and zip the back. I guide her legs into the pants and force the material up to her waist. With my arm wrapped around her, I help her stand.

"We're going home," I tell her. Fright Night is exactly that—a terrible fright.

Tremors shake her as we head down the hall. I call for a teacher, an adult, someone, anyone. We need help, and they need to know what happened at their school. They need to take measures to ensure something like this doesn't happen again. But we make it to the parking lot without catching anyone's notice, because these hallways are cordoned off; the school's way of preventing anyone unauthorized from entering the building.

A whimper escapes her when we come to Bobby and

his group. Bobby—whose face is now cut and bruised, I notice with satisfaction. He's gathered an even larger group of friends, who have surrounded Clarik with a wall of testosterone.

Clarik is far from intimidated. In fact, he's grinning with cold calculation.

Bobby has provoked a bear, but he probably feels invincible with his friends around.

I don't want to move away from Mercedes, but I don't want to leave Clarik on his own, either. "You've done enough damage, Bobby. Stop this."

His attention never veers from Clarik. "Not yet. I'm going to prove to your *boyfriend*—" he sneers the word "—that he isn't as tough as he thinks he is."

"By having your friends gang up on him? All that proves is how weak and cowardly *you* are." Where are our chaperones, the teachers and staff paid to be here? Principal Hatcher? Martha?

"Get your sister to my truck, Jade." Clarik doesn't spare me a glance, either. "You don't need to stay for this."

"Yeah, it's gonna be a bloodbath." Bobby pops his knuckles.

People gather around us, Fright Night forgotten. Everyone wants to watch a down-and-dirty slaughter.

"Fight, fight, fight," they chant.

A new flood of tears streaks down Mercedes's cheek. Her tremors intensify.

"Someone go get Hatcher," I call. "Now."

"No." Clarik gives a single shake of his head. "Bobby hasn't learned his lesson, so I'm going to make sure he does this time. He won't be walking away—he'll be crawling."

Bobby bristles, and I wonder if this reality shift has turned him into his worst villain self, or if he is truly this bad in real life.

"Go get help," I command the girl who stands a few feet away. "Now."

When she takes a step, Bobby points an accusing finger at her, and she stills. "Do it, and you'll regret it," he snaps.

Dang him! What should I do?

"Intimidating people who are smaller than you. Look how brave and strong you are," Clarik says, mocking him as he steps forward. "If you want a piece of me, come and get it."

Bobby, too, steps forward. His friends remain a flank at his sides. Not all of them are as cocky, however. Some are visibly frightened, pale and trembling. But not one of them backs down, probably too afraid of being ridiculed.

They can dish it, but they don't want to eat it.

The two opposing forces converge. I gasp, and Mercedes cries out. Fists are thrown. Legs are kicked. Grunts of pain blend together. Clarik… Clarik knows what he's doing, as if he was born in a boxing ring. He's in total control. He ducks when he needs to duck, spins out of the way when necessary and throws a well-placed punch at every opportunity.

Anyone he hits falls.

It doesn't take Bobby long to realize he's outmatched. He does his best to throw his friends at Clarik in order to keep himself out of the strike zone, but Clarik knocks out every…single…one. All the while, his gaze continually returns to Bobby, the main target.

When one of Clarik's victims regains consciousness, he jumps to his feet and runs out of the fight circle, knocking into Mercedes and me. We stumble backward, and I lose my grip on her. People scramble out of our way, and in the chaos, I tumble into a wall—headfirst. Sharp pain explodes through my temples.

Mercedes is pushed into a bronzed scarecrow and screams as if she's been ripped from her mental reverie. Though my vision is hazy, I'm able to see her through the legs of the people in the crowd. Blood pours from a wound in her ankle. She must have scraped the ends of the scarecrow's pitchfork as she fell.

All she can do is press a shaky hand against the gaping flesh to hopefully stanch the flow. I crawl over to her, rip the hem from my skirt and wind the material around her ankle.

"You are going to be okay," I assure her.

A car parks at the curb. Despite the violence taking place around us, Linnie and Kimberly don't hesitate to rush out of the vehicle and straight to Mercedes's side.

"Sorry, sorry. She told us to leave without her, but we didn't feel right about it so we just stayed in the car, debating what to do, then we saw the fight," Linnie babbles. "Just…leave her alone, Jade." She pushes me out of the way. "You and your friends have done enough damage. We'll get her to a hospital."

"I didn't do this. Her mom is a doctor." I move in front of Mercedes. "I'll take her home."

"No," Kimberly spits at me. "You aren't—"

"It's okay," Mercedes tells her. "I trust Jade."

Both girls look like they want to argue, but concern for her well-being overshadows everything else, and they nod.

Working together, we get her to her feet. Ahead of us, kids are moving with Clarik and Bobby, who are still fighting. Bobby throws a punch, but Clarik dodges and throws one of his own. His strike has a lot more power behind it. His knuckles collide with Bobby's nose. Blood sprays, and he topples backward.

Clarik pins Bobby to the ground—and punches one final time.

Knowing the girls have Mercedes anchored in place, I let go and push through the crowd, reaching Clarik as he stands, throwing my arms around him. He's panting, a stream of crimson trickling from his cracked lip. Blood coats his hands—Bobby's and his own. His knuckles are split open.

"What's going on out here?" Principal Hatcher winds through the now-gaping onlookers, three men at her sides. Two are security guards—and one of those guards is Clarik's uncle. Mr. Parton is the third man.

They reach us seconds later. The security guard who isn't related to Clarik grabs him, despite his uncle's protests. I cling to Clarik, refusing to let go.

Hatcher crouches beside Bobby to assess the damage and check his vitals.

I'm horrified as my boyfriend's hands are cuffed behind his back. "He was protecting Mercedes," I say, refusing to release him.

What should I do? This is a lose-lose situation.

"Let him explain what happened," Tag demands.

"I'll tell you what happened," I shout. "Bobby and his friends stole a female student's clothing and threatened to violate her. Clarik protected her from further harm. Protected us all by knocking them out, preventing them from causing more trouble or escaping. He should be rewarded!"

Looking shell-shocked, Hatcher scans the crowd for confirmation.

"Jade." Clarik nuzzles my cheek with his own, everyone else forgotten. It is a gesture of comfort. "I'll be all right. Don't worry about me. Take care of Mercedes. She needs you right now."

Brutal tremors rock me, nearly knocking me off my feet. "I don't want to let you go," I whisper. I'm not talking about this moment exactly, but tomorrow and the next day and the next.

"I know, Jaybird, but you must."

"He's known for fighting," the security guard grates at Tag. "He was warned what would happen the next time he resorted to violence." Then, glaring daggers at me, he adds, "Let him go, Miss Leighton. Now."

"It's okay," Clarik tells me. "Everything will be okay."

"If what Miss Leighton said is true," Hatcher announces, "Clarik was acting in the defense of another. Get him inside. Keep him there until the proper authorities arrive and sort everything out."

Behind us, Mercedes whimpers. If not for her mental trauma, I would have gone toe-to-toe with the adults. She's seen enough brutality for one day. So I do it. I release Clarik at last.

He's hauled into the building. I watch him until the last possible second. Just before disappearing behind the door, he glances at me over his shoulder, and my heart breaks. This wasn't supposed to happen. I'm fighting for better. This isn't better.

When has life ever done what I expected, though?

Tag hangs back. "Don't worry, Jade. I'll see that he's taken care of." Then he, too, is gone.

"All right, everyone," Hatcher calls. "An ambulance has been called. So have the police. Do not, under any circumstances, leave this area."

I return to Mercedes's side. "Let me have her," I say to Linnie and Kimberly. "I'll get her to our car." Suddenly, I'm feeling pulled toward home. To get there now, now, now. "Please tell Hatcher and Parton what you witnessed, what Bobby and his friends did. If the authorities need to speak with Mercedes, they can come to the house, or call."

"You're not leaving with her," Linnie says with an adamant shake of her head. "Not without us."

"Not without us," Kimberly reiterates. "Where she goes, we go."

"Please." Mercedes's eyes well with tears again, her chin trembling. "Let Jade take me home. I just want to go home. My mother will patch me up, okay, all right? I'll talk to you guys tomorrow, promise."

They share a reluctant look before passing Mercedes on to me. I wind my arm around her waist, saying, "I'll take good care of her, you have my word." This girl…she is my sister. Once, I lived for her misery, but no longer. Acting as her crutch, I lead her toward the parking lot.

"Mr. Parton," Kimberly calls, doing her part. "You need to know what happened tonight from my point of view."

"Mrs. Hatcher," Linnie calls next. "Let me tell you what else Bobby and company have done."

Without garnering anyone's notice, I get Mercedes buckled in the passenger seat of our car—and then I take the wheel. My blood chills. As I key the ignition, old fears rear their ugly head. As soon as the car moves, I'm responsible for Mercedes's life. I'm responsible for *every* life out on the road today.

Do not vomit. Or pass out!

"I can do this." Breath wheezes from my throat. "I *can* do this." I grip the wheel so tightly my knuckles bleach of color. What if someone slams into us? What if—

"Just drive, grandma," Mercedes says. "You can do this."

"Drive. Yes, right." I gulp and place the car in Reverse…only to jam my foot on the brake the instant we're in motion. Using the back of my wrist, I wipe the sweat from my brow.

"You can do this," she repeats, encouraging me despite her pain. "You are Jade Leighton. You can do anything."

"I'm so sorry about what happened." Tears well in *my* eyes. "I'm so sorry for what Bobby and the others did to you. I'm so sorry I wasn't there—"

A sob leaves her, and she turns away from me, staring out the window. "It wasn't your fault. Your mom wanted me torn down, remember?"

"Not like this." Never this.

"Face it, Jade. I deserved this betrayal. What goes

around comes around. I shared your journal entries, which was a violation of your privacy. Tonight, Bobby did the same to my pride."

"No! You did *not* deserve this, and you had better not think something like that ever again. *Nothing* you did or said makes you culpable in this. What Bobby did is wrong in every way, shape and form, but it's *his* wrong, not yours. Got it?"

After a lengthy pause, she nods.

"Good." Finally, I ease off the brakes. A little more… still more… Okay. The car is moving.

Oh, crap, the car is moving!

I slam my foot against the brake once again, and the car jerks to a stop. "I'm brave," I say with false confidence. Chin up, shoulders back. I can do anything, just like Mercedes said.

Sweat pours from me as I ease my foot off the brake, and the car inches into motion. We roll forward…soon, we're on the road. With other cars. One car after another passes us. I'm going too slow, but I'm not having a panic attack, so I consider this a win.

"At this rate," Mercedes mutters, "I'm going to bleed out."

"Sorry not sorry." I press a little harder, speeding us up, but not by much.

"You drive like my grandma," Mercedes says on a sigh.

"Then your granny is an excellent driver. She's probably won multiple safety awards."

Cars honk and swerve around me, but finally, blessedly, we arrive home.

I help Mercedes out…help her hobble inside and shout

for her mother. My dad and Nadine come flying out of their bedroom.

Nadine is tying her robe. When she spies Mercedes's bloody ankle, she pales. "What happened?" She returns to the bedroom, only to reappear a few seconds later with a bag of medical supplies. "Why can't you go one night without—"

"Enough!" Mercedes shouts. "You shouldn't speak until you know all the facts, Mom. And you don't have to worry. I'm a problem child. The message has been received, trust me. I'm not perfect, and I'm done trying to be. I don't need your approval to be happy with who I am."

"I didn't mean… I wasn't…" Nadine pales as she works on cleaning, numbing and stitching Mercedes's torn flesh.

"Tell her what happened," I say to Mercedes. Then I tug my dad into the hall, so we can give the mother/daughter duo a little privacy. Besides, my head still hurts from my encounter with the wall.

"Are you all right?" Dad asks. "What happened? *You* tell *me*."

I do. I tell him what the boys did to Mercedes, and his features twist with anger.

"Thank you for telling me," he says. "A lot of kids wouldn't open up like that, would try to handle the situation on their own. I'll make sure to follow up with Principal Hatcher."

"Thank you." I give him a hug and say, "I'm going to my room now, okay? I need a little rest."

"Sure. Holler if you need me."

I hole up in my bedroom and ease onto the edge of the bed, inhaling, exhaling, trying to steady my thoughts.

We've come so far, Mercedes and me. Learned so much. It kind of sucks that our hard work didn't make everything perfect, but I guess every day is a new battle and another chance for victory. We're stronger now, and we're fighting the good fight.

A light tap on my window gets me on my feet and padding across the room. I move the curtains and gasp. Clarik is here! I open the pane, and he climbs inside. He must have come straight from the school. Blood is dried on his hands, and his shirt is torn.

The second he's steady on his feet, I throw my arms around him, my headache forgotten.

"They let me go," he says softly.

"I'm so glad!"

"Jade."

I gasp at the sound of my mother's voice and jolt from Clarik's arms.

"What's wrong?" Clarik asks.

I step in front of him, acting as a shield. Mom is standing in front of the window, the curtains blowing through her.

Her expression is somber. "It's time."

Time…time… "You're here to take me back." Whether I'm ready or not.

"Jade?" Clarik's hands settle on my waist. Good thing. He becomes my anchor, the only thing holding me upright.

"I'm here to offer you a choice," Mom says.

In the distance, a voice whispers, "Come on. Don't do

this. You're too young. Come back to us." This time, I can't blame a TV show or a radio.

I don't know what's happening exactly, or what it means, but I do know I'm at the precipice of something big.

"You can stay here," she continues, "or you can go back. The choice is yours."

"I can stay?" My heart races, fast, so very fast. With anticipation?

"You can, but I need to know your decision," she says. "Now."

Not yet! "Just…give me a second to think."

"Think about what?" Clarik asks. "Jade, what's going on? And what did you mean, you can stay? Are you telling me you have a chance to stay here, with me, in this reality?"

A light flashes before my eyes. More voices sound in the distance as the pain in my head returns and redoubles.

My mom reaches out her hand. "There's no time, sweetheart. Make your choice. Here or there?"

I whirl, facing Clarik, clinging to him, really. How can I leave? I've built a good life here. Things aren't perfect, but what is? Things aren't perfect in the real world, either. Here, at least, I'm on the right track, headed in the right direction.

But how can I stay? Sometimes you have to let go of something good to grab onto something great.

"I am telling you I can stay here, yes," I say as tears stream down my cheeks.

He cups my jaw and gently wipes away the teardrops

with his thumbs. "But you're also telling me you have to go back." A statement, not a question.

"Yes," I whisper. "I have to go back." I won't let fear make another decision for me and hold me back. I may not know what awaits me on the other side, but whatever it is, I will face it, and I will prevail.

"I love you." His gaze searches mine before he leans down and presses our foreheads together. "And I *will* find a way back to you, Jaybird."

"I love you, too. And, Clarie? You had better." Our breaths mingle, and as I inhale, infusing his essence in my every cell, a wave of darkness sweeps over me, and I know nothing more.

Chapter 17

Our reality should never be limited
to the things we see and feel.
There's always more to the story.

—Jade Leighton

Beep, beep. Beep, beep, beep. Beeeeeep.

My head! Oh, my throbbing head. It's worse than ever before. And my body. Every inch of me aches. And dang it, there's something stuck in my throat. I struggle to remove it, but no part of me wants to cooperate, and all I do is flail.

Someone looms over me, but my vision is blurry, so I can't make out his features. "Jade. Jade. My name is Dr. Weller. I'm one of the members of your recovery team. You were hit by a car."

That voice. I know it. The radio DJ.

Wait. He's a doctor. On my recovery team? I was hit by a car?

"You've been in a coma," he continues, "and you're just now waking up. I know you're scared, and I know you're in pain, but I need you to be still, okay? There's a tube in your throat. It's been helping you breathe. I'm going to remove it, but you have to be still."

What? A coma? No, no. I was in my bedroom, talking to Clarik and my mom…

My mom! She sent me back. I've returned to my real life.

Beepbeepbeep. I need to see Mercedes. And Clarik. Does he remember our time together? I need to see my dad. And Fiona! Is she here? How's Ruby? I want to see Linnie, Kimberly and Robb. Robb! He's still alive. He must be!

"Jade, honey. Please, settle down. I don't want you to injure yourself further."

My dad's voice penetrates my awareness, and I fight to turn my head. He's blurry to me, but I can tell he's standing beside my bed, being pushed away by a woman in scrubs and a lab coat. He's here, but not Fiona? They're still married, right?

Panic sweeps me up, and I struggle against my bonds more stridently.

"All right," the doctor says. "We'll try again in a bit."

One of my arms goes cold, as if someone just filled the veins with ice water. Black clouds instantly envelop me, and I drift away.

Beep. Beep. Beep.

The steady sound drags me from sleep. I pry open tired, burning eyes. My vision is blurry, but the more I blink, the clearer my surroundings become. A small room filled with medical equipment.

My head throbs more with every move I make, but I manage to turn to the left without wishing for death. A non-Goth version of my dad is sleeping in a chair next to my hospital bed; his upper body is slumped over, his dark hair disheveled. His white T-shirt is wrinkled, and his jeans have...coffee stains?

How long has he been here, watching over me?

Hospital. That's right! Memories flood me. Hit by a car. Coma. Breathing tube.

The beeping increases in speed as I reach up to pat my mouth. Oh, thank the good Lord. The tube has been removed. I'm breathing on my own—though every breath makes it feel as if needles are piercing my lungs.

My dad jerks upright, his eyelids popping open. When he realizes I'm awake, he smiles—and then he bursts into tears.

The sight brings tears to *my* eyes. I try to speak, but my throat is too raw, and the soft rasp that escapes is absolute agony.

He grabs my hand, careful not to disrupt my IV. "Shh, shh. Don't try to speak. Do you remember anything? Do you want me to tell you what happened?"

A slight incline of my chin is all I can manage.

"The night after you went out with Clarik, you came home, asked me about Nadine and shut yourself in your room, and I thought you went to bed, so I went to bed, too. You snuck out of the house to go for a jog, I assume. I truly hope you weren't running away. You came upon Mercedes along the way. A car was about to hit her, but you pushed her out of the way. The car ended up clipping her leg and ramming you. A boy named Bobby Bay was behind the wheel. He left the scene, but Mercedes was able to identify him and he was arrested just a few days later."

The car actually hit us? But…but… I remember diving out of the way and smacking into the flower bed.

"Though her leg was injured, she managed to crawl to Clarik's house. He called 911." A sob. A sob he fights to control. "You had massive cranial swelling, a few broken bones and a ton of other stuff. I can't remember all the details, I'm sorry. All I know is that you slipped into a coma, and I've never been more scared in my life." He lifts my hand, kisses the center. "You've been here about three weeks."

In my foggy, drugged state, I struggle to make sense of things. My mom visited me *before* the accident. Unless, of course, coma-brain rearranged the timeline. Which is entirely possible, and far more probable than a ghost going all *A Christmas Carol* meets *Matrix* on me.

Which means my mother never actually visited me. Mercedes never became my ally, and Clarik and I never dated. We had our nondate date and nothing more.

The other reality was never created to teach me the error of my ways. Instead, it was a construct of my own making—of my imagination. And yet…

Deep down in my heart I believe the things I learned about my mom are true. My subconscious must have unveiled the details little by little, helping me cope.

"Grandma Beers drove up from Tulsa," my dad says. "She's staying at our house. Your friends have visited every day. Linnie, Kimberly and Robb. They've been so worried."

Robb! He *is* alive. I'm so… I can't wait… He must be…

Hot tears pour down my cheeks. My temples throb, fragmenting my thoughts, even as relief floods me. Relief and happiness. A thousand things might be wrong, but this…this is right.

"Even Mercedes came to see you," Dad adds. "She

would read to you and hold your hand. And Clarik. I think he's visited you more than anyone. Yesterday he brought a keyboard and, for the first time, you responded to stimuli. The doctors prepared us for the worst, but finally, we had hope." He pauses as another sob overtakes him. When he calms, he gives me a smile that is big, wide and toothy, and melts my heart.

So much to process! Here I am, back in the real world. Mercedes and Clarik came to see me, even though they know nothing about the past we share inside my head. Mercedes, my enemy. Clarik, my crush. Clarik even played a song for me. Probably the one I heard in the other reality, my mind weaving a story to explain what I heard in real life.

My tears fall faster. *Release the pain, embrace the joy.*

"Nadine has been part of your team, acting as your primary physician," Dad says now. "She and Fiona were like hissing cats at first, but then your condition changed and suddenly they were like long-lost best friends."

Fiona. Sweet, gentle Fiona. I let the darkness of my past cast a shadow over her, never really giving her a chance, always pushing her away. I might not have lashed out at her, but cruelty comes in many forms. My coldness must have been a constant dagger in her heart.

She deserves so much better than what I gave her.

"We think Ruby sensed something was wrong with her big sister." Dad smooths a damp strand of hair from my face. "She wasn't moving around as much, but, oh, baby, did she start kicking up a storm when you woke up yesterday."

A sob shakes my entire body, and almost chokes me,

then another and another. A tidal wave of anguish spills from my heart, crashing through me, and I offer no resistance.

Dad rubs my back and mutters encouragement. "That's it, sweetheart. Let it out, let it all out…everything is going to be okay… I'm here for you, I'll always be here for you… I love you so much."

Had I opted to stay in coma-world, where things were easy—well, easier—I would have chosen death. I see that now. *See so clearly.* But I decided to live. This is my second chance, and I will not waste it.

I take my dad's hand and squeeze, using what little strength I have. Never again will I give this man cause to doubt my love for him or think I'm running away from him.

I feel a thousand pounds lighter when I calm, but there's no time to enjoy it. A nurse comes in, shoos him out and takes my vitals while asking me a thousand questions about pain and mobility; she has me blink once for *yes* and twice for *no.*

For the first time, I realize a cast binds my non-IV hand, and a brace hugs one of my ankles.

When the nurse leaves, my dad returns. He's on the phone with Fiona, giving her an update. He is glowing. "Fiona's on her way," he tells me when they hang up. "She's so excited to see you. You're not going to believe how big she's gotten so quickly."

I desperately want to see her and find a way to tell her I'm sorry for the past, and that I love and appreciate her, that I look forward to a future together. But my eyelids seem to weigh ten thousand pounds now. Fatigue is racing me toward a finish line I can't see.

Finally, my eyes close, and there's nothing I can do about it. I just don't have the strength.

"Sleep, honey." Dad pats my hand. "We'll be here when you wake up, I promise."

In the ensuing days, I'm given so many tests—both mental and physical—I don't have time for visitors. Only my dad and Fiona are allowed in the room between those tests, and we talk about my mother.

I was right. My subconscious unveiled the truth.

I expect confirmation to fill me with anger or hurt, but I realize *another* startling truth. I've already forgiven her.

"I know you're eager to go home," Nadine says when she enters the room, "and today we make it happen."

Home...the one I've missed, with colorful walls, lace doilies and country chic furnishings. I'm eager to see my friends, and a little nervous to speak with Clarik, *if* he even comes to see me. What am I going to say to him?

I give Nadine a thumbs-up. She isn't the she-beast I portrayed her to be in the other reality. Or what I'm calling CPR: Coma Provided Reality. CPR versus IRL. In real life.

Anyway. Nadine is actually courteous, professional and kind. Yesterday she told me that my near-death helped her appreciate her daughter as never before and value the time they have together. She thanked me for saving Mercedes, and apologized for the things she said all those years ago.

Nadine—who is wearing a pink top and brown slacks—types into the computer beside the bed and smiles at me. "You're looking great, kiddo."

"Thank you." Every day, speaking is easier. The first time I caught sight of my reflection in the bathroom mirror, I was pleasantly surprised. I expected a swollen and bruised face, but time has been kind to me.

A nurse comes in with my dad, and together they help me get settled in a wheelchair. Putting any weight on my injured ankle isn't fun—yet.

Fiona is waiting for us outside, sitting in the driver side of her sedan, parked in the roundabout just beyond the emergency entrance doors. She smiles when she spots us, and I smile back.

I know what life is like without her, and I never want to experience such a loss again.

My dad opens the passenger door, helps me stand and hobble to the car and watches as I buckle my belt, ready to swoop in and take over if I weaken.

"Hey, Mom," I say, and I do not use the term lightly. Fiona *has* been a wonderful mother to me, loving me when I was unlovable, supporting me even when I resisted and refusing to ever give up on me.

Tears of happiness well in her eyes. "Hey, sweetie."

Waves of affection warm my heart. "How's our girl?"

Beaming now, she rubs her stomach. "Still kicking up a storm."

My dad shakes the nurse's hand before settling in the front passenger seat. He flicks me glance after glance over his shoulder as we motor down the road.

"Dad, I'm fine. Promise."

"I know, sweetheart." And still he glances over his shoulder.

I chuckle as I peer out the window, enjoying the early December scenery. Gray sky, red leaves. Signs advertising pumpkin *everything*. Yeah, this is real life.

I haven't told anyone about my CPR, and I'm not sure I will. Robb won't be happy that I killed him off in my dreams, and Linnie and Kimberly will want to barf about their wardrobe choices. Mercedes... I don't know what she'll say. I know only that I *miss* the friendship we built, and the strong, brave girl she became. Clarik might think I'm a creepy stalker chick.

Plus, everyone will laugh about an experience that has changed me on a fundamental level, laugh at memories that are as real and precious to me as any others. No, thanks.

These memories...they *are* precious to me. I'll guard them like the treasure they are.

"Home at last." My dad helps me out of the car and prepares to act as my crutch.

"I promise not to run, or try to jump any hurdles," I say, and kiss his cheek. "I'd love a chance to walk on my own." Gotta start sometime.

He holds up his hands, palms out. Though my gait is slow, every step measured, I manage to limp to my bedroom on my own. Of course, Dad and Fiona remain nearby, just in case.

While Dad gathers everything he thinks I'll need—junk food, a bottle of water, an iPad, iPhone, black marker and TV remote—Fiona tucks me into bed.

Before she can leave, I clasp her hand. "I'm sorry for

all the times I ignored you. I'm sorry for all the times I acted as if you didn't matter." My voice wobbles. "You matter to me."

"You matter to me, too." She presses my hand against her heart. "Always have, always will."

My dad comes up beside her and drapes an arm around her waist, gazing at me as if I'm a cross between fungus and a check for one million dollars. "Pod person! Who are you and what have you done with my little girl?"

Fiona playfully slaps his shoulder. "She survived a major trauma. Of course she's changed." She smiles at me. "Feel free to ignore the garbage your dad just placed on the nightstand. While you were in the hospital, I cooked and froze a thousand different meals so that you'd have plenty of food to choose from when you got home. Food that is nutritious *and* delicious. No mushrooms, you have my word."

"I would love one of your casseroles," I say, grateful for her thoughtfulness. "Yes, please, and thank you."

"I'll go heat something up." Still smiling, she waddles off.

My dad leans down to kiss my forehead. "You've made her year."

"Well, she's a wonderful person. You couldn't have picked a better partner." And that's the truth.

He bops my nose before striding from the room. Giggles jumps onto the bed and stretches out on the pillow beside mine, then looks at me with pleading eyes, practically *begging* me to pet him.

I reach out—and he claws my hand, drawing blood. A

laugh bubbles from me. Some things never change. "I'm glad to see you, too, devil-cat."

Grandma Beers visits later that day, and I love that she's back to her normal self. Her hair is completely gray and styled into a perfect beehive shape. She's wearing an orange muumuu with yellow flowers and green socks. We talk about my mom, about her depression, and mourn together for what could have been.

Throughout the day, I receive other visitors. Every time Dad or Fiona escorts someone to my bedroom, I'm reminded to stay put, and my friends are warned not to jostle me.

Linnie is the first, Goth once again, and my heart nearly bursts with love as she sits in the chair that's been placed at the side of my bed. I beckon her closer and closer until I'm able to hug her. She hugs me back, careful not to squeeze me too tightly. Giggles hisses at her, but doesn't try to maim her. I guess his attacks are saved for me and me alone.

"What was that for?" she asks, her eyes watering.

"I love you, that's all."

Her mouth hangs open as she studies me more intently. "Be honest. Did an alien take over your body?"

I toss a potato chip at her—which she catches and pops into her mouth.

I ask her about her day. Actually, her weeks. I want to know every detail about her life. At first, she offers scant details, because I've never really shown such an interest before. But it isn't long before she's gabbing about everything and nothing.

Before long, Kimberly and Robb arrive and join us.

They, too, are back to normal, and it makes me smile so wide the muscles in my jaw begin to ache. I give them both hugs, and they're as surprised as Linnie.

"I love you guys, and I missed you," I tell them. They'll never know how much, but I will delight in proving it. "And, Robb," I add, taking his hand. I peer deep into his eyes so he'll know how serious I am. "I don't know if you've been planning to maybe say goodbye to us… forever."

He looks ready to cry. Heck, at this rate I'm going to make everyone who comes into contact with me sob.

Yes. He had. And the realization hurts. "You are one of the best people I know. Whatever trials you're facing, they can't, they won't, last forever. This is a storm, and storms pass. Flowers bloom." I think of the time I ridiculed the philosophy and want to shake Old Jade. "I know those words won't fix the pain inside you, but they are true nonetheless. And you are loved. You are valued. You are a treasure, and there's not another one like you."

"Thank you," he croaks, then he clears his throat. "I don't know who you are or what you've done with our Jade, but I like you and I've decided I'm keeping you."

Everyone snickers. Including me! As we talk and laugh, happy to be together, my dad brings us each a bowl of the homemade chicken noodle soup Fiona heated up. I eat until I feel like I'm going to burst at the seams, loving each bite more than the last.

But with food in my belly, fatigue threatens to overtake me and I know I'm running out of time. There's so much more to say. "You guys have always been kind to me, even when I didn't deserve it. I took you for granted, and that stops now."

"You had your moments," Kimberly says as she draws on my cast. "And you always defended us. No one dared attack while the machine queen was there with her icy stares."

Machine queen. Ice princess. Robot. Without emotion, I'd been hollow. A shell of myself…

"You were worth waiting for," Linnie tells me with a fond smile.

My thoughts jump to Mercedes. She was worth waiting for, too, and I want her back. "Have you guys spoken with Mercedes?" I can't help but ask.

"We have. Believe it or not, she's been nice to us," Linnie says. "At lunch one day, Charlee Ann told Robb the world would be a better place without him, and Mercedes went off. Like, she had a legit hissy and said she and her group weren't better than everyone else."

He nods the entire time Linnie speaks, and even the memory seems to leave him a bit shell-shocked. "It was pretty awesome."

Oh, Mercedes. Sister. Like me, you've changed. But why? She wasn't in a coma. And even if she had been, there's no way our minds could create the same alternate reality.

"What about Clarik?" I ask.

"You mean the brand-new slice of beefcake?" Kimberly pauses her artwork long enough to wiggle her brows.

My beefcake! "The very one."

Linnie fans herself, but there's a guarded look on her face. "He's, uh, good. He's good."

"What's wrong?" I insist.

"Do you have a crush on him? I'm guessing yes." Kimberly sets the marker aside, revealing a skull and crossbones. "I think he had a crush on you, too, but...since your accident, he's been hanging out with Mercedes."

My stomach sinks. "Are they dating?"

Linnie licks her lips before admitting, "No one knows for sure."

Disappointment stabs me, a quick *jab, jab* that leaves me bleeding on the inside. I knew things would be different when I returned, but this is... Wow. This hurts.

The old Jade wouldn't have cared—much. She would have gone numb. What she wouldn't do? Hurt every time she spotted Clarik and Mercedes together. But I am New Jade, and I won't go numb. If they *are* together, well, I'll just have to find a way to deal. I love them both, and I want them in my life—in whatever capacity I can get them.

We chat a little longer, until my head begins to fog and throb. Ugh. It's time for a pain pill. Which means it's time for a nap. I won't be able to fight sleep any longer.

I don't want my friends to go, but asking them to watch me sleep is too much, and creepy, so I hug everyone goodbye and settle into the covers. Giggles curls into my side.

"Planning to protect me or kill me while I'm defenseless?" I ask him.

Amid his purrs, I drift off to sleep and dream of Clarik.

Two days pass. Two days of homework and physical therapy, but the two people I most want to see never visit me.

Why are Clarik and Mercedes staying away? I know they don't remember our time together—why would they? It never really happened. But they came to see me while I was in the hospital. Why not now, when I'm at home?

I *need* to make things right with Mercedes. Her friendship is a lifeline. And I want Clarik in my life. Want to hold his hand and lean against him, the way Fiona leans against my dad. I want to hug him and kiss him. I want to calm him if the rage comes—

Did I make up his background, or did he talk to me while I slept?

Most of all, I want answers.

When I'm cleared for active duty—meaning I can leave the bed for more than potty breaks and physical therapy—I perch on a bar stool at the kitchen counter while Fiona warms up hamburger casserole, and beg her to let me drive to Mercedes's house.

"You're still taking pain meds, honey," she says. "You *can't* drive."

"*You* drive me to Mercedes's house, then."

"I don't know." She chews on her bottom lip. "I don't want to overtax you. Let me call your dad."

He's currently at work, making up for the time he spent at the hospital. I don't want to take a chance that he'll say no. "Please, Mom. Please."

Everything about her softens. "All right. Yes. But only if you sit down while you're talking to her."

"I will. I promise. Thank you, thank you, thank you." I stand, hiding a grimace as weight settles on my foot, and close the distance. For the thousandth time since my return, I hug her. These hugs…they aren't just for others. They help me, too. And they are like medicine to me. Better than admiration! When I'm in her arms, or my dad's or my friends', I'm cocooned by love.

In life, there are no guarantees about who will live long and strong and who will go early. There's going to be loss. Loving people doesn't make their loss unbearable; loving people just makes dealing with their loss worth it.

Fiona puts our leftovers in the fridge. "When do you want to—"

"Now," I interject. "Please, please, please."

She sighs. "Very well. I'll get my keys."

Chapter 18

If you want a different life,
you have to do something different.

—Jade Leighton,
today

Nerves threaten to get the better of me as I knock on Mercedes's door. Nadine is still at work, but I know my sister—my hands curl into fists. She's not my stepsister, not here. But...

We could be sisters-by-choice. I choose her. Will she choose me?

I know she's here. Her car takes up prime real estate in the driveway.

Knock, knock. No response, but a shadow moves along the bottom door crack.

From the car, Fiona calls, "She's not here, hon. Let's go home, rest for a few hours, and I'll bring you back, I promise."

With the lift of my index finger, I ask for another minute. "Please, Mercedes." I knock again. "I know you're in there. What I don't know is why you're avoiding me now."

Finally, the door swings open, hinges creaking. She stands before me, pale hair tangled, dark circles under her eyes. Despite the evening hour, she's still wearing pj's. A Star Wars tank and short set.

"Jade Leighton." She crosses her arms over her middle. "What do you want?"

There's no affection in her expression or tone, and the lack is like a dagger in the gut. I'd been so hopeful some part of her had grown to like me; I just hadn't realized it until now.

"May I come in?" My heartbeat springs into a wild race. "I'd like to talk with you."

Panic flares in her eyes, gone before I have time to wonder about its source. "Fine." She waves me in.

With a glance over my shoulder, I tell Fiona, "I'll text you when we're done, if you want to go home."

"I'll stay here in case you need me," she responds. "I brought a book. But don't take too long, okay?"

Darling woman. She is a precious treasure!

Mercedes leads me into the living room, where every wall and every piece of furniture is white. There isn't a speck of color. Everything is sleek and modern, like Nadine herself.

Mercedes plops onto the couch, where multiple bags of potato chips await. Crumbs dust the cushions around her. On the coffee table, empty soda cans are stacked in what looks to be a house.

"So." She stretches out and palms a remote, flipping channels as if she's alone and bored. "What do you want?"

"What's wrong with you, Mercedes?" Concern gets the better of me. "Are you sick?"

A bitter laugh escapes her, but she never offers a reply.

Before, I might have left then and there. Actually, I never would have approached her. But this isn't before, and I'm not the girl I used to be. I stand, limp to the coffee table, swipe the remote, switch off the TV and knock the cans to the floor. I sit in front of her, forcing her to face me.

"Thanks a lot. You ruined an hour of hard work." She scowls at me. "What are you doing here, Jade? Seriously."

"You came to visit me in the hospital."

"Yeah. So?"

"So. You care about my well-being, and you can't deny it."

Her gaze slides away from me. "Or," she says with more bite, "I felt guilty that you took a hit meant for me."

"That's something at least."

"Be honest. You're here to tell me to stay away from Clarik."

No. If they want to be together, I won't stand in their way. I love them both too much. "I'm here for you, because *I* care about *you*, too. Because I regret telling you I didn't want to be your friend the day you and Nadine moved out. I want to be your friend."

Some of the animosity drains from her, and she peers at me with something akin to hope. Hope she dislodges with a single shake of her head. Her expression hardens. "I don't like Clarik romantically. You don't have to worry."

"Oh, thank goodness." The words leave me in a rush, unstoppable.

"You care about me, huh?"

Sheepish, I say, "I won't deny I'm happy to hear you two aren't dating, but even if the answer had been different, I would still care for you."

"No, you wouldn't. Not about me." The words are

thrown at me as if they are weapons. "You never have, and you never will."

All right. Now we're getting somewhere. Such *feeling.* "I should have fought to stay with you. I'd lost my mother, and I feared losing someone else I loved, so I shut down and pushed everyone away. I can't go back and change what happened, but I *can* change how I act today. And today I'm here. I'm ready to fight for you and our friendship."

"Just…screw you, Jade. I mean, why now? Huh?"

"I learned firsthand how short life can be. Learned I need to value the things I have, or I'll lose them."

"And you value me?"

"I do."

Ashen, she anchors her elbows on her knees and rests her face in her upraised hands. "I have something to tell you, but I don't want to. You'll laugh."

"I won't, you have my word."

One minutes bleeds into another, but she says nothing more.

Finally, I crack. "Tell me! I'm staying here until you do, moving in if I need to. Tell. Me. Telllllll meeeeeee. Come on, Mercedes. Woman-up. Show off your ovaries of steel. Tell me, tell me, *tell me.*"

She looks up, her gaze spitting fire at me. "You want to know? Fine. I… Jade, I dreamed about you. The entire time you were in a coma, I dreamed we were living a secret life. It was you and me against the whole world. A world gone Goth. Crazy, right?" A laugh that borders on hysterical fills the air. "Everyone I know and love betrayed me, except…except…"

"Me, Linnie and Kimberly," I say softly. She was there. How? How is that possible? How was she pulled into a reality created by my unconscious mind? Unless…

No. Absolutely not. But…what if I *did* see my mom's ghost before Bobby's car hit me?

"We hated each other at first," I say, even as a lump grows in my throat. "But things began to change when you accompanied me to my grandmother's house."

Her eyes are wide as saucers as she says, "Grandma Beers. How intoxicating."

A jolt slams through me. *How intoxicating.* The same words she used in the CPR.

Impossible, my mind screams.

Still, I continue. "You made friends with Linnie and Kimberly. You would have made friends with Robb, but he'd died right before our arrival."

She looks entranced as she nods. "Charlee Ann and Bobby were unkind to me. And at the end at…

"Fright Night," we say in unison.

"He lured you into the boys' locker room," I say, "and stole your clothes."

A hand flutters over her mouth. "You *were* there."

Impossible…and yet probable.

"You were elected class president, and everyone adored you. You found out your mother had killed herself and—" She winces before pressing her lips together. "I'm sorry, Jade."

I give her a nod. "It's all right," I repeat. "My sister helped me deal."

"Sister," she echoes, and a tear cascades down her cheek. "Since you woke up… I've been in mourning. I loved you, but I lost you again. The dreams just stopped. You weren't my friend anymore. I couldn't sit in your bedroom and talk to you, couldn't lean on you."

"You can *always* lean on me."

She reaches over to take my hand, linking our fingers. Suddenly, I'm unable to speak; a sob is too busy rising from deep inside me…escaping. Then Mercedes and I are holding on to each other, both of us crying.

For some reason, my mind is flung back to the day my mom died. She sits behind the wheel of her car. Over and over she glances at me, her eyes wild, her hair a mess. But there, at the end, just before we soar over the railing, she looks at me and smiles.

"It's going to be okay, sweetheart. Everything is going to be okay now."

Our car hits the railing. Impact jars me, and the air is sucked from my lungs. I experience the sensation of falling, of flying…my seat belt is the only thing keeping me from dropping onto roof. I want to scream, but I don't. Momma said everything is going to be okay, and I believe her.

Boom! Another impact, this one more forceful, accompanied by a macabre soundtrack: grinding metal and crumbling cement. My head thrashes around as if I'm a rag doll—or nothing is attached the way it's supposed to be. I'm afraid to look down. What if my seat belt has split me in two?

Then everything goes still. My mom is lying on the dash, her head twisted so that she's facing me. One of her eyes has been gouged out, a thin piece of metal in its place. Her clothes are ripped, and there's blood everywhere. A metal spike protrudes from her torso. Bones protrude from her collar, her arm and both legs...one of her feet is severed.

Death isn't beautiful. Death is ugly and horrifying. Death is loss and regret.

Death is the enemy.

Momma. Momma. I scream for her. When she doesn't respond, I scream louder and louder, and try to fight my way free. I'm stuck. And I hurt. Oh, do I hurt. I'm cut and bruised and broken, and I'm hanging upside down, my blood dripping onto my mother, blending with hers.

At some point, though, I go still. I stop fighting. I stop crying for the mother who doesn't respond. My mind is what split in two—the girl I used to be, and the girl I am now. The one who can look at the carnage, as if it's a scene from a cartoon or a page from a coloring book, rather than real life.

Now, in the present, those two parts of me are reconnecting, finally weaving back together. Like a bone that's been reset. I cry harder. My entire body shudders. The tears are so plenteous and scalding that they soon make my cheeks feel like raw meat. All the while, Mercedes clings to me, her warm breath fanning my tearstained face, silky strands of her hair tickling my overly sensitive skin.

She doesn't tell me to be quiet, or to calm down. No, she tells me, "I've got you. I've got you, and I'm not letting go. Not ever again." But eventually she does let go to reach for her cell phone.

At some point, Fiona comes in and hugs me. Sometime after that, hinges squeak and footsteps sound, and then…new arms wrap around me. Stronger arms. A familiar scent fills my stuffy nose. Chocolate, cinnamon and vanilla. Familiar heat envelops me.

"I'm here, Jaybird."

Clarik? He's here, and he remembers me, too?

I clutch the collar of his shirt and cry even harder. As strong as he is, he lifts me onto his lap smoothly, then rocks us forward and back.

I almost died before I ever had a chance to live.

When I'm too drained to shed another tear, my burning eyes too puffy to open, my nose now too swollen to breathe, I sag against Clarik's chest.

Mercedes tells him something in hushed tones, then leads Fiona away to the kitchen. The only words I can make out are "real" and "knows."

His hold on me tightens. Against my ear, he says, "Jade, I dreamed of the Goth world, too."

He *did*? My fingers clench and unclench before pressing against his chest. His heartbeat races in time to mine.

A memory…something he said to me after our first kiss. *This feels like a dream. I don't want to wake up.*

"We dated," he added, "and I had more fun with you than I've ever had with anyone else. You smiled and laughed with me, and I felt like I was king of the world."

Maybe the CPR *was* more than a CPR. Wait. No maybe about it. It was. How else would Mercedes and Clarik have dreamed of me, of our time together, with details perfectly matched to my experiences…experiences that never really happened?

Clarik kisses my temple. "While you were in the coma, Mercedes and I ran into each other in the hospital. I heard her talking to you, telling you what was going on. I admitted the same thing was happening to me. After that, we met every day at lunch to discuss our dreams."

No wonder people had assumed they were dating.

"I wanted so badly for the dreams to be real," he says. "I was falling in love with you, Jaybird. I know, everyone is going to tell me it's too soon, and it happened too fast. But it's true. I love you. I love the sound of your laughter—how it was rusty at first, but by the end had become natural. I love your wit, and your capacity to forgive those who have wronged you. I love the way your eyes crinkle at the corners when you give me the smile I've been craving. The smile very few people get to see. I love your kindness toward a new boy at school, your willingness to help whoever needs you, even without being asked or appreciated."

Well. The well of tears hadn't dried up, after all. Another drop slides down my cheek. I want to tell him all the reasons I love him. And there are many. But exhaustion invades every muscle and cell in my body and I slump against him, no longer able to hold myself up in any way. Eyelids the weight of boulders close and the lights dim in my head. I drift away.

Chapter 19

Life is not about surviving. Life is about love.
The reason we are here. Love never fails.

—*Jade Leighton*

"Jade?"

I blink open tired eyes, and, oh, wow, do they burn. I stretch and roll to my back, wanting to sleep a thousand more hours, but something holds me in the realm of wakefulness. My limbs are heavy, but it's a good heavy. As if I've climbed a mountain, a whole world of possibilities now awaiting me.

"Jade, honey. Can you hear me? It's time for us to go home."

"Dad?" I blink up at him. He hovers over the side of my bed—

No, not my bed. An unfamiliar bed. In an unfamiliar room. White walls. White furniture. White covers. My dad and I are the only spots of color.

No, that's not true, either. Mercedes sleeps beside me. Clarik is asleep in a rocking chair by the window.

Fiona paces in front of the door, her hands rubbing her belly. "Did she overexert herself? I knew I should have made her stay home."

Memories flood me. The accident. The coma. The

CPR. The dreams shared by Mercedes and Clarik. Crying as if the world had come to an end, because, in a way, it had. The one I used to know at least. Being held and comforted. Healing.

I must still be inside Mercedes's house.

I expect another influx of pain, another bout of tears, but…the sun is shining inside me, the storm clouds finally chased away for good.

A smile blooms as I sit up. "What a glorious day."

"Jade?" my dad says again, his shock a beacon. "You're… you…"

Fiona moves to his side and takes his hand. She, too, stares at me as if she can't believe what she's seeing.

Another weight has been lifted from me. A terrible weight I hadn't known I carried. I hadn't understood the toll it had taken on me, until now. Now, I'm light and free and happy.

Yes, *this* is happiness.

Clarik—awake now—stands and, like the others, stares at me.

"Dad, Fiona, you've met Clarik. My boyfriend. At least, I think. I hope."

Clarik smiles at me. "Boyfriend. Definitely." He closes the distance, passing my parents, and sits beside me on the bed. He takes my hand and, uncaring about our audience, kisses my knuckles. Then he combs his fingers through my hair. The way he likes. The way I adore.

"I love you," I tell him, and I swear, fireworks explode in his eyes.

"Jade," my dad says, and I hear the underlying moan

of distress. "Can this wait until I'm out of the room? Not that I want you two staying in a room alone together."

No more waiting. Life is precious, and I'm not wasting another second of mine.

"Put your hands over your ears, Dad. Things are about to get sickeningly romantic."

He does moan this time. He also covers his ears.

To Clarik, I say, "I love your sense of humor. It never tears others down but always manages to lift them up. I love how fiercely protective you are. Bullies aren't allowed to bully on your watch. I love your determination. You saw a girl who never smiled and did everything in your power to give her a reason to turn her frown upside down. I love the care you showed me. The patience. I love the music you play, not just on a piano but with your actions. You make my heart sing."

He kisses me. Soft and swift, but a promise just the same: we're in this together. Now and always.

Fiona sighs dreamily.

"Talk, talk, talk," Mercedes mutters from her side of the bed. "Doesn't anyone have a romantic declaration for me? I'm pretty amazing, too, you know." She winks at me. "Maybe we should consider a sister-wife situation."

I snort. "I'm not sharing Clarik, but I'm not giving you up, either. With or without a marriage, we're family."

"What! Who said anything about marriage?" my dad shouts.

"Oh, hush up." Fiona pats his chest. "Magic is happening. Let's give these kids a moment of privacy." She drags him from the room and shuts the door behind them.

"Everything's going to change, you know." Mercedes

climbs over the mattress to sit on the other side of me. "Some of our friends won't like our friendship."

Too bad, so sad—for them. "I'm not going to hide my feelings for you. For either of you. Everyone else can deal. Or not. Their choice. But if their happiness is based on our decisions, they've got a sad life ahead."

"This." Clarik gives my knuckles another kiss. "This is one of the reasons I love you."

"Yeah, yeah, yeah. Enough mush. There's only one way to handle this situation." Mercedes leans her head on my shoulder and rubs her hands together. "We've got a coming-out party to plan."

Our "coming out" party ends up being a Light Night redo that Saturday evening. Mercedes admits she hated that I missed the first one, that it wasn't complete without me. She also tells me, "*I'm* Madam President in this reality, Miss Leighton, so you have to—one—agree with everything I say, and—two—suck it."

Dang, I like her.

She invites every kid at school, except Bobby, who is now being homeschooled. Charlee Ann refuses to come, and that's okay.

Linnie, Kimberly and Robb are the first to arrive. They're still not 100 percent comfortable around Mercedes, but they don't avoid her or give her a hard time, either. Well, not much of a hard time.

Linnie tells her, "When did you stop sucking so hard? Asking for a friend." But she gives a half grin and bumps Mercedes on the shoulder.

"You're okay. I guess," Kimberly says in her rumbling, grumbling tone.

Robb smiles a smile that is bright, zero sadness. "You're growing on me…like fungus."

Everyone laughs, even Mercedes. I hug and kiss them all, and maybe I cling to Robb a little longer than the others. But just a little!

"You are a treasure," I tell him.

He squeezes me tighter. "Right back at ya."

"Is this a lovefest?" Linnie says and claps. "Let me join, let me join!"

She wraps her arms around us, then pulls in Kimberly… who pulls in Mercedes. We are rocking this love and acceptance thing.

Martha comes, and so does Principal Hatcher and Mr. Parton. I returned to school earlier in the week, and he has been surprisingly…not horrible. Whether the changes occurred because of my near-death experience or the intensely protective stare Clarik laid on him anytime he glanced in my direction, I was too happy to care.

Even Nadine takes time off from work to attend. Yesterday she had a heart-to-heart with Mercedes about the disintegration of their relationship. Mercedes admitted she would very much like to work to repair the damage, and that her mother's constant criticisms hurt her and torch her self-esteem.

The two are a bit more at ease now, I've noticed. They are still finding their way, but they're finally on the right path. Also, Mercedes is seeing a therapist now, working on her personal issues and getting healthy. There's a long, hard journey ahead, but every step forward will be worth it. I'm so proud of her.

"Hey, guys. So glad you could come," I say. I'm part of the welcoming committee. Clarik and I stand in front of the house, directing everyone to the backyard. "If you'll go right through there..."

I'm wearing a black fit-and-flare dress with a ruffled skirt, and on that ruffled skirt are eight roses. White, yellow. Pink, red. Blue and green. Orange and violet. My rainbow.

I lean into my boyfriend.

He wraps a strong arm around my waist, his fingers toying with the ends of my hair. "Have I told you how beautiful you look tonight?"

"You have, but I'll never tire of hearing the words." Not because outward appearance matters most. It doesn't and never will. But because he sees the real me. Clarik loves me no matter the outer casing.

His mother, Evelyn, is here. I liked her at first sight. She's a lovely woman with Clarik's dark hair and blue eyes, though they share no other similar features. She carries an air of delicacy, while he is a tower of strength.

She took one look at me and said, "I've heard so many lovely things about you, and with only a glance, I know they are all true."

His uncle Tag came with her, and he gave me a gruff smile. As soon as Evelyn and Clarik turned their heads, he leaned down to whisper, "The boy has a heart of gold. I hope you'll treat it with care."

His family loves him dearly.

"You're doing it again," Clarik says.

"Doing what?"

"Smiling."

"Am I?" I pat my mouth, and sure enough, the corners are upturned. "I am. Well. I suppose you'll have to deal."

"Oh, the travesty," he mutters, and I laugh. A big, booming laugh that make his eyes sparkle like freshly polished sapphires.

"Funny man."

"And you wouldn't have me any other way."

So, so true. "By the way, I've decided I'm going to be a demanding girlfriend and expect you to serenade me '80s style at least once a week." I can't wait to hear him play IRL.

He gives a mock shudder. "If I must—"

"You must."

"Then I will. In return, I'm going to expect a reward every time I do."

"A reward, huh?"

"Oh, yes. A kiss. You still need practice." He gives me a smile.

I step up to his chest so that we are flush against one another. "You're so kind, allowing me to practice my wiles on you."

"And me alone," he says, then draws my bottom lip between his teeth, making me shiver.

"On the front lawn, Jade? Really?"

My dad's quip snaps me from my reverie. Jolting, I glance over to see his truck idling beside the curb, the window rolled down.

"First, I thought you wanted me to be more touchy-feely," I say. "Second, find a parking spot before they're all taken."

He shakes his head and mumbles under his breath as he eases down the road. After a few minutes, he finds a parking space for his truck at the end of the road, and helps Fiona climb out.

As they walk toward us, I wave them over and call, "Mom, tell Dad to give me a break."

"Give our daughter a break," she says, and we share a smile.

Smug, I motion to the backyard. "Come on. We'll show you the way."

"Clarik," my dad says with a nod. "Nice to see you again."

"And you, sir."

"I want to thank you, again, for the kitchen table," my dad says. "Your talent amazes me."

I squeeze Clarik's hand. Deliverymen brought it over this morning, the same table from my CPR. It is even more exquisite than I remember.

"Thank you, sir," he says.

The next few hours are spent mingling with the crowd, drinking the sherbet punch Mercedes made and eating the snicker doodle cookies I attempted to make. Pinterest fail! Clarik is the only one kind enough to finish his, and I think it's because he has a sweet tooth—the reason he always smells like dessert.

As the sun sets, a beautiful blaze of pink, gold and orange in the horizon, Mercedes passes out paper lanterns.

"It's time," she tells me. A lighter is passed around until every paper lantern is aglow.

It's time. The same words my mother spoke to me before my entire world changed—twice. I'm ready.

Mercedes shouts, "Release!"

In unison, we obey. Up, up the lanterns float, and I laugh with delight, watching, mesmerized. And what a sight to behold. Absolutely magnificent. The sky is an endless stretch of black velvet, now lit up with hundreds of lanterns, beacons of light in a world of darkness.

Hope.

"This is what you are to me," Clarik whispers to me.

I take his hand and once again lean against him, my head resting on his shoulder. Contentment fills my veins, flows to every part of me. The road behind me was rocky, and no matter where I turned, there were potholes. The road ahead isn't completely smooth—it never is, there are always surprises along the way—but it is worth traveling.

I'm not alone. Not anymore. I have family, friends… and love. So much love.

"To Jade Leighton," Mercedes calls.

"To us," I say. "To life." And oh my Goth. Life is good.

★ ★ ★ ★ ★

Thank you for reading
Oh My Goth
by Gena Showalter!
We hope you enjoyed this journey to
embrace life along with Jade, Mercedes and Clarik.

Be sure to look for more teen fiction stories
from Gena Showalter!

Mirror, mirror
on the wall...
who will perish
when I call?

Don't miss the next fantastic series from
New York Times *bestselling author*
Gena Showalter

The Forest of Good and Evil
Book 1
The Evil Queen

Thank you for reading Oh My Goth*!*
Now please enjoy excerpts from the first books
in Gena Showalter's bestselling series
The White Rabbit Chronicles
and
The Everlife Novels,
available now at your favorite retailers.
Don't miss a single exhilarating moment!

Alice Bell always thought her father had delusions.
Until the night she learned for herself…the monsters are real.
Read on for an excerpt from chapter 1 of
Alice in Zombieland
Book 1 of The White Rabbit Chronicles
by Gena Showalter.

All through her performance, Em *glowed*. She also dominated that stage, kicking butt and not bothering with names. Honestly, she put the other girls to shame. And that wasn't sibling pride talking. That was just plain fact.

She twirled and smiled and utterly dazzled, and everyone who watched her was as enraptured as I was. Surely. By the time the curtain closed two hours later, I was so happy for her I could have burst. And maybe I did burst the eardrums of the people in front of me. I think I clapped louder than anyone, and I definitely whistled shrilly enough to cause brain bleeds.

Those people would just have to deal. This was the *best. Birthday. Ever.* For once, the Bells had attended an event like a normal family.

Of course, my dad almost ruined everything by continually glancing at his wristwatch and turning to eye the back door as if he expected someone to volley in an H-bomb. So, by the time the crowd jumped up for a standing O, and despite my mad rush of happiness, he'd made me so tense my bones were practically vibrating.

Even still, I wasn't going to utter a single word of complaint. Miracle of miracles, he'd come. And all right, okay, so the miracle had been heralded by a bottle of his favorite whiskey, and he'd had to be stuffed in the passenger seat of the car like the cream filling in a Twinkie, but whatever. He had come!

"We need to leave," he said, already edging his way to the back door. At six-four, he was a tall man, and he loomed over everyone around him. "Grab Em and let's go."

Despite his shortcomings, despite how tired his self-medication had become, I loved him, and I knew he couldn't help his paranoia. He'd tried legitimate medication with no luck. He'd tried therapy and gotten worse. He saw monsters no one else could see, and he refused to believe they weren't actually there—or trying to eat him and kill all those he loved.

In a way, I even understood him. One night, about a year ago, Em had been crying about the injustice of missing yet another slumber party. I, in turn, had raged at our mother, and she had been so shocked by my atypical outburst that she'd explained what she called "the beginning of your father's battle with evil."

As a kid, my dad had witnessed the brutal murder of his own father. A murder that had happened at night, in a cemetery, while his father had been visiting Grandmother Alice's grave. The event had traumatized my dad. So, yes, I got it.

Did that make me feel any better right now? No. He

was an adult. Shouldn't he handle his problems with wisdom and maturity? I mean, how many times had I heard, "Act like an adult, Alice." Or, "Only a child would do something like that, Alice."

My take on that? Practice what you preach, people. But what did I know? I wasn't an ever-knowing *adult*; I was just expected to act like one. And, yeah. A real nice family tree I had. Murder and mayhem on every gnarled branch. Hardly seemed fair.

"Come on," he snapped now.

My mom rushed to his side, all comfort and soothing pats. "Calm down, darling. Everything's going to be okay."

"We can't stay here. We have to get home where it's safe."

"I'll grab Em," I said. The first flickers of guilt hit me, stinging my chest. Maybe I'd asked too much of him. And of my mom, who would have to peel him from the roof of the car when we finally pulled into our monster-proof garage. "Don't worry."

My skirt tangled around my legs as I shoved my way through the crowd and raced past the stage curtain. Little girls were everywhere, each of them wearing more makeup, ribbons and glitter than the few strippers I'd seen on TV. When I'd been innocently flipping channels. And accidentally stopped on stations I wasn't supposed to watch. Moms and dads were hugging their daughters, praising them, handing them flowers, all about the congratulations on a job-well-done thing. Me, I had to grab my sister's hand and beat feet, dragging her behind me.

"Dad?" she asked, sounding unsurprised.

I threw her a glance over my shoulder. She had paled, those golden eyes too old and knowledgeable for her angel face. "Yeah."

"What's the damage?"

"Nothing too bad. You'll still be able to venture into public without shame."

"Then I consider this a win."

Me, too.

People swarmed and buzzed in the lobby like bees, half of them lingering, half of them working their way to the doors. That's where I found my dad. He'd stopped at the glass, his gaze panning the parking lot. Halogens were placed throughout, lighting the way to our Tahoe, which my mom had parked illegally in the closest handicapped space for an easy in, easy out. His skin had taken on a grayish cast, and his hair now stood on end, as if he'd scrambled his fingers through the strands one too many times.

Mom was still trying to soothe him. Thank goodness she'd managed to disarm him before we'd left the house. Usually he carried guns, knives and throwing stars whenever he dared to venture out.

The moment I reached him, he turned and gripped me by the forearms, shaking me. "You see anything in the shadows, anything at all, you pick up your sister and run. Do you hear me? Pick her up and run back inside. Lock the doors, hide and call for help." His eyes were an electric blue, wild, his pupils pulsing over his irises.

The guilt, well, it stopped flickering and kicked into a hard-core blaze. "I will," I promised, and patted both of his hands. "Don't worry about us. You taught me how to protect myself. Remember? I'll keep Em safe. No matter what."

"Okay," he said, but he looked far from satisfied. "Okay, then."

I'd spoken the truth. I didn't know how many hours I'd logged in the backyard with him, learning how to stop an attacker. Sure, those lessons had been all about protecting my vital organs from becoming some mindless being's dinner, but self-defense was self-defense, right?

Somehow my mom convinced him to release me and brave the terrifying outdoors. All the while people shot us weird looks that I tried to ignore. We walked together, as a family, our feet flying one in front of the other. Mom and Dad were in front, with me and Em a few steps behind them, holding hands as the crickets sang and provided us with an eerie soundtrack.

I glanced around, trying to see the world as my dad must. I saw a long stretch of black tar—camouflage? I saw a sea of cars—places to hide? I saw the forest beyond, rising from the hills—a breeding ground for nightmares?

Above, I saw the moon, high and full and beautifully transparent. Clouds still puffed through the sky, orange now and kind of creepy. And was that…surely not…but I blinked, slowed my pace. Yep. It was. The cloud shaped like a rabbit had followed me. Fancy that.

"Look at the clouds," I said. "Notice anything cool?"

A pause, then, "A…rabbit?"

"Exactly. I saw him this morning. He must think we're pretty awesome."

"Because we are, duh."

My dad realized we'd lagged behind, sprinted the distance between us, grabbed onto my wrist and jerked me faster…faster still…while I maintained my grip on Emma and jerked *her* along. I'd rather dislocate her shoulder than leave her behind, even for a second. Dad loved us, but part of me feared he'd drive off without us if he thought it necessary.

He opened the car door and practically tossed me in like a football. Emma was next, and we shared a moment of silent communication after we settled.

Fun times, I mouthed.

Happy birthday to you, she mouthed back.

The instant my dad was in the passenger seat he threw the locks. He was shaking too hard to buckle his belt, and finally gave up. "Don't drive by the cemetery," he told Mom, "but get us home as fast as you can."

We'd avoided the cemetery on the way here, too—despite the daylight—adding unnecessary time to an already lengthy drive.

"I will. No worries." The Tahoe roared to life, and Mom yanked the shifter into Reverse.

"Dad," I said, my voice as reasonable as I could make it. "If we take the long way, we'll be snailing it along construction." We lived just outside big, beautiful Birmingham and traffic could be a nasty monster on its own. "That'll add at least half an hour to our trip. You don't want us to stay in the dark, at a standstill, for that long, do you?" He'd work himself into such a panic we'd all be clawing at the doors to escape.

"Honey?" Mom asked. The car eased to the edge of the lot, where she had to go left or right. If she went left, we'd never make it home. Seriously. If I had to listen to my dad for more than thirty minutes, I'd jump out the window and as an act of mercy I'd take Emma with me. If Mom went right, we'd have a short ride, a short anxiety attack to deal with, but a quick recovery. "I'll drive so fast you won't even be able to *see* the cemetery."

"No. Too risky."

"Please, Daddy," I said, not above manipulation. As I'd already proved. "For me. On my birthday. I won't ask for anything else, I promise, even though you guys forgot the last one and I never got a present."

"I... I..." His gaze shifted continually, scanning the nearby trees for movement.

"Please. Em needs to be tucked into bed, like, soon, or she'll morph into Lily of the Valley of Thorns." As we'd long ago dubbed her. My sis got tired, and she left carnage in her wake.

Lips pursed, Em slapped my arm. I shrugged, the universal sign for *well, it's true.*

Dad pushed out a heavy breath. "Okay. Okay. Just... break the sound barrier, babe," he said, kissing my mom's hand.

"I will. You have my word."

My parents shared a soft smile. I felt like a voyeur for noticing; used to be they'd enjoyed these kinds of moments all the time, but the smiles had become less and less frequent over the years.

"All right, here we go." Mom swung the vehicle right, and to my utter astonishment, she really did try to break the sound barrier, weaving in and out of lanes, honking at the slower cars, riding bumpers.

I was impressed. The few driving lessons she'd given

me, she'd been a nervous wreck, which had turned *me* into a nervous wreck. We hadn't gone far or cranked the speed above twenty-five, even outside our neighborhood.

She kept up a steady stream of chatter, and I watched the clock on my phone. The minutes ticked by, until we'd gone ten without a single incident. Only twenty more to go.

Dad kept his nose pressed to the window, his frantic breaths leaving puffs of mist on the glass. Maybe he was enjoying the mountains, valleys and lush green trees highlighted by the streetlamps, rather than searching for monsters.

Yeah. Right.

"So how'd I do?" Emma whispered in my direction.

I reached over and squeezed her hand. "You were amazing."

Her dark brows knit together, and I knew what was coming next. Suspicion. "You swear?"

"Swear. You rocked the house hard-core. In comparison, the other girls *sucked*."

She covered her mouth to stop herself from giggling.

I couldn't help but add, "The boy who twirled you around? I think he was considering pushing you off the stage, just so people would finally look at him. Honestly, every eye was riveted on you."

The giggle bubbled out this time, unstoppable. "So what you're saying is, when I tripped over my own feet, everyone noticed."

"Trip? What trip? You mean that wasn't part of the routine?"

She gave me a high five. "Good answer."

"Honey," Mom said, apprehension straining her voice. "Find some music for us to listen to, okay?"

Uh-oh. She must want him distracted.

I leaned over and glanced out the front windshield. Sure enough. We were approaching the cemetery. At least there were no other cars around, so no one would witness my dad's oncoming breakdown. And he *would* have one. I could feel the tension thickening the air.

"No music," he said. "I need to concentrate, remain on alert. I have to—" He stiffened, gripped the armrests on his seat until his knuckles whitened.

A moment of silence passed, such thick, heavy silence.

His panting breaths emerged faster and faster—until he roared so piercingly I cringed. "They're out there! They're going to attack us!" He grabbed the wheel and yanked. "Don't you see them? We're headed right for them. Turn around! You have to turn around."

The Tahoe swerved, hard, and Emma screamed. I grabbed her hand, gave her another squeeze, but I refused to let go. My heart was pounding against my ribs, a cold sweat beading over my skin. I'd promised to protect her tonight, and I would.

"It's gonna be okay," I told her.

Her tremors were so violent they even shook me.

"Honey, listen to me," Mom soothed. "We're safe in the car. No one can hurt us. We have to—"

"No! If we don't turn around they'll follow us home!" My dad was thoroughly freaked, and nothing Mom said had registered. "We have to turn around." He made another play for the wheel, gave another, harder yank, and this time, we didn't just swerve, we spun.

Round and round, round and round. My grip on Emma tightened.

"Alice," she cried.

"It's okay, it's okay," I chanted. The world was whizzing, blurring…the car teetering…my dad shouting a curse…my mom gasping…the car tilting…tilting…

FREEZE FRAME.

I remember when Em and I used to play that game. We'd crank the volume of our iPod dock—loud, pounding rock—and boogie like we were having seizures. One of us would shout *freeze frame* and we'd instantly stop moving, totally frozen, trying not to laugh, until one of us yelled the magic word to shoot us back into motion. *Dance.*

I wish I could have shouted *freeze frame* in just that moment and rearranged the scenery, the players. But life isn't a game, is it?

DANCE.

We went airborne, flipping over, crashing into the road upside down, then flipping over again. The sound of crunching metal, shattering glass and pained screams filled my ears. I was thrown back and forth in my seat, my brain becoming a cherry slushie in my head as different impacts jarred me and stole my breath.

When we finally landed, I was so dazed, so fogged, I felt like I was still in motion. The screams had stopped, at least. All I heard was a slight ringing in my ears.

"Mom? Dad?" A pause. No response. "Em?" Again, nothing.

I frowned, looked around. My eyesight was hazy, something warm and wet in my lashes, but I could see well enough.

And what I saw utterly destroyed me.

I screamed. My mom was slashed to ribbons, her body covered in blood. Emma was slumped over in her seat, her head at an odd angle, her cheek split open. No. No, no, no.

"Dad, help me. We have to get them out!"

Silence.

"Dad?" I searched—and realized he was no longer in the car. The front windshield was gone, and he was lying motionless on the pieces a few yards away. There were three men standing over his body, the car's headlights illuminating them.

No, they weren't men, I realized. They couldn't be. They had sagging pockmarked skin and dirty, ripped clothing. Their hair hung in clumps on their spotted scalps, and their teeth…so sharp as they…as they…fell upon my dad and disappeared *inside* him, only to reappear a second later and…and…eat him.

Monsters.

I fought for my freedom, desperate to drag Em to safety—Em, who hadn't moved and wasn't crying—desperate to get to my dad, to help him. In the process, I banged my head against something hard and sharp. A horrible pain ravaged me, but still I fought, even as my strength waned…my eyesight dimmed…

Then it was night-night for Alice, and I knew nothing more.

At least, for a little while…

Tenley "Ten" Lockwood just wants the right to choose for herself where she'll live...after she dies.
Read on for an excerpt from chapter 1 of
Firstlife
Book 1 of The Everlife Novels
by Gena Showalter.

"You are better off Unsigned than a slave to Troikan law."
—Myriad

I've been locked inside the Prynne Asylum—where happiness comes to die—for three hundred and seventy-eight days. (Or nine thousand and seventy-two hours.) I know the exact time frame, not because I watched the sun rise and set in the sky, but because I mark my walls in blood every time the lights in the good-girls-gone-bad wing of thc facility turn on.

There are no windows in the building. At least, none that I've found. And I've never been allowed outside. None of the inmates have. To be honest, I don't even know what country we're in, or if we're buried far underground. Before being flown, driven, shipped or dropped here, we were heavily sedated. Wherever we are, though, it's bone-deep cold beyond the walls. Every day, hour, second, our air is heated.

I've heard friends and enemies alike ask the staff for details, but the response has always been the same. *Answers have to be earned.*

No, thanks. For me, the price—cooperation—is simply too high.

With a wince, I rise from bed and make my way to the far corner of my cell. Every step is agony. My back hates me, but the muscles are too sore to go on strike. Last night I was caned *just because.*

I stop in front of my pride and joy. My calendar. A new day means a new mark.

I have no chalk, no pen or marker, so I drive the tip of an index finger over a jagged stone protruding from the floor, slicing through the flesh and drawing a well of blood.

I hate the sting, but if I'm honest, I'll love the scar it leaves behind. My scars give me something to count.

Counting is my passion, and numerology my favorite addiction. Maybe because every breath we take is another tick on our clock, putting us one step closer to death…and a new beginning. Maybe because my name is Tenley—Ten to my friends.

Ten, a representation of completion.

We have ten fingers and ten toes. Ten is the standard beginning for any countdown.

I was born on the tenth day of the tenth month at 10:10 a.m. And, okay. All right. Maybe I'm obsessed with numbers because they always tell a story and unlike people, they never lie.

Here's my story in a nutshell:

Seventeen—the number of years I've existed. In my case, *lived* is too strong a word.

One—the number of boys I've dated.

Two—the number of friends I've made and lost since my incarceration.

Two—the number of lives I'll live. The number of lives we'll *all* live.

Our Firstlife, then our Everlife.

Two—the number of choices I have for my eternal future.

(1) Do as my parents command or (2) suffer.

I've chosen to suffer.

I use the blood to create another mark on the stones. Satisfied, I head to the "bathroom." There are no doors to provide even a modicum of privacy, just a small, open shower stall next to a toilet. For our safety, we're told. For the amusement of others, I suspect. All cells are monitored 24/7, which means at any given time during any given day, staff members are allowed and even encouraged to watch live camera feed.

Dr. Vans, the head of the asylum, likes to taunt us. *I see and know everything.*

A good portion of teachers scold us. *Time waster!*

Orderlies belittle us. *Put on a little weight, haven't we?*

Most of the guards leer at us. They hail from all over the world, and though their language varies, their sentiment is always the same. *You are begging for it and one day I'll give it.*

Just some of the many perks offered at chez Prynne.

Not everyone is horrible, I admit. A small handful

even strive to keep the others from going too far. But it's no secret every staff member is paid to make us hate our stay, to make us want to leave *more than anything.* Because the more we want to leave, the more likely we are to do whatever our parents sent us here to do.

My friend Marlowe dared to pawn her mother's jewelry to buy groceries, and she needed help with her "kleptomania." My friend Clay, a drug addict, needed to get clean.

The institution failed them both. A few months ago, Marlowe killed herself, and Clay… I don't know what happened to him. He planned an escape, and I haven't heard from him since.

I miss them both. Every. Single. Day.

I begged Clay not to risk a breakout. I tried to leave once, and I had help. My boyfriend, James, a guard high on the totem, arranged for cameras to be shut down, certain doors to be unlocked and other guards to sleep on the job. Still I proved unsuccessful.

For his efforts, James was shot in the head. While I watched.

Hot tears well in my eyes and trickle down my cheeks as I slowly strip out of my jumpsuit. Every motion comes with another blast of agony. When finally I'm naked, I step under a tepid spray of water. Modesty has long since been beaten out of me—literally!—but I wash as fast as I can. We're given a small ration of water a day. If we run out, we run out. Too bad, so sad. Something we're never given? Razors. I keep my legs and underarms smooth with threads I've pulled from old uniforms. I already feel like an animal; there's no reason to resemble one, too.

Not that a well-groomed appearance matters. While we're allowed to socialize with the opposite sex during mealtimes, I'd rather dig my heart out of my chest with a rusty spoon than date again. Yes, the rewards are tremendous, but the risks are more so. When everything comes crashing down and it will I'll be shattered into a million pieces. I'll have to rebuild. Again.

I should have resisted James's pursuit of me, but I'd been at a low point, desperate for any show of affection. He'd risked his job every time he'd disabled the cameras to sneak inside my room. He sneaked in so many times, in fact, his memory still lives here. Every night when I climb into my twin-size bed, I'm reminded of the way he teased me out of my initial shyness. Of the way he cleaned my wounds whenever I was hurt. Of the way he held me in his arms, offering comfort and kisses. He'd wanted to do more. I hadn't. Not here. Not with a potential audience.

Forget the past. Concentrate on the present. Right.

I shut off the water and towel dry as best I can. I step into a clean, peed-in-the-snow-yellow jumpsuit, but only manage to bring the material to my waist, my arms refusing to work properly, my shoulder muscles giving up.

What am I going to do? I can't leave my cell like this.

The door suddenly slides open with a quiet *snick*. My blood flashes ice-cold as two guards march inside my cell, a flailing girl between them.

I gasp, my surprise giving me the strength I need to lift my hands and cover my breasts.

No, I'm not modest, but this is a special kind of humiliating.

The guards release the girl and push her in my direction. The first thing I notice about her? She has unevenly cropped pink hair.

"New roomie," one of them says to me. When he notices my partial state of undress, he grins. "Well, well. Vhat we have here?"

His Russian accent is as thick as ever, one of the many reasons I refer to him as Comrade Douche. Though my cheeks burn, I strive for a confident tone. "Vhat we have here is an underage girl who, upon her release, will ensure you rot in prison."

His grin only widens as he takes a step toward me. The pink-haired girl kicks him in the stomach, surprising me.

He focuses on her, raising his hand to deliver a strike. *"Suka!"*

Bitch in Russian. A word that's been thrown at me, as well.

She smiles and crooks her fingers at him, the universal sign for *bring it*.

The other guard grabs Comrade Douche by the arm and drags him into the hallway. Both men frown at me as the door slides shut.

Without missing a beat, the girl waves at me, looking almost…giddy. I blink in confusion. She's happy rather than scared? Really?

"Hello," she says, and I detect a slight British accent. "I'm Bow, your new best friend."

She's crazy. Got it. "I'm not in the market for a new friend." I hoped I'd remain solo. I don't like sleeping in front of another person but I have to steal catnaps to function. My last roommate told me I toss and turn, screaming about the torture I've endured or singing a number song my aunt taught me as a child.

Ten tears fall, and I call...nine hundred trees, but only one is for me. Eight—

Oh, no. I'm not getting lost in my head right now.

"Here." Bow stalks toward me, her stride long and strong. Up close, I can tell her eyes are the color of freshly polished pennies. They're odd yet captivating, smoldering with an intensity that should be too much to contain. "Let me help you."

Out of habit, I step out of range when she reaches for me. But...zero! My favorite four-letter curse word. I don't think I can finish getting dressed without her.

She cups her breasts in a mimic of me and beams. "Boobs are awesome, yeah? Literal fun-bags. I don't know what you girls are always complaining about."

"Don't you mean *us girls*?"

Her hands fall away from her *fun-bags*. "Dude. There's nothing wrong with enjoying the equipment and getting a little some-some of my own goods and services. Seriously. I'm so hot even *I* want a piece of me."

Hot? Debatable. Bizarre, narcissistic and pervy? Unquestionably. She's the trifecta. In other words, I hit the probably-gonna-get-murdered jackpot this go-round. Yay, me.

"I'd rather not talk about your goods and services, thanks." Slowly I pivot, placing her at my back. This is a rarity for me. A low point, a moment of utter desperation. If she attempts a hit-and-run or a grab-and-stab—*anything* dirty—I'll make sure she regrets it.

She inhales sharply, and I assume she's studying the wealth of bruises I'm sporting.

"Sometime today," I snap, horrified by the perceived weakness.

She gently works my arms through the sleeves. "I hope you're prepared for the Everlife. Another beating like this could kill you."

Doubtful. Dr. Vans has the torture thing nailed. He knows when he's about to push a body too far. "Trust me. Death isn't the worst thing that can happen to me."

"Of course it isn't. If you haven't made the right plans for the Unending, you'll wish you ceased to exist."

The Unending, where Myriad and Troika—the two realms in power in the afterlife…aka the Everlife—are located. Where "real" life is said to begin.

Over the years, the world has been divided into two factions. Those who support Myriad, and those who support Troika. No one ever supports both. How can they? The realms are too fundamentally opposed—about everything!

Myriad boasts about autonomy…bliss…indulgence. To them, Firstlife is merely a stepping stone into the Everlife, everything happens for a fated reason and, when we experience Second-death—death in the Everlife—our spirit returns to Earth, the Land of the Harvest, to Fuse with another—brand-new—spirit.

They are willing to negotiate covenant terms to win over a human.

Troika, on the other hand, is known for structure… constant study…absolute conformity. To them, Firstlife matters just as much as Everlife, fate is a myth and, when we experience Second-death, we enter into the Rest, never to be seen by human or spirit again.

Troikans refuse to negotiate covenant terms, offering the same benefits to everyone everywhere without exception. The same laws, too. To them, what is right is right and what is wrong is wrong, for one and for all. Everyone on equal footing.

If one realm says the sky is cloudless, the other will say a storm is brewing.

They've been at war for centuries, the other's destruction the ultimate goal. That's why they fight so hard to win souls. That's also why picking the right side is so important. Someday, someone is going to lose.

Here on Earth, the Myriad and Troika supporters aren't segregated…exactly. They try to coexist, but it's in imperfect harmony and there's always an underlying hum of tension.

Sometimes riots break out, and the government is forced to execute martial law to prevent an all-out brawl.

A rare few people, like me, have no idea which side to back. We see merits to both sets of beliefs. We also see downsides.

We are called the Unsigned.

For us, there are rumors of a third spirit realm, the place we'll end up after Firstdeath. My parents used to tell me horror stories about it, stories whispered in the dark of night. The Realm of Many Ends, where nightmares come to life.

I've often wondered… Is Many Ends a made-up place intended to scare kids straight?

"Do you?" Bow asks as she zips up my jumpsuit. "Have plans for the Unending, I mean?"

"I'm not talking Everlife with you."

Her features scrunch with disappointment. "Why not?"

"I'll be here another three hundred and fifty-two days."

3 + 5 + 2 = 10

"And?"

And she will leave sooner rather than later. I recognize her type. Extremely optimistic until something goes wrong. After her first beating, she'll cave and do whatever her parents want, guaranteed.

"Forget the next life. What about this one? Tell me why you're here." I motion to our illustrious cell with a tilt of my chin.

"My guardian sent me." She strides to the second twin bed and sits, and there's nothing graceful or feminine about her. "Told me to be a light."

Ugh. What I hear? Absolute conformity. "You signed with Troika, then." Not a question.

Her nod contains a thread of pride. "I did."

We're going to clash *so* hard. "What is light, exactly?" What's she going to be pushing on me?

"Whatever is needed to help someone find a way out of darkness."

Darkness. "Meaning Myriad."

She ignores my dry tone. "Meaning a problem, any problem."

Well, I've got plenty of those—though I tell myself

this situation is fertilizer, and something good must grow from it.

"Why are *you* here?" she asks me.

"I refuse to make covenant with Myriad." Covenant—the equivalent of signing a contract in blood.

Sometimes, in an attempt to convince me to sign away my rights, I'm pampered. *Isn't this nice? This is what awaits you in Myriad.* Most times I'm tortured. *This is only the beginning of what you'll endure in Many Ends.* Not knowing what awaits me is the worst.

"Prynne is supposed to be unaffiliated with either realm," she says with a frown.

"It is." How else could Dr. Vans convince one kid to sign with Myriad and another to sign with Troika? Which he does. All the time.

She meets my gaze, a little surprised, a lot hopeful. "Do you want to make covenant with Troika?"

"Not even a little." As her shoulders droop, I add, "I hate to break it to you, but your guardian sucks. He—she?—sentenced you to hell. For nothing! No one here will accept your *light*." *Trust no one. Question everything.*

"Maybe not, but I'll still make the offer. Yesterday, today and tomorrow, my actions matter."

In that, I agree with her. I'll even take it a step further. The most destructive or constructive actions begin with a single thought. And, ultimately, a single action can decide the direction our lives take. And our deaths.

I will choose my path. Me alone. My choice will affect no eternal future but my own.

She opens her mouth to say more, but I shake my head. Subject closed.

She hops up and walks around the room, studying every nook and cranny, finally stopping to gape at my calendar. "Seriously? You're using a finger pen? No wonder everyone calls you Nutter. You're the biggest nut in the whack shack."

She just got here. How does she know what I'm called? "Everyone calls me Nutter because of the size of my lady balls. That, and I tend to smear my opponents across the floor like peanut butter."

She thinks for a moment, frowns. "If your lady balls are so big, why don't they call you Hairy Cherries? Or Furry Meatballs?" She taps her chin. "Well, duh. Because neither name describes your explosive temper. Oh! I know. I'll call you Sperm Bank! It covers the balls *and* the explosions."

I snort-laugh. She's brave, so gold star for that. In a place like this, lack of fear is rare and precious. Of course, if she threatens me in the slightest way, I won't hesitate to end her. Survival first, nothing else second.

"If anyone calls me Sperm Bank, my temper is going to explode all over *you*," I say. "Meanwhile, I'll be sure to call you Hatchet. The tool used to cut your hair, I'm guessing."

She fluffs the ragged ends of her *style*. "I used a kitchen knife, thank you very much. I'm confident the trim properly highlights my beauty."

Have to admire her positivity.

My internal clock suddenly goes off, the conversation forgotten. "Breakfast!"

She sighs. "Mealtime. Yay."

"Our cell will open in three...two...one."

The double doors slide apart.

"We have thirty seconds to exit the room," I explain. "If the door closes while we're still inside, we'll miss the meal." The food sucks, nothing but slop, but that slop has enough vitamins to keep us somewhat healthy. And really, anything is better than starving.

"So we're like dogs in a crate, taken out only at scheduled times so we won't crap on something important or chew on the furniture. Awesome."

Together, we dart into the hall. Our blockmates do the same. In total, there are twelve of us.

Twelve: the number of months in a year, members on a jury, and the hours on the face of a clock.

For a moment, we take each other's measure. Anyone going to uncage the rage today?

When no one makes a lewd or violent gesture—hey, this might be a good day—we head for the exit at the end of the hall.

Jane, one of the older inmates, mutters to herself and stops to bang her forehead against the wall. Skin splits at her hairline and blood trickles down her cheek. Everyone else keeps walking, head down and arms wrapped around the torso, as if to protect the vitals—or stop an avalanche of pain and misery from spilling out.

I march determinedly beside Bow, for the first time noticing she exudes a fragrant mix of wildflowers and lemon drops. I like it, but I know it won't last. Our water smells like chemicals, and the soap we're given smells like grease.

A high-pitched whistle cuts through the air, making me cringe. “Well, well,” a voice says from behind me. “I just lost a bet I’d assumed was a *sure thing*.”

“Like Becky,” someone else calls, and snickers erupt.

I don’t have to glance over my shoulder to ID the first speaker. Sloan “don’t hate me because I’m beautiful, hate me because I plan to murder you” Aubuchon. She is Dr. Vans’s favorite inmate, even though she’s tried to kill him, oh, a dozen times.

From the things I’ve heard the good doc say to her, she’s here because either (a) she can’t control her temper or (b) she refuses to marry the old fart who will save her grandparents’ estate. I’ve always leaned toward A. Arranged marriages still happen, but not often.

“Tenley didn’t kill her new roommate at first sight, y’all,” she continues, her Southern twang ridiculously adorable even while she’s sneering. “Meaning, the newbie wasn’t eaten—at least not literally.”

Charming.

A few boos ring out, but so do a couple of cheers.

Bow turns and smiles at the girl. “What’d you lose? A few more IQ points?”

I almost sigh, because I can guess what’s coming next.

A volcanic Sloan races forward to grab Bow by the collar of her jumpsuit, forcing her to stop.

Yeah. That.

I stop, too, unsure how I’ll proceed. I’ve seen this song and dance before—eleven times, to be exact—and my reactions always differ. I’ve pretended to be blind and deaf, but I’ve also thrown a punch while screaming obscenities.

Sloan and I live by different philosophies. While I lash out only when provoked (usually), she attacks newcomers at the first opportunity to prevent challengers later.

Life sucks. We've adapted.

"Bless your heart." Sloan releases Bow to plant her hands on her hips. Tall, blonde and model-pretty, she's the girl every other longs to be. Until she opens her mouth, and her outer beauty can no longer compensate for her inner bitch. "You're not smart enough to realize I run this shit show. You'll keep your eyes down and your tongue quiet…or you'll lose both."

Bow flicks me an amused glance. "Hey, what do you call a blonde with only half a brain? Gifted!"

Am I really caught in the middle of this? "Have you forgotten that *you* are a blonde?" And Troikan! Forgive and move on.

"So," Bow says, tapping her chin. "You're suggesting I blow in her ear for a data transfer?"

"That's it! Say goodbye to your tongue." Sloan pushes Bow with enough force to make the girl stumble.

Before she can do anything else, I react without thought, slapping her arm away. "Hands off." Guess I'm going to protest today. Which might do more harm than good. Like the rest of us, Bow has to learn to defend herself. There's no other way to survive.

Sloan's narrowed gaze focuses on me. "What are you gonna do, Nutter? Huh?"

"Do you really want to know?" I ask softly. Being the crazy girl in a place full of crazy girls certainly has its advantages. No one is ever able to anticipate my next move. "What I say, I'll do. No take-backs."

We've thrown down before, Sloan and I, and it wasn't pretty. Forget scratching and pulling hair, the quintessential "catfight." We punched and kicked and ripped at each other like animals.

We both bear the scars.

I'm not afraid of physical pain. Not anymore.

I'm hit with surprise when my roommate says, "Dude. Do you have any idea how funny this is? Sloaner the Moaner has a mouthful of number two while she's talking to Ten."

Another round of boos and cheers ring out.

Sloan forgets all about me, baring her teeth in a scowl. "Maybe I won't remove your tongue and eyes…yet. I want you to see what I do to you, and beg for mercy I won't give you."

"Enough!" A harsh voice booms from overhead speakers. "You know the rules, girls. There's no loitering in the hallways. Go to the cafeteria or go to the whipping post. Your choice."

I look at Sloan, who's glaring at Bow, who's smirking at Sloan.

Sloan bares her teeth and says to me, "You do know your boyfriend wasn't the only one capable of paying the guards to shut off the cameras, right? If I were you, I'd start sleeping with one eye open." With that, she turns on her heel and flounces off. Or tries to.

I grab her arm, stopping her, and get in her face. I keep my voice low as I say, "You sneak into my room, and I'll fillet you like a fish. No one will pay attention to your screams. *You* know *that*, right?"

You scream, I scream, we all scream. No one cares. The asylum's unofficial anthem.

Sloan jerks free and stalks away.

I cast Bow a humorless smile. "Welcome to Prynne."

Excerpt from *Firstlife*